i

Wrath of Wolf

Louise Furley

WRATH OF WOLF

ISBN- 978-1-7363452-6-9 (Paperback)
ISBN- 978-1-7363452-5-2 (eBook)

Cover design by Pixel Mischief Design

ALSO BY LOUISE FURLEY

A Mafia Romance series

Distilled Duplicity
His Winnings
Adara
Jozadak

Satan's Brood series

Devil's Prince
Devil's Seed

Dutch Military Special Forces series

Jungle Treasure
Jancarlo

Stand alone titles

Jezábel and the Assassin

Solitar

Halo Valley

WRATH
OF
WOLF

Chapter One

"*F*or cripe's sake, Ollie," Annabella groused from the passenger seat, "slow down. We have an hour before we have to be at dinner with your stupid family. I wanna stop for a drink. I need fortification to spend even a minute with your pompous father and his imbecilic friends."

Her bulbous bosom rounding over the seatbelt jostled like mad from the swerves and bumps as the car cruised the uneven road.

The Lincoln SUV easily hugged the ancient winding road as it coiled down and around the mountain like a thin black snake. The last of the dropped autumn leaves whooshed behind the vehicle like a confetti tail.

The night pitch black, there was nothing to illuminate the shrouded asphalt except the beaming headlights. Even the bordering trees were just dark craggy phantoms looming along both sides of the narrow two-lane road.

Ollie Duncan let out a loud, beleaguered sigh. Thumping a thumb irritably on the steering wheel, he grumbled, "Will you shut it for just one damned second? Nag, nag, nag, I'm tired of your incessant complaining. And FYI, my brothers aren't coming until Christmas."

Her double chin wobbling, Annabella retorted nastily, "Screw you, Ollie, and your father, and Talon DeMar that insists on having their special retreats at the lodge. Just because all of your father's frat brothers grew up together doesn't mean we have to spend every blasted minute of our time with them. I'm bored out of my tree with the McShanes, Ansberrys and the Burtons and the others."

Ollie nodded, peering into the dark night ensuring he kept the car on his side of the twisting road. "Yeah, the king himself, Talon DeMar and his clan will already be there, and of course Talon's right-hand knight, Stone Cash will be present as well."

"Oh just great." Annabella tipped her head back with a scowl. "That bitch Ketherine will be hanging about then, won't she? When Caralina passed, Talon dragged her daughter from her schooling in Italy to run the company with him per Caralina's will. From archeology to building bridges, I bet Ketherine hates every second of it." The scowl turned into a gloating smile.

Ollie shot her a quick frown. "Keti is not a bitch, she's just...kind of...cold."

"Uh huh," Annabella grunted. "Glacier kitten the men call her, Glitty for short." Her coarse laugh a piggish sound, she said, "Glitty Kitty. Even though so much older than Keti, as soon as her little tits sprouted you boys were on her like barbeque sauce on ribs."

Her pudgy lips twisted in antipathy. "They say she's beautiful like a soft icy statue. Michael McShane says a goddess statue. Huh. I think she's butt ugly and too- too-"

"Dainty?" Ollie smiled.

Her eyes narrowed at him, she spat, "No. I was thinking brittle, too slender for most men's tastes. Stick thin as if she's still in her teens for Pete's sake. Those green eyes unattractively too big for her fragile face."

A small chuckle, Ollie remarked, "I think you mean delicate. Or even ethereal."

Annabella snorted. "Come on, that is so over-used, so cliché. She's hardly a wraith. Unfortunately her damned curves have filled out since she suddenly left home at 13. She's nothing but ignorant trailer trash from her mother's side of the family. Talon, her stepfather put the kibosh on her archeological studies, and rightly so.

"Honestly, rooting around in the dirt like a sow. I heard he's planning an arranged marriage for her. Good thing. Keep her away from all you horndogs." A jealous sneer pinched Annabella's melon round face.

She prattled on, "I hear Talon wants her to marry Rein van Baer. That old perv was sniffing after the girl when she was barely out of diapers."

His shoulders hunched, Ollie tugged the wheel tightly to the right to keep on the serpentine roadway. He agreed, "I know. Poor Keti did not want to come home to Talon…her bastard of a father, rather stepfather, and be forced to work with him. Her mother left her half of the business to Keti. But they each have 50-50 of the company and all documents have to be signed by both."

Annabella snickered. "Yeah. Remember that time Talon tried to forge Keti's signature and he got caught? He was lucky, he only got a slap on the wrist. But he learned his lesson, I'll say."

Ollie leaned over the wheel squinting into the dark. "And Rein van Baer is not that old. Like my dad, he's in his fifties." He shrugged one shoulder. "But compared to young Keti, yeah, he's old."

There was silence in the car for a few minutes. Annabella rummaged in her huge purse for her cigarettes.

At the sound Ollie made, she huffed and slammed the pack back in the bag and tossed the purse on the floor with an annoyed sigh.

"Second hand smoke is just a stupid myth, Ollie, for people to put guilt complexes on smokers." She pulled out a package of Twinkies instead.

His head swiveling as he struggled to follow the dark road, Ollie tried to cajole his wife. "It won't be as crowded this year though. Most of the other siblings won't be there. They have work and other shit to attend to. It'll just be the older generation, the basic fathers, their wives and one or two of their children, the younger generation like me at the lodge."

"Yeah, I hear as usual the guys are bringing a plus one." After a minute of unsuccessfully trying to open the package of Twinkies, Annabella used her teeth to tear the wrapping apart.

Ollie nodded. Speaking over the loud crinkling of wrapping as Annabella fought with it, he said, "Yes, a wife, fiancée and a girlfriend or two."

"God," his wife groaned. "I hate this mountain we have to get around to get to the mansion. It's damp and chilling this far north of Oregon. Listen," her whining voice turned to a fake, but gentle coaxing. "There's that bar just past the exit off this ghastly hill. O'Shareef's, we can get a cocktail there."

Rolling his eyes, her husband sniped, "Oh sure. We want to join the party reeking of booze. Leave it to you to know where every watering hole in the Northwest is. Of course everyone is used to you and your all-consuming love of food and alcohol. You just-"

"Look out!" Annabella screeched.

A truck suddenly emerged from the gloaming darkness and was barreling straight at them right in their lane.

"Omigod! Omigod!" Ollie yelled as he wrenched the wheel to the right to avoid the truck. But the truck clipped the front bumper and the Duncans' SUV veered sharply off the road.

Annabella's screams were so loud they almost drowned out Ollie's frightened wails as the SUV went flying out of control and crashed through the wooden fence.

Pieces of wood shot out in all directions like brown fireworks. Their screams mingled as the car careened wildly for several yards before it flew off the side of the mountain.

The car rolled and bashed over rocks and grass as it tore down the mountain then it suddenly smashed into a tree and that stopped it dead.

Metal clanking against the stalwart tree proved Mother Nature was stronger than mankind as the car wrapped around the redwood's thick trunk like a paperclip.

The mangled Lincoln wheezed and rattled then whistling steam plumed from under the crushed hood.

****

He pulled off to the side of the road and carefully parked the stolen tow-truck far over on the shoulder.

Climbing out, he closed the door then trod across the grass. "Boy," he muttered, "what a bitch stopping the truck and getting turned around in that skinny driveway. Now, let's see how I did."

Stepping over the pieces of broken fence, he sauntered to the rim of the grassy area and looked down.

"Yowzer," he let out a whistle. "I didn't mean to smash 'em up so much. I thought the fence would stop the car. Shit, I hope they're still breathing or this won't be any fun at all. Now," he put a finger to his chin and pondered.

Mumbling to himself, he said, "Gonna be rough getting them and the car up. Especially that Porky Pig Annabella.

5

Thank God the car's descent was halted so near from the road. Tree ain't looking too happy though," he grinned.

"I guess I can tie a rope around ol' Ollie and the pig and to my truck and drag 'em up the side of the mountain. Okay then, off to work!" He spun around to grab the rope from his vehicle.

****

Ollie's head was pounding, and Annabella's screams weren't helping any. *What the hell is the matter with her now?*

He didn't move for a minute trying to get his bearings. "Ahh," the groan scraped out as pain hit, everywhere. Dizziness flooded his brain making him slightly nauseous.

"What the-" He was lying in a funny position. On his stomach but his hips were pushed up over a pillow, oddly shoving his ass up in the air.

He moved an arm, then started when he realized he couldn't budge it. His arms were splayed out to the side, and they were bound to a bed frame. He tugged at his legs only to find they were spread apart and also immobilized.

Blinking rapidly, he took in the closest wall. The room had a cabin feel to it with the rough wood walls, and the cowboy lamp on the nightstand beside the bed, he didn't recognize where he was.

On the table Ollie saw a box. Squinting at it, he read the title on the lid, it said 'wood burning kit.'

Annabella's screaming went on and on. Only his wife could shriek that piercingly, sound goes right through a man's head. How can he think with her caterwauling?

"Annabella, for crying out loud, shut the hell up!" He cranked his head so he could see more than the mattress he was lying on. "What kind of game are you playing tying me up like-" His eyes widened in confusion.

On the floor beside the bed, Annabella was on her back, it appeared that her hands were bound behind her. Naked as a beached whale, she was writhing and squirming, and peeling paint with her screams.

Covered with scrapes and bruises, her hair was matted with dirt and dead leaves, and a man was on top of her, banging her. Hard.

Seeing red, the wooziness clearing, Ollie shouted, "Hey! Annabella you slut, what's the matter with you?" His own yelling made his head hurt worse. "You're so freakin' obnoxious to be screwing him while I'm right here! I want no part of your sick fantasy."

He could now feel his entire body ached. The SUV crashing through the fence flashed in his mind. Remembering the car going over a cliff, the last thing he recalled was the Lincoln rolling over and over and-

Annabella stopped screaming, but now she was making gagging, gurgling sounds.

"What-"

The man screwing his wife turned his head and grinned at Ollie. "Oh, took you long enough to come around, Ol." His hands were wrapped around Annabella's throat, and he was squeezing the very life out of her, even as his hips pounded between her sausage fat kicking legs.

"Hey! Stop that!" Ollie could see Annabella's face turning scarlet, her eyes bulging out of her head. "Shit, man, you're killing her! Stop!" Ollie jerked at his binds, struggling to get free and get the freak off his wife.

It was too late. Annabella made no more sounds, no more movements. Her now bone-white face was frozen with

the terrified eyes bulging, her tongue lolled out the side of her open mouth.

Ollie's brain fizzled and went blank as confusion and horror took his breath. He stared blankly as the man ejaculated into his wife with a moan.

Grunting as he pulled from her, the man carefully peeled the condom off, tied it and then bustled to his feet doing his pants up.

Ollie couldn't form a sentence, he stammered, "Wha, wha, wha…"

The man's head fell back honking out a laugh. He grinned at Ollie with dark mirth. "Aren't you the lucky ones I came upon first?" His grin widened at the bound Ollie's bewilderment. "Ah, you're curious to know what's gonna happen next?"

With gloved hands, he pulled a plastic baggie from his pocket. He dropped the condom in the bag, sealed it and tucked it in his pocket.

Ollie blinked at him, his mouth opening and closing like a gasping fish.

"Well," the man said, rolling down the long sleeves of his white shirt and smoothed the cuffs. He chuckled. "I won't keep you in suspense, Ol. I'm going to do the same thing to you as I did to Annabella," he jerked his head at Ollie's dead wife lying like a trussed hog on the floor.

Frowning at her, he remarked, "I don't care much for the fat ones, but," he shrugged, "a man's gotta do what a man's gotta do for the cause, you know what I mean?"

If possible, Ollie's eyes rounded even wider at the man. His gaze lowered to the man's zipper and he gulped. "Y-you're going to- to rape me?"

The man turned to him and nodded gleefully. "Yep. And kill you." He frowned at the dead woman, his lips pulled in.

He looked back to Ollie and smiled. "Oh, don't worry, I'm not going to rape you with my dick, ew, no," he grimaced and shook his head. "I am not a homosexual. You know very well I like the ladies. No, I'll be using that," he looked pointedly towards a wall.

Painfully, Ollie angled his head to see what the man was talking about, and he blanched. His stomach revolted at the sight of the iron rod leaning against the wall. "Wha-" he choked.

His eyes twitched back to the male who had just killed his wife. He said, "Bro," swallowing trying to wet his dry throat, "we- we're practically family! Why?" His voice an anguished cry, tears poured down his cheeks wetting the sheet beneath him.

The man deliberately stepped over Annabella as if she was just a crumpled piece of trash left on the floor and ambled over to the wall and picked up the iron bar.

Tapping the bar against his palm, his eyes gleaming with tormenting delight he moved to where Ollie lay trembling.

That was when Ollie fully comprehended that he was buck-naked, his bound legs spread, with his butt pushed up in the air.

"Since you asked so nicely, Ol, I'm gonna tell you why I'm doing this." The man's eyes darkened as the torturous doom of hell stalked into them. He lifted the iron rod and placed it near Ollie's rear end.

Ollie started screaming.

Shaking his head, the man said blithely, "Now Ol, my bro, how can I tell you my story over all that yowling? You need to hush now. So," he began, pushing the bar, speaking like he was telling a fairytale, "a long, long time ago, there was this little boy," he pushed harder.

Ollie screamed so loud the windows rattled.
"Quiet now, Ol, I can't think with all that noise."

Chapter Two

"*H*e's calling for you," hanging up the landline, Griselda Borda, Talon DeMar's administrative assistant told Ketherine as the young woman snagged her coat off a hook by the door.

Watching Ketherine, Griselda crossed her arms, and said, "Nigel, his snooty majordomo said everyone else except for the younger Duncans have been there for several days and you'd best get your behind on the way tout de suite."

Slipping the coat on, Ketherine tugged her long hair out from under the collar and picked her purse up off the desk. With a stressed sigh, she replied, "I know. He commanded me to be there to help serve cocktails as the others arrived."

Griselda shook her head with a, "Tsk tsk." The fortyish woman with short curly dark hair said kindly, "Honey, I shouldn't say this against your dad, but it's terrible how he treats you. Like you're a servant, not his daughter, and certainly not as his partner. I don't understand why you put up with it? You're what, 22, 23 now?"

Ketherine buttoned the cashmere coat so dark blue it looked black, a gift from her late mother. Her smile dim, she replied, "He made sure the Santatini University cancelled my scholarships forcing me to leave the dorms as well as the school. I worked for the school and therefore I had no income or home. I had to return to Blackslade, Father's estate. My mom..."

She swallowed the lump of sadness the thought of her mother always brought. "She made sure I was her beneficiary because Father was always pulling dirty deals that hurt innocent people, and my mother hoped I could counteract them like she always had. It's a tough job, he's such a sly bully."

The older woman agreed with a sad frown. She asked, "But why do you stay with him? Why do you do his bidding? Like going to the lodge for the holiday season? He expects everyone to continue their work from there. Why don't you refuse and stay here?"

Slipping a blue and red silk scarf under the collar of the coat, Ketherine smoothed the scarf tails making sure both sides were even.

The averseness evident in her voice, she explained, "It was a codicil of the will that my stepfather insisted my mother add. He wanted to be able to keep his...thumb, make that fist, over me. He deliberately ruined my credit and made false accusations of embezzlement against me to keep me in his clutches.

"He's made it so I can't work anywhere else but at the company. Not even a burger joint will hire me. He thinks if he holds these things over my head I'll do everything he dictates."

Her faced wreathed in commiseration, Griselda said, "But, honey, why don't you fight him? Tell the law what happened, tell them what's going on?"

Ketherine's expression turned dour, plush lips curved down with devastating remembrance of when she was a child under Talon DeMar's care.

Her mother had married Talon when Ketherine was less than two, and Caralina had been grateful that Talon adopted her baby. Keti had gained two much older stepbrothers in the blended marriage.

A shiver of horror rolled through Ketherine's body. She pushed out of her brain the reason why at thirteen she had begged her mother to send her out of the country to a boarding school.

Somewhere where she would be safe from the shattering horror that made her forever shut herself off from people. Out of reach of Satan's claws.

Ever since then she'd kept herself walled up in self-protection, she learned the hard way that she couldn't trust anyone.

"Honey?" Griselda brought her out of her painful musings.

Ketherine gave the secretary a vague smile that didn't reach her eyes. "Father has Constable Carmichael on his payroll. He only says the word and I'm tossed into prison for…forever."

Before Griselda could respond, Ketherine forced a cheerful, "Have a good evening, Gris, I'll see you I'm sure at some point at the lodge."

She turned quickly and strode out the door. She didn't need pity, or false hope, she needed strength, everything she had to keep herself together to face the demons that were waiting for her.

Chapter Three

*T*he rain hammered at the partially opened window screaming for entrance. The shutters slammed wide open letting it in, instantly the counter beneath the window was soaked.

A middle-aged woman hurried over to stop the gushing water. Cursing at the wild wind battering her face, Diana Ansberry shut the window and wrestled with the old fashioned shutters, forcing them to close and lock against the raging elements.

"Damned rain," she muttered under her breath as she locked the clasps to hold the shutters closed. "Where the hell is the Help for Pete's sake? Why am I even in the kitchen?"

Savory smells leaked from the commercial oven and the unattended large pots bubbling on several burners.

Stepping from the window, she scowled down at her wet dress. "Great. I need to change. I'm going to give the housekeeper a piece of my mind...Mrs. Brady or Bradley, whatever..."

She continued muttering curses as she traipsed out of the kitchen and around the corner to the back staircase.

Last thing she needed was for someone to see her looking like a drowned rat. After all, she has a reputation to uphold. As the wife of a retired astronaut, Andrew Ansberry, Diana was a prominent presence in their city of Gladonia. People kowtowed to her, rushed to fill her every demand.

Even here in countrified Diggler's Rock, the damned woodlands where the men had insisted on building the lodge, she held top status.

At least the commercial and residential area nearby was upscale. Small like Aspen, but just as prestigious. One had to be relatively wealthy to reside, or vacation in Diggler's Rock.

Shaking her head she griped, "What the hell kind of name is Diggler anyway? It's so ugly for such a picturesque land. Some fool named the pretty village after an old miner that had struck it rich. If it'd been me it would have been called Luxuryville or Chic City something savvy like that."

She continued muttering and cursing as she marched up the stairs to change her clothes.

In the main building, the men were sprawled around the spacious grand room.

Rustic with wood beams crisscrossing the ceiling, landscape paintings hung on the stone walls. Elk antlers held court over the enormous stone fireplace.

On either side of the fireplace were arched openings trimmed in brick that led to other hallways.

The flooring of polished planks was covered with thick scattered rugs embossed in reds and blues that matched throw pillows and scattered afghans.

Decorations left over from Halloween still remained. Scarecrows and wagon wheels nestled in corners. The servants had been adding Thanksgiving decorations to the room such as wooden turkeys, and corncob and straw concoctions.

Most of the men were semi-retired, but they all had duties in the business.

As usual, they were meeting for the entire fall quarter at the lodge where no one could look over their shoulders or listen in on private conversations, they could privately compare the year's notes etc.

And they could toss paperwork that they don't want disclosed into the blazing orange fire.

Among other enterprises, McMaster Lexington Inc. builds bridges in foreign countries. A lot of their deals were made treading the thin line between legal, and not always so much.

McMaster was Talon DeMar's great uncle's first name, and Lexington was Caralina Reniere's grandfather's last name. McMaster DeMar and Marco Lexington started the company.

The widowed Talon married Caralina, thereby completely merging the families, each owning 50% of the company. He had headed the company then, and more so now since her death. His friends, all former frat buddies, had hands and toes in the business.

The large room held clusters of overstuffed furniture and cushioned benches. Knickknacks, bowels of mixed nuts and numerous candles covered coffee tables, end tables and sideboards.

Comfortably ensconced in thick leather chairs, or on the huge, semi-circle leather sofa that could easily seat ten, each man held a glass of liquor, a few toked on cigars.

Stone Cash stared at the burning end of his cigar and flicked the ashes with his fingernail near the large crystal ashtray next to his elbow. "Where's your lovely daughter,

Talon? You said she would be here." At 54 he maintained his physique and was genetically blessed with thick sandy hair. Blue eyes canted in annoyed question at Talon DeMar.

"Yeah," a burly, auburn-haired man agreed, taking a slug of the long-necked beer he held with a few very thick fingers.

Gulping loudly, he complained, "You promised she'd be present the entire time. Otherwise I wouldn't have come all this way. I've been busy readying my estate in Germany for Keti's eventual arrival as my bride." Rein van Baer, a bear of a man frowned at Talon. Although most of the men were dressed like casual Friday, Rein wore a suit and tie.

Leaning a broad shoulder against a corner of the fireplace, Talon DeMar sipped his drink and bumped a casual shoulder.

"She will be here. She does as she's told," DeMar responded. He would be described as suave with black hair slicked straight back. Winged brows over hooded dark eyes made him appear as if he was rich and powerful, cunningly dangerous, and that he looked down on the rest of the world. All of which were true.

Refilling his own drink at the bar near the front of the room, on the short stocky side, Devis McShane rubbed the end of his round red nose, pushed his glasses up the bridge and sniffed. "Where'd the boys go today?" He had a squarish head with curls on top and shaved on the sides.

His legs stuck out in front of him, Garrett Griggs' barrel chest puffed, he said with pride filling his voice, "They took out one of the sailboats. My boy Kyle's been dying to get those sails up. They're back now, in their rooms changing for dinner."

"Bit chilly doncha think to be out on the water?" An ex-astronaut, Andrew Ansberry chugged his drink then plunked the empty glass down on the table next to his floral patterned chair. His long, angular bony body looked incongruous in the big fluffy chair.

He avoided leather finding it too stiff and sticky on bare skin in the summer seasons and too cool in the winter. Shiny thinning black hair was parted low on one side to sweep over and cover the bare spots on his gaunt head. He twisted his long neck seeking a refill from a servant.

The last man present, very balding with a big round belly, Miles Burton, spoke from the plush sofa he half sat, half slumped on. "Their girls go too? I think it's too windy for them to be out on the lake."

Garrett Griggs tossed his drink down his throat and let out such a large belch the other men shot him disgusted grimaces. "My boy Kyle looks out for them. He's always safety first, you know."

"Plus he's way too chicken-livered to take any daring risks." Stone Cash ribbed his frat brother.

Dense greying brows drawn down, Griggs pushed his heavy chest out and waved his glass at Cash with pinky out, the diamond ring sparkled on his thick finger, he snapped, "He ain't a coward, Stone, he's just careful."

"So," as the men started to bicker, Rein van Baer interrupted. "The older women, your wives, I've barely seen hide nor hair of them the past two days until an hour ago. What's up with them?"

Cigar chomped out of the corner of his fleshy mouth, Devis McShane answered him with an exasperated grunt, "They've been shopping of course. This rustic crap drives them insane. They'd gone into town to shop, lunch, peruse the art galleries." He swiped at the end of his round nose, sniffed and adjusted his glasses.

The door opened abruptly, a gale of cold wind and pellets of rain burst in. Jared Duncan stepped inside.

Closing the door on the combative elements, he flung his head back and forth like he'd popped up from the lake, and ran his fingers smoothing his damp hair back. He looked to Talon DeMar. "Is there any word?"

Talon shook his head in response. "No. I've had Nigel calling every one of their friends, Annabella's relatives, their clubs, their neighbors, the police, hospitals, there's nothing. Your son, they just…"

He looked up at his friend through a lock of black hair that had fallen over one eye. Pushing it back, a shade of concern in his voice, Talon finished, "Disappeared. Vanished. There's been nothing since Ollie called as they were leaving. You've been out looking?"

Jared nodded, wiping raindrops out of his eyes. His shoulders hunched, rigid with worry. "I've gone up and down and around the whole damned mountain. I called Sheriff Dutch Kross, he's got men searching. He says there are many places where the security fence is broken on the mountain.

"He," his voice cracked, he dragged stiff fingers through his hair. "The sheriff says hikers are always finding, uh, cars that have crashed through the fence and- and plummeted, down…"

Stone Cash trod over to him and shoved a strong drink in his hand. "I'm sure they're fine, Jared. They'll turn up."

"Maybe Annabella ate Ollie," Devis McShane suggested. He ducked his head with a grin at the frowns the other males sent his way.

"Not funny," Jared growled.

19

"Vulgar and uncalled for," Talon commented, his brows down, he firmed his mouth hiding his own grin at McShane's deprecatory quip.

Garrett Griggs said, "Everyone knows Annabella would eat this lodge if she could stick a fork in it. But it doesn't explain where they would be." He let out another crass belch as if he were the pig instead of Annabella.

The door opened, the men all paused, every eye turned to it.

Chapter Four

*T*he earlier rain had turned to sleet that now softened into fat snowflakes falling gently.

Ketherine Nicoletta DeMar hesitated outside the huge double doors and took a long deep breath. It took several deep breaths to calm the shaking in her hands, quell the butterflies in her stomach.

Last place she wanted to be was Caesar Peak Lodge. Every person who had ever harmed her was inside, behind the big doors. She didn't knock, the less attention she drew the better.

She wore a professional suit and pumps. Beneath the cashmere coat Keti smoothed the skirt, pretending she wasn't wiping the perspiration from her palms on it.

Brushing a few snowflakes off her shoulders, as she turned the knob, she thought, *Perhaps I can slide in and slip quickly to my room without anyone seeing me.*

The problem was, the main doors opened to a lavish marbled foyer that spread wider to the rustically designed grand room.

Her gut sank, the butterflies took flight. They were all there, most of them anyway, the older generation of males and they were all gawking at her. A few lounged, two stood sipping their drinks.

"Glitty!" Devis McShane crowed then winced when Rein van Baer chucked him on his arm. The rest of the men snickered.

Unhinging his bulk from his chair, Rein hurried across the vast room to Keti, his loafers thumping on the colorful throw rug. "Darling!" he greeted her.

Before she could step away, he wrapped big thick arms around her slender form and yanked her in for a bear hug. He bent to kiss her, but she turned her head in time and his lips landed on her high rounded cheek.

He tried to hold her with his grizzly paws, but she maneuvered out of his grasp.

"About damned time, Keti," her stepfather's deep voice carried, full of angry rebuke. He approached the pair and nudged Rein aside. "What took you so goddamned long to get here?"

Keti winced at his cursing. "There was some paperwork that needed completion, Father."

He harrumphed his annoyance. "Griselda and your brother Roger could have covered all that. Roger isn't expected here until the end of the week." His voice lowered, an angry grate in his tone, he chastised her, "I told you to be here on Monday."

He leaned in and whispered harshly in her ear, "There will be no more stalling, no stonewalling me this time. You are here until New Years, and we have papers to sign. I will not tolerate any resistance from you. None. You understand me?"

A flashback struck her so hard she stumbled. The memory flowed as clear and sharp as if it had happened yesterday.

Almost a year ago when Talon had initially brought her back home to Blackslade and forced her to be involved in the company, he had thrust a document in front of her to sign and handed her a pen. She had balked.

The bridge McMaster Lexington planned to build would pass over a village in Sierra Leone. The bridge would bring the main road above and beyond, virtually diverting all traffic from the town.

It would only be a short time before the rural shops would wither and close, the indigenous people, too poor to move would starve. It would be devastating. She had flat out refused to sign.

All arguing, demanding and coercion Talon tried failed to change her mind. Until. He had dragged one of the servant's young son into his study where he had Keti waiting.

Keti was puzzled, what did the child have to do with business? "Father, why is Kenny-"

"He is an instrument of incentive, my dear Ketherine." Talon's mouth thinned smugly at her confused look.

Suddenly, he grasped the boy's arm and slammed it over his raised knee. The thin arm snapped instantly and the boy screamed in agony.

"Father!" Keti had cried in stunned disbelief. She moved to stop Talon as he grabbed the boy's other arm. "No! Stop!" she shouted frantically over the boy's screams.

Talon gripped the child's arm and hovered it over his knee. "You can't stop me, Keti. You sign those goddamned papers right now or I'll continue until every bone in the kid's body is dust."

Keti came to a horrified halt. "No, you can't, you can't mean-"

He smirked with angry determination. "Oh yes I can. I have already and I will continue. Now, are you going to sign or shall I…" he raised the boy's arm preparing to slam it down over his knee. The child was wailing and sobbing.

Keti held both hands out and cried, "No, stop. I- I'll sign." Tears raced down her face as she reached for the pen. Half the servants were undocumented so there would be no complaining to the authorities of the atrocities Talon committed upon them.

Talon shook her arm roughly and snarled, "You hear me, Keti?"

His roughness snapped Keti back from the horrific memory. Her eyes closed, she nodded silently. Talon's fingers dug deeply into her arm showing he meant business. She didn't doubt him.

Talon DeMar was ruthless and as cold-blooded as a rattlesnake with skin-puncturing fangs, lacking an iota of mercy. For anyone. Least of all a stepdaughter he could sell on the open market.

Rein van Baer wasn't the only millionaire to ask for her hand. But he was a close friend, an old frat buddy, so he got first dibs.

Rein would have married her as soon as she turned of age but she had hidden out at her college out of the country. And ever since Talon had brought her back home to stay, she had managed to avoid him. But, she was trapped now.

"Good." Talon released her arm. "Thanksgiving Dinner is about ready, go freshen up. Nigel will have a porter bring your bags in. The rest of the group has moved on into the drawing room with their third cocktail."

Shoving his face into hers, he snarled tersely, "You've made us wait enough already. I won't abide any more of your stalling."

His smile as ugly as his soul, he said, "Rein has been on tenterhooks waiting for you to arrive. You be nice to him, eh? You hear me? You've put him off long enough. He will be giving you a ring before the end of this retreat, and you will accept it. You got it? I think a spring wedding will be perfect. All those blossoms and shit makes it nice."

She nodded mutely, half-turning away from him.

He snatched her arm again and squeezed hard. Getting back in her face he told her, "I mean it, Keti. I won't brook any disobedience from you. Not anymore. There are plenty more of the Illegals' children running around I can use to induce your cooperation."

Releasing her, he smiled meanly, watching her rub her arm as she hurried without response to the staircase at the far end of the room.

The men that were still present and enjoying the scene, followed her fleeing figure with amused eyes.

Keti murmured rushed greetings as she strode quickly past them, her heels clicking unevenly over polished planks and plush rugs.

Their gazes turned to a self-satisfied Talon DeMar. He stood with his hands clasped behind his back, feet planted akimbo, a triumphant smile on his cold face.

Thirty minutes later, Keti had washed her face, unpacked and changed into black slacks and a yellow blouse with a frilly collar. She bought clothes that were a size too big to hide her figure. Her luxuriant mahogany hair was pinned up tight in a prim bun.

Last thing she needed was to encourage Rein, or any of the other males present. Over the past year since Talon had brought her home, she'd had to endure gropings and disgusting innuendoes along with raunchy offers to private, personal parties.

The grand room was now empty and she could hear voices coming from the dining room.

She moved quickly through the archway to the dining room and took a seat next to her brother, Tommy, ignoring Rein's frown when she didn't sit next to him in the chair he'd obviously saved for her.

Her efforts at dressing primly didn't alter the way the males' attention continually shifted back to her every few minutes. And judging by the sour looks on the females' faces, they were not oblivious to their men's wandering lustful gazes.

Heavens, she thought miserably, she's known them all since her birth. So tight with each other they were almost family. Why did they all either despise her or harbor carnal desires for the use of her body, when she should have been treated with love and dignity of a daughter or sister?

The depressing thoughts did nothing to dispel the gloom that clung to Keti's soul. She was trapped with people that wanted to assault her albeit in different manners. She tried to shrug off the wretchedness of her situation and focus her attention on the others seated at the grand table.

Several of the younger generation were involved in excited discourse over their third day sailing on Wogtail Lake.

The only males not eyeing Keti with lascivious interest were her father and her stepbrother, Tommy.

Rein got up from his chair, marched over to where Andrew Ansberry's thirty-year-old son Eddie was seated and told him to move.

Eddie opened his mouth to object, then saw the glower on the older man's face and let out a loud sigh then vacated the seat. Rein plopped down in the now empty chair that was next to Keti.

On Keti's other side, Tommy leaned over and whispered, "Hang in there, sis, it's only a couple of months and we're outta here. I hate this as much as you."

Her stepfather Talon and his frat brothers had brought their spouses, all were in their fifties. Their offspring were all 8 to 15 years older than Keti, except for Tommy, or Tomasso as he was legally named.

Her stepbrother was only 6 years Keti's senior. He tried to be a buffer between Keti and their father, and also Rein's advances, but he wasn't around that much.

Tommy worked at the company as well, but was in charge of a different area than where Keti was located and he didn't reside at the Blackslade estate with them.

Hair as light as corn silk and sky blue eyes, with his boyish looks, Tommy was as handsome as he was shy. Still, the girls flocked to him. "Hey," he growled when Devis McShane's son Michael slapped him on the side of his head.

"Where the hell were you today you little pissant?" Michael's snide voice matched an equally snide face.

They were all wealthy, and Michael was one of those that loved to flaunt it and make people bow down to him. His lip curled in a perpetual sneer. "We were all on the boat, you said you'd be there."

Tommy muttered a curse and said, "I have other friends in town you know, asshole."

"Oh yeah." Michael snickered maliciously. "Another sissy, your friend Renner Zigfried, the pussy with the pussy name. Isn't Zigfried a circus or some shit?"

"Fuck off," Tommy muttered at him smoothing the hair Michael had mussed with his slap.

"Ha," Chester Cash snorted. "That's Siegfried. Siegfried and Roy with the white tigers, remember they-"

Michael spoke over him off with a nasty snarl, "Don't you talk to me like that, Tomasso you little shit, I'll take you outside and-"

"Michael, really, you're such a bully, lay off him," Keti couldn't help breaking in. She didn't want Tommy injured. They hadn't grown up together because she'd been out of the country in school and he was so much older, but still, he was her kin even if he was a stepbrother and not really blood.

Not that Tommy couldn't handle himself, he was just as muscular as his father Talon and brother Roger.

Michael's face burst with red. His eyes squinted into harpoons at her, he threatened, "Screw you, Glitty Kitty. Miss Trailer Trash, don't make me put you in your place."

"That's enough," Talon barked from the head of the table. "I know it's tough to be civilized, but please try. All of you." He cut a piece of roast turkey, speared it with stuffing and chewed elegantly as he turned to Stone Cash who sat at his right and resumed their conversation.

Michael fumed but knew better than to disregard Talon DeMar's orders. They had all learned that painful lesson when they were toddlers. Making a revolting sound of aggravation, Michael stabbed a maple yam, shoved it in his mouth then noisily chomped.

His mother, Patricia McShane threw him a frown and shake of her head. He set his fork down and picked up his beer, guzzling most of it noisily before slamming the bottle on the table.

Keti kept her head bowed to her plate as she pushed the food around. Her appetite had soured the instant she pulled into the long curving driveway canopied by oak trees leading to the lodge. It didn't matter, no one spoke to her except for Rein van Baer and Tommy.

For the entire unbearable evening, she'd had to shove Rein's beefy palm off her thigh, avoid his hand as it brushed against her breast when he reached for something, and lean away from his thick lips as he tried to kiss her as every other course was served.

Tall, thin and angular, Nigel stood in the doorway and announced with precise diction, "Master Kyle and Miss Bonnie Boyco have returned."

Garrett Griggs' son Kyle and his girlfriend had gone into town to meet up with old friends and had returned late to dinner. A big no no.

Talon's lips pressed tightly as he glared at Garrett. Garrett flushed and scowled at his son as he entered the dining room.

Garrett's wife Jeanie frowned at the young couple then caught Talon's fierce reprimanding glower. She snatched up her wine glass and gulped down half of it. Her cheeks bloomed crimson from the alcohol. The children weren't the only ones Talon physically vented his anger on.

The tardy red-faced couple quickly sat at the table and a maid brought them plates of salad.

They could then help themselves to traditional turkey and stuffing, mashed potatoes and gravy, green bean and sweet potato casseroles, numerous other dishes along with homemade cranberry sauce. Platters of deviled eggs, honey glazed carrots, creamed corn and dinner rolls were also on the table.

Bonnie didn't look quite as abashed as her boyfriend, she glanced over at Keti and winked. The pretty Bonnie with strawberry blonde waves and big brown eyes was eight years older than Keti. But on the rare times Keti was home they had gotten along famously.

Keti grinned at her. She had been disappointed when she had arrived and her only friend, Bonnie, was not present. She hadn't had an opportunity to ask if she was coming. Thank the Lord, there she was. At least one supporter in the bunch. Of course Tommy was always on her side too.

As alcoholic beverages continued to pour, conversation flowed somewhat drunkenly around the room. Talon and Stone Cash kept their heads together talking business as usual.

Stone Cash was divorced, his only son, Chester, a blobby carrot-top was with him. The young man had his father's blue eyes, but did not inherit Stone's muscular boxer's build and hard features.

Neither did he acquire his father's cutthroat approach to business as well as to life. Chester was only two years older than Tommy so he was closer to Keti's age than the others but they had nothing in common. Chester was too shy to hit on her, and Keti avoided everyone including him.

Eddie Ansberry was making mooneyes at his fiancée Sabine while his mother Diana chastened them at the same time she was complaining to her husband Andrew about the size of their cabin. They were all pretty identical, huge and opulently designed, but still all the women felt someone got a better deal than them.

Next to them, Marc and Libbie Burton were engaged in conversation with their father Miles and their mother Alice.

Down the table, Devis McShane was arguing with his wife Patricia while his son Michael had turned his back on Keti and Tommy and was now rudely making out with his girlfriend, Audrey.

Behind Michael's back the other young men called her Tawdry Audrey. Audrey had slept with half of them and Michael hadn't a clue.

His eyes leveled at Audrey, Talon leaned close to Stone Cash. "Stone," he whispered under his breath, he bent his head so only Stone could hear him. "Devis told me his kid Michael came to him somewhat distraught. He said Audrey overheard Devis and Miles a little while back talking about the...you know."

His head down, Stone's blue eyes slanted towards the rest of the group, they were involved in their own conversations. "She knows what we did?"

Talon nodded. "Yeah. Devis is worried she might try to blackmail us. Something needs to be done."

Very quietly, Stone told him, "I'll take care of it." The two men exchanged a nod then sat back and let the chit-chat flow around them as they washed down rich food with high-priced liquor.

Jared Duncan sat swirling a glass of bourbon in his hand, his eyes glued to the entrance of the dining room. His son Ollie and daughter-in-law Annabella still had yet to show.

Jared was getting more and more worried as time passed. He absently patted his wife Rachel's hand as she struggled to hold back her own panic.

Diana Ansberry, her thin aristocratic nose in the air, plumped her stiff blonde bob and stared at Keti. She said loudly over the din of conversation, "So, Ketherine, what was so important to have kept you away this past week?

What could be more important than us?" She waved a hand indicating the rest of the room.

Miles Burton's daughter Libbie grinned nastily at Keti adding her two cents, "Yeah, you think you're better than us?" Libbie's face was smushed in like a Persian cat. The blonde had been head cheerleader in high school and she still played the snobby Prom Queen.

Approaching thirty-two, Libbie was starting to purchase body enhances along with cosmetic surgery with her daddy's bucks. Her new breasts spilled out of the low cut blouse. Baby-doll blue eyes glared with jealous spite at the much younger, fresh looking Keti before she turned and gave Diana an ass-kissing big smile.

"Um…" Keti glanced over at Bonnie who gave her an encouraging smile. "I had business to finish, ma'am," she said to Diana Ansberry. "I apologize for being so late."

Keti was much younger than Diana's son Eddie, but still Diana resented Keti calling her ma'am.

As always, Keti was cool and unfailingly polite. And it burned Diana's flat ass. "You little snot, you think your shit doesn't stink like the rest of ours-"

At the open arched doorway, Nigel interrupted her. His face was white as a sheet, his voice shook out some of his rigid bearing. "Ah, sir," he spoke, glancing at Talon. His gaze flicked to Jared Duncan then returned to Talon.

The majordomo was tall and built like a steel light-post, precisely groomed, dark-haired with silver at his temples and regal. Normally unflappable in his professionalism, at the moment he appeared to be about to jump out of his skin.

Chapter Five

*N*ot hiding his annoyance, Talon snapped, "What is so vital, Nigel that you would interrupt us at dinner?"

A deep voice broke in from the doorway. A man wearing a uniform and badge stepped around Nigel. "I'm afraid that I have bad news, DeMar," the man stated as he removed his Stetson.

Conversation halted, everyone looked at him.

Talon wiped his mouth with his napkin then set the napkin beside his plate. He rose, his chair scraped back along the carpet.

"Sheriff Kross, shall we take this in my study?" Silent question was in Talon's arched brow, he wore a displeased frown and his tone perturbed.

"Ah." Sheriff Dutch Kross glanced again at Jared then cleared his throat. "That would be fine." He nodded to the Duncans, and said quietly, "Mr. and Mrs. Duncan, would you join us?" Then he spun and stalked off, he knew the way to Talon's study.

The sheriff had been invited to several parties at the lodge over the last few years. He wasn't close to Talon as the man was old enough to be his father, but DeMar was a dangerous man and Dutch Kross was of the mindset as they say, 'keep your friends close and enemies closer.'

"Would you like something to drink, Dutch?" Talon offered as he went to push a bell by the study door to summon a maid.

Hovering just inside the room, Jared and Rachel Duncan clung to each other.

"No thanks, DeMar. Mr. and Mrs. Duncan, why don't you two sit down." The sheriff motioned to a dark blue sofa.

The austere room was done in navy blues and browns, it was clearly a masculine room. Dark-blond Dutch Kross fit right in with the room.

He was quite young for a sheriff in charge of the rural area spread far and wide around the small glitzy town, and the marina at Wogtail Lake.

It was hard to keep people employed in a basically vacation land. Summer season was for sailing and swimming, horseback riding and hiking; winter for skiing, ice skating and snow mobiles. Springtime brought the annual pink dogwood tree festival.

The forest was teeming with deer, bear, elk, bobcat and turkey for fall hunting. The wide lake at the center of the county went on for miles, wreathed by cabins as well as mansions and resorts tucked into endless whorls of mottled forest.

Well above average height, the strapping sheriff could have been created right out of the rugged rock of the mountains. Chiseled strong features and dark blue eyes that were hard and shrewd toughened up the blond exterior.

He wore the beige and brown sheriff's uniform shirt but with jeans. A brown leather jacket hugged his broad shoulders, and he wore sturdy hiking boots as most people did in the organically tough environment.

Jared Duncan pulled his wife to the sofa, he sat and tugged her down beside him. "Sheriff, what's going on? Don't keep us in suspense, it's Ollie, isn't it?"

Rachel gasped at his words. She clasped his hand in a death grip, her other hand covered her mouth. Rachel doted on her youngest son.

She made no secret of her dislike for her daughter-in-law. Annabella was loud, boorish and ate anything she could wrap her blubbery mouth around. She never hesitated to take the last cookie or last piece of pie. Or the last four pieces of cake.

This was the toughest part of Dutch's job. His bearing and tone deeply somber, he said, "Well, I'm sorry to have to inform you that your son-" Rachel's cry out broke in- "ah, Ollie, and his wife Annabella were found a short time ago."

Talon moved to stand beside Dutch who stood tall and confident. He said to the sheriff, "They are...?"

"Deceased," Dutch said flatly. He clutched his Stetson in both hands in front of him.

A shriek caught in Rachel's throat as she doubled over.

His arm around his wife, Jared's face stricken white, his voice scraped out, "You- are you sure, Sheriff? A mis-mistake, it must be a- a-" His eyes pleaded with Dutch to deny what he'd said.

A sharp nod, Dutch replied, "No. I'm sorry. There's no doubt. Their ID's were in the car. Of course we'll need you, um, one of you to come down to the, ah, morgue for a positive identification."

Rachel's agonizing sobs scored the air in the room suddenly weighing heavy with sorrow.

Talon took control of the situation. "I'll have Andre bring the car around to take you." He raised his brows at Dutch. "Was it, um, a car crash?"

"Ah, no. Well, partly." The sheriff shook his head. He murmured, "They were...murdered."

A horrified squeak burst from Rachel, a wounded cry lurched from Jared. Their faces mutual masks of disbelief, shock, confusion, and despair.

Dutch and Talon walked the grieving couple to the waiting limo.

Once they were bundled inside and the car drove off, Talon turned to Dutch. "What the hell happened to them?"

Several yards behind the two big men, people gathered in the open doorway, hair blowing in the brisk wind, clothes whipping. The snow had disappeared but the chill remained. They didn't know what was going on, they were waiting for Talon to fill them in.

Black night glared quiet and cold around them. Placing his hat on his head, his voice low so their audience couldn't hear, Dutch said, "It'll be in the papers tomorrow so I might as well prepare you, so you can gently tell the others." He took a breath, let it out slow.

"It appears Ollie and Annabella Duncan had crashed through one of the guard fences and went off a cliff. A big tree stopped their momentum."

Talon nodded grimly as he pictured what happened. "How dreadful, to die like that in a car accident. But," he looked puzzled. "You said, murder?"

"It doesn't appear to have been an accident, DeMar. There were skid marks and fragments of metal strewn on the road. Ah," Dutch took a breath, "the crash was nothing compared to what else we think happened to the Duncans."

His forehead furrowed in confusion, Talon asked, "What happened to them?"

Dutch lifted his Stetson and dragged his hand through his dark blond hair. Taking another deep breath, he set the hat back down. "Ah, they weren't killed in the crash." His lips pulled in as he recalled the scene.

Dutch had waited for the medical examiner to complete his preliminaries before he had come to fetch the senior Duncans.

"What killed them, then?" Talon prompted him to spill the gruesome details.

With Talon's resources, Dutch knew every detail would be blared out in the media by tomorrow so there was no point in trying to keep the murders on the down low. "Yeah, well, the doc thinks they were both sexually assaulted before likely being strangled."

Shock widened Talon's eyes, his mouth dropped open. "Rape? Ollie? That's absurd."

"I agree. It's absurd, cruel and sick. But, the two of them had been brutally violated. Ollie's, ah, backside was drenched in blood. We could see gouges from, whatever was used to sodomize him. And, ah, Ollie's penis had been...butchered."

He paused at the stricken look on Talon's face, waited until the man swallowed down his nausea.

Then Dutch went on, "Purple bruising ringed their necks, and petechial in their eyes indicated death by asphyxiation. I'm sure the ME will find their hyoid bones were broken. Doc said Annabella was attacked from the front, and Ollie strangled from behind."

Talon's mouth snapped shut, he narrowed his eyes. His voice rough with shock and horror, he demanded, "Who the hell would kill Ollie Duncan? He's one of the mildest young men I know. He works hard, doesn't drink, smoke or do drugs. There's no way he'd be involved in- in kinky shit."

Dutch's lips pursed, he pulled at them with his fingers. "It doesn't look like sex play, DeMar. It looks like they were taken someplace else after the car crash where they were violently savaged then killed, and returned to their destroyed car where they were then posed."

A little green around the gills, Talon grimaced. "Posed?"

"Yeah. It was sick shit, DeMar. Both were naked. Ollie was spread eagle on his stomach over what was left of the car, and Annabella was on the ground slumped against the side of it. Her beefy legs had purposefully been obscenely pushed wide apart."

He kept the other bit of description to himself, only he and the ME knew about it. They didn't want it blasted in the media. There had been marks carved, or branded in Ollie's chest. Forensics would study them to see if they had any meaning.

"You recognize this?" The sheriff held his palm out. In it lay a gold pin with a curlicued K inside a heart-shaped circle, it was contained in a plastic baggie.

Talon's chin jerked up, his eyes flit to Keti standing with the watching and waiting group. "Ah…"

"It's hers," Dutch said for him. "Last July she was here for the fireworks. I remember it." His gaze cut over to Keti and back to Talon. "She didn't join in the festivities but she was briefly present. No one could miss that gal."

"Yeah," Talon admitted, "her mother gave it to her for one of her birthdays. I had objected, thing is real gold, you know. I thought the girl was too young for expensive jewelry."

"Okay. Call her over here."

Talon bristled at being ordered around, but he waved and called out, "Ketherine, come here."

There was no missing the unhappy look on her face at being beckoned. Keti's idea of a good time is hiding in her room studying the science she favored. She didn't hurry, but she didn't move too slowly either to incur Talon's impatient wrath.

When she reached the two men, Dutch held his palm out. "Is this yours, Miss DeMar?"

Her eyes widened in delight. She reached a hand out to take it exclaiming, "Yes, that's mine! Where did you find it? I been looking everywhere for it."

Dutch closed his hand preventing her from taking it. "It was found at a crime scene, Ketherine. I need you to verify your whereabouts for the past two days?"

"Hey, Sheriff," Talon broke in. "What the hell?"

His lids low over sharp blue eyes, Dutch said, "It was found in the back seat of Ollie Duncan's car. You ever been in his car, Miss DeMar?"

Her mouth dropped open. "What? I- no. Never. What is going on?" Her confused eyes bounced back and forth between the two men.

Talon snapped, "Okay, that's enough, Kross. Any more questions and Keti will have a lawyer present."

"All right, DeMar. Better call him, we'll be questioning everyone here."

Stone Cash strode up and joined them. "Is there trouble, Talon?" Taking measure of the young sheriff, Stone's mouth pressed in scorn as if Dutch didn't measure up to his staunch idea of a sheriff, even one of a small rural town.

"Later," Talon muttered.

"So." Dutch gave a small cough and shifted his stance. "For now, no one leaves the lodge. I'll have a couple of deputies come by tomorrow, early, to question everyone."

He glanced at his watch. "I have to get going. I want to meet with Jared and Rachel Duncan before they leave the morgue. I'll be in touch." He tapped two fingers on the brim of his hat and made for his cruiser.

As he opened the car door, he heard Ketherine gasp, "The morgue?"

Chapter Six

The next morning everyone was atwitter with the news. They theorized a dozen causes of the Duncans' demise. Robbery, road rage, kinky sex like Talon had considered.

"Hey," Diana Ansberry suggested, "maybe Ollie, or- or Annabella had a secret gambling addiction and owed bad guys big bucks."

Patricia McShane indelicately snorted. "More like Annabella had a drug addiction and owed her dealer." As much as her husband Devis was short and stocky, Patricia was stick thin with short, straight brown hair and eyes, and she was an inch taller than Devis. They both wore round framed glasses.

"What would she be addicted to? Certainly not cocaine, not a flabby as she was," Devis joked.

"No," Diana smiled slyly. "I would go for marijuana. Potheads eat obsessively. That would fit Annabella."

"Come on you guys, that's not nice," Alice Burton gently rebuked the crowd. "Annabella had a problem, she couldn't help it."

"Yeah," Miles Burton piped in, "her problem was she never met a food she didn't like, or couldn't not eat a ton of it." A few of the group snickered along with the hypocrite who stretched his own clothes with his inability to put his own fork down. He rubbed his bald head pleased that people laughed at his joke. His tubby belly bounced against the rim of the table with his guffaws.

Keti darted past the door to the grand room and headed for a side exit so she didn't have to pass through and sit with the rest of the gang while they waited for the police and made nasty jokes about poor Annabella. Talk about speaking ill of the dead.

Hurrying down a carpeted hall, her head down, she ran straight into Rein van Baer, literally. She would have bounced backwards and fallen if he hadn't reached out and grabbed her arms.

Catching a hold of her, he wrapped large fingers around her slender arms, and didn't let go when she steadied.

"Hey there, darling, I've been looking all over for you," he crooned, while pulling her closer to him even as she struggled to be rid of his grasp. "If I didn't know better I'd think you were avoiding me."

He let go of one of her arms to grip her chin. His grip was not gentle, neither was the way he lifted her jaw so he could look her in the eye.

"And, I know you wouldn't think of avoiding me. Talon promised me that you were finally on with the program. He said you had agreed to marry me and we can start planning the wedding. Isn't that right, my little Keti flower?"

When she didn't answer, he gave her chin a sharp jerk. Lowering his face to get in hers, he growled, "You'd better answer me now, little miss, and in the affirmative or we're going straight to see your father." His thick auburn hair waved over a large, square-jawed head.

Angry cobalt blue eyes narrowed at her. He held her close enough the lower half of his thick chest pushed against her breasts. He had over a hundred pounds and stood at least a foot over her.

Rein was the same age as Talon. He disgusted Keti, his presence prickled goose-bumps of gross dread up her arms. Even as a child, before she left home at thirteen, the man had taken every opportunity to fondle her, touch her.

She'd rather jump off the roof than marry him. But, she sighed with hopeless resignation, she would actually have to die to get away without marrying him.

Talon would run right out and grab another innocent child and torture him or her until Keti gave in. She had no choice. She tried to break his grip on her jaw, but Rein's strong fingers only tightened, if he squeezed any harder she'd have bruises.

"Keti," he warned.

She raised her huge green eyes up at him and instantly lowered them. The flagrant lust she saw in his heated gaze made her stomach revolt. But, again, she had no choice.

"Okay, Mr. van Baer," she felt his fingers stiffen. He hated when she called him by his surname, it kept him level with her father, and it made him feel old. Yet that didn't stop him from pursuing her.

His brows daggered down. "Keti, I told you about that. I can't hit you until we're wedded but I'll have your daddy take his belt to that fine ass real hard if you keep it up. Speaking of up," a lurid grin creased his heavy face.

He rubbed his erection against her then leaned in and licked the side of her face. "I can show you hard, right now. How about we take this conversation to my room?" His fingers still wound around her arm, he started dragging her down the hall.

"Keti!" Michael McShane's girlfriend Audrey called out from the top of the hall.

Rein and Keti stopped and turned to look at her.

Audrey said, "The police are asking for you."

Saved by the bell, Keti sighed gratefully. She extricated her arm from Rein's indomitable grasp and started towards Audrey. Rein's angry curses followed her down the hall.

Audrey grinned at him when Keti reached her.

Rein glared darkly at Keti's back as she hurried away from him.

Audrey said, "You go on, Keti, I'll entertain Mr. van Baer for you," and she strolled to the frustrated man.

When Audrey reached him, she brazenly stretched her hand out and gripped the hard-on Keti had caused. She whispered, "Let me help you with your little, I mean, big problem my red-headed grizzly."

Rein still frowned at Keti getting away from him, yet again, but, he wasn't one to look a gift horse in the mouth. "Yeah, sure, the cops done with you? We can hit my room," he tacked on lewdly, "Tawdry Audrey."

She laughed, and he curled his arm around her waist as they walked to the staircase. By the time they reached the steps his hand was under her blouse and squeezing her breast.

Keti was led by a policewoman to the den where another officer waited. He sat on the sofa holding a notebook, and a recorder set on the coffee table in front of him.

Leaning his hip against a wall, Sheriff Dutch Kross looked up at her entrance. A smile fought his grim mouth, he battled it down. "Myron, I'll take this one," he said, and gestured for Keti to sit on a chair at a small round table. Snapping up the recorder, he took a seat opposite her.

Twenty minutes later, after answering questions about herself, her family, job, where she was the last couple of days and why she had initially arrived days after everyone else, she was free to go.

Although he remained purely professional, his gaze cool, voice calm and steady, Keti felt the sheriff's distinct interest. His dark blue eyes never left her during the entire questioning. His gaze flowed from her eyes to her lips to her breasts to her lips to her eyes.

Sheriff Kross was a manly man, roughly attractive, but Keti didn't need any more problems. When he concluded the interview she nodded at his thanks, left the room and scurried back down the hallway she'd started on before Rein had accosted her.

"Keti!" Kyle Grigg's girlfriend, Bonnie Boyco called out just as Keti reached the hall.

When Bonnie reached Keti her smile was big and glorious and commiserating. "How's it going, girl? I know how much you hate this, being here."

Keti returned her friendly smile. "It's okay. Not so much for Ollie and Annabella, though." Her smile fell.

Bonnie was much older than Keti as were all the prodigy of the frat men, but she and Keti had always gotten on well the few times Keti was home for holidays.

"I know, can you believe it? The word is that they were both naked and viciously assaulted." A thin shiver rolled across Bonnie's shoulders. She pushed wavy strawberry blonde hair off her shoulders. "The news said it was…sordid, and grisly. How awful. I'm a little afraid to be alone, you know?"

Keti nodded. "I know. Let's hope they catch whoever did it quickly. The whole attack sounds so horrible, so unbelievable, how they must have suffered."

"Yeah, if they'd go after Ollie and Annabella, none of us are safe, right?"

"At least you have Kyle to protect you. How are things between you two? Are we hearing wedding bells soon?"

Bonnie giggled, her shoulders rose then lowered coyly. "Maybe. He's been pretty lovey dovey this trip. Maybe he has the ring burning a hole in his pocket right now."

"Let's hope." Keti crossed her fingers and they laughed together. Keti's future looked bleak but she could be happy that her friend found true love and will live happily ever after. "Where is the lucky groom?"

Bonnie giggled again. "He was getting dressed. We're going to a vineyard for a wine tour. He promised he'd buy a case of whatever I like. Hey, you want to come with us? They give a bunch of different wine tasting and the landscape is lovely, all rolling green hills and plump purple berries ready to be picked."

Keti said, "That's nice of you to ask, but," she looked to the door that would lead to the corridor to the grand room. "I think Kyle probably wants this to be a romantic rendezvous for the two of you. I don't want to be a third wheel."

"Oh you know you wouldn't be, Kyle would love to tote you around too."

"It's okay. I'm going to go out and hit the hills on horseback. Oh, there's Kyle now. You guys have fun." She gave Bonnie a quick hug and flapped a friendly wave at Kyle.

"All right. But it's you and me later tonight for drinks. We can stow away in the library. No one ever goes in there. Except for you of course, little bookworm." Bonnie's nose wrinkled as she teased her friend.

"It's a date." Keti grinned at her and waved again at Kyle who was making his way down the hall towards them, then she took off in the opposite direction.

After escaping out the side door, Keti strode quickly to the stables.

Foreman over the stable hands, Ben Dandashi was mucking the hay. Since the rain had stopped and no snow flurries recently, the mud had hardened and the grass yellowed.

Ben set his rake aside when she said hello. A wide grin split his ruddy face. Ben was pushing his late sixties. Long and lean, he wore overalls and wiped a red bandana across the sweat gathered on his weathered forehead.

"Hey Miss Keti, how you doin'? There's a lot of activity goin' on at the big house, eh?" He looked over at the lodge then back to her. All staff had also been interviewed by the police.

"Yeah, busy. That's why I'm here. I need to escape the…activity. Can you saddle Sassy for me?"

"Sure nuff, Miss Keti, anything for you." He stuffed the bandana in his pocket and traipsed deeper in the stable to retrieve the mare. Loose straw crunched and cracked under his scuffing old boots as he made his way to the stalls.

Because Talon allows other business associates and their families to use the lodge, as well as he conducts his own occasional business deals there, and his friends and family vacation all year round in Diggler's Rock, everything remains open. A skeleton staff stays on when the lodge is empty.

As soon as Ben brought Sassy, Keti mounted her. The second Keti gave Sassy a slight kick, the horse took off, galloping across the pasture. The mare was just as happy as Keti to be out running in the brisk air and roaming the open meadows.

Chapter Seven

*K*eti spent the next three days on horseback. She knew the land well enough she could take a picnic lunch and find plenty of secluded places that if any of the others came looking for her they would have a hard time finding her.

She made sure she came into dinner at the last split second, ducked in and out of hallways to avoid people, mostly Rein, and her father, and, don't forget Stone Cash.

He acted like he was discreetly wandering the corridors, but his path crossed in front of her closed and locked bedroom door frequently. She recognized the strutting thump of his dress snakeskin boots on the carpet. It was just a thin runner in the hall over planked flooring.

Keti knew her luck wouldn't hold. It was too soon before her father's hard rapid knock banged on her door suddenly and so loud she about had a heart attack.

"Keti, open the goddamned door, it's time we talk." He waited.

She held her breath.

He barked, "You know I can take this door down, so you open up or I'll whip your ass with my belt when I break the door in. You have three seconds."

Letting out her breath, Keti set her laptop on the desk and plodded across the colorfully braided rug to the door.

Sucking in another bracing breath, she opened the door.

Talon's foot was raised, his face blared angry red, he appeared to be preparing to kick her door in.

"Father," she said quietly.

Fuming, Talon pushed past her and marched inside.

Keti left the door wide open, none of the males in the lodge and cabins could be trusted.

Talon stomped across the floor and pointed a rigid finger at the desk chair, "Sit," he commanded.

Keti knew from experience Talon had no reservations about striking her. He'd never hesitated before to use his fists to illustrate his ire. So she eased by him and sat on the chair he indicated.

Talon moved to stand in front of her. He crossed his muscular arms and spread his legs in an unrelenting aggressive stance. "Now," he started, "you've had your fun. It's time to get down to business. You did not sign the papers for the location of the Gangspoort Bridge, and you conveniently left them at the office."

Her silence damned her. It didn't matter, he would ignore any protests, denials, arguments she raised.

Glaring hard, he informed her, "Well, I had Griselda mail them to me, they're on the way. We're too far out for FedEx so we have to wait for the snail mail. Which just makes me angrier, Keti."

His solid jaw grit, eyes mean and narrowed, he threatened, "You don't want to push me, girl."

He moved closer. Lowering his head, he set his hands on his hips and said, "No more fooling around. You will sign the papers. Giovanni Rana is planning on coming here by the end of the week."

He paused and took a breath. He stood directly in front of her ensuring she wasn't leaving without his permission. "They call him Johnnie Frog as frog is rana in Spanish. But don't take his name lightly or as a joke."

"I've heard of him, Father," Keti murmured quietly, staring off to the side. Talon had done some shady business with the man on occasion, and word was, Rana was a dangerous man to cross. She had heard people that got in his way tended to disappear.

"Yeah, so, anyway, Johnny Frog does not want you to sign the papers for my bridge. He wants it built in another location. He's coming by to convince me to give up my site."

"Why does he want to build his bridge away from yours? Why can't you both just build one bridge together?"

Talon rubbed the back of his neck and looked away. "Not that it's any of your business, but, he has money tied into the highway that is planned to be built near his location, and there are developers with big money intending to build around that location.

"He also owns some of the land where the development is being blueprinted. On the other hand, our company wants to build across Elephant Bay where we can do the developing ourselves, which means bigger bucks for us."

"So, why don't you both build your bridges?" Keti wasn't happy with any of it. Like other times, both bridges would take tons of business from the natives leading to destruction of their habitats and villages. She wanted no part of either bridge.

She had requested for Talon to build where it would benefit the natives the most, but Talon had told her to keep her opinions and ideas to herself. They were there to make money, not help humankind. The indigenous people can fend for themselves.

Talon's head bent back as he rolled his eyes. "Because, Miss Interference, the government in that region will only allow permits to build one bridge. Two bridges would cause havoc on the land, making it unstable. So, as I was saying, you need to sign the papers before Johnny Frog arrives."

His lips pulled in a grim grimace, he continued with sarcasm, "Because honey, the man will kill to get his way. That would be kill you, not me. He needs me alive for other deals we have going on together. If he can prevent you from signing off on the paperwork then I get stalled and he builds his bridge."

"Huh, I would think that's what you would want. Mr. Rana kills me and you can inherit the entire company and do as you please without my hindrance."

"Yeah well…" Talon paced a few steps rubbing his neck. He stopped and looked down at her under calculating lids. "One would think that would make my life simpler," he grimaced and his lips bunched.

"Except then every relative known and unknown would flock here like locusts and try to get their piece of the pie. It would be years of chaos as the lawyers bashed out who gets what and how much. Then instead of fighting one little controllable girl," he sneered at her, "I'd have dozens of people with shares to battle, and the attorneys would sit and rake in the dough.

"Plus, this would all get tied up in the court for ad infinitum and we would be prevented from doing any business at all while it got settled. After lawyer fees we'd be lucky if we still owned our shirts."

"Maybe those people would care about the natives you devastate and be better able to fight you than me." She sounded hopeful, there had to be relatives that cared more about people than money.

His barked laugh made her jump. Hands on his hips he shook his head at his stepdaughter's ingenuous perception of the world. "Don't be ridiculous, sweetheart, they would be just as greedy and bloodthirsty and merciless as me and Rana."

He jutted his chin at her. "You think I'm bad, they don't get any more bloodthirsty than Johnnie Frog, and," his smile curved vindictively, "he's coming for you."

Keti was appalled at the way these men played with people's lives like they were just tiny ants they could crush at will with no remorse. They were all about the money. And she was in the middle of a tug-o-war.

"Therefore, sweetheart," he spoke through his teeth, "it would behoove you to sign with me as soon as the paperwork arrives. You can either save your life and sign with me before he gets here and it'll be too late then for him to do anything about it, or lose your life and save a bunch of worthless migrants' livelihood. Besides all that, it's time, I've told you, you need to get with our lawyers and make out that goddamned will. You'll designate your brothers your beneficiaries."

Stepbrothers. Then Talon would have 100% control of the company. He would love for her to create that will then have her disposed of. Keti lowered her head, she couldn't bear to look at the man who had helped raise her.

Well, he gave her his name but that was because he needed to appease her mother. Caralina had inherited half the business from her grandfather, Lexington Raneire, and Talon had received his half from his great-uncle, McMaster DeMar.

Talon had wooed Caralina so fast the woman never suspected he married her to get hold of her half of the company. He never dreamed he'd have to fight his wife on many of the deals he brokered. She was as soft-hearted as her daughter. Such a nuisance.

At least he obtained a mother for his sons. If he thought Keti would be easier to deal with than his wife, Talon had quickly learned differently, and it pissed him off royally.

Talon suddenly slapped Keti across the face.

Her head whipped to the side as she cried out. She put her hand on her cheek to cover the burn.

"That was to get your attention, you were drifting off. I swear, Keti, you are so much more trouble than you're worth."

Ignoring her shock at the slap, he said, "Speaking of worth, Rein tells me, well he whines and complains that you have been avoiding him. We talked about that, remember?" He looked about to hit her again, she quickly nodded, tears of pain welled in her eyes.

Tears were just simple salt water to Talon, they didn't faze him. "Yeah, so, like I said before, you let the man propose and accept his ring. I don't want to have another discussion about it. That slap will be like the pelt of a butterfly wing compared to what I'll do if I have to go over this with you one more time.

"And, any more stalling on the paperwork for the bridge and I'll have Nigel pluck up a kid from home and bring him here for incentive. Am I clear?"

Hands on his hips, he dug his fingers in hard as if to keep from striking her again. With the cops around he didn't dare leave marks on her. He scowled down at the top of her lowered head.

Her palm against her burning cheek, Keti nodded numbly. She was trapped, there was no way out for her, or for the poor people of Gangspoort. Whether she signed with Talon or Rana, either bridge would bypass the villages.

Talon waited, she said nothing, didn't look up at him. He huffed, "Fine then. We're done here." Without another word he stomped out slamming the door behind him.

Chapter Eight

A few days later, Talon sent a servant into town to retrieve the mail. He was expecting the bridge paperwork.

The police had come up with nothing in their investigation of Ollie and Annabella's murders. The town was small and homicides weren't common, the police had little experience in investigating them. Dutch stopped by twice to check in, but he had nothing to tell them.

"Hey Keti," Devis McShane hailed her when he saw her near the grand room.

"Hi Mr. McShane," she smiled her greeting. She kept walking, intent on sneaking out to the stables when he stopped her.

"Keti, honey." McShane resembled the no-neck Dilbert cartoon with the curls on top of his head and the tiny eyes behind the round glasses. He stood up and ambled over to her. He was short and stocky yet still had several inches on her.

Peering with worry at her through the glasses, he asked, "Listen, have you seen Michael and Audrey around? They never came home last night. I figured they were out partying with townie friends and maybe crashed with one of them, but, hell, it's almost two in the afternoon and no one has heard from them. Neither of them answers their cells, calls go straight to voice mail."

The last time Keti had seen Audrey was when she was skipping down the hall with Rein on the way to his bedroom.

She hadn't seen Michael in almost a week. The young men were always off hiking or hunting, they went alone or in groups and came and went. They didn't all show up at every dinner, they often just grabbed supplies and took off.

Some of the couples went into town for dinner or a show, hit the bowling lanes or played billiards. Heck, Keti hadn't even seen her own brother Tommy since that first dinner. Her other stepbrother Roger had yet to put in an appearance.

"No, I'm sorry, Mr. McShane, I haven't seen either of them." She didn't think it would help matters to tell Audrey's boyfriend's father that she'd seen Audrey go off to have sex with Keti's soon to be fiancé.

His face fell with concern. "Oh, okay. Keep an eye out though will you? Let me know if you hear from them?" The side of his mouth rose in a worried smile. He gave a quick swipe at his round red nose and twitched his glasses up with an anxious snuffle.

"Sure, of course, Mr. McShane. I'm sure they're just fine." Keti zipped out the door before anyone else could grab her.

****

"Damn Mikey, you fucker, you need to lay off the carbs, man, you weigh a ton," he grunted as he hauled an unconscious Michael McShane into the cabin. "Hell, your brakes worked a lot longer than I expected before they failed from the slash I made. The crash wasn't enough to knock

56

you two out, I had to Taser you. But it was still fun," he chuckled.

"Tawdry Audrey dropped like a zapped bag of shit. She was no fun. But, you were hilarious, Mikey, you shook and gagged and hummed, and your eyes were like bulging golf balls before you hit the ground. I'd like to do it again just for shits and giggles."

He dragged Michael across the wooden floor by his feet, laughing when his head bumped into a chair leg. He smiled in approval when he neared the bed.

Audrey lay where he'd left her. She was naked and hogtied. She was a bit more athletic than Annabella so he had extra ropes around her ankles that in a few moments he'll tie down to keep her legs apart and from kicking him during the rape.

She'd likely put up quite a fight when he got to strangling her. He grinned, that would actually be more fun than strangling that lump of fat flesh that had just laid there while he did his deeds. "Boring," he sniffed, thinking about Annabella.

He said to Audrey, "Fat bitch barely squirmed." His eyes lit up. "She did scream a lot though, that was good. But it was Ollie who was the most entertaining. Let's see if ol' Mikey here can beat Ollie's drama."

Audrey's eyes were bugged-out wide and terrified. He'd gagged her just in case some hikers happened by. They were in a remote area so the chances of that were slim, but still, one did have to be careful when engaged in murder.

He'd done Ollie in the nighttime, right now it was broad daylight and a better chance of someone being near enough to hear her scream.

Besides, he really just didn't want to hear her run her mouth. She cursed him and called him every filthy name in the book instead of giving him the more fun screams he enjoyed. Girl was a real ball buster. But he'd have the last laugh.

He had covered the cabin with as much leaf and branch camouflage as he could, and made sure prickly briar bushes were scattered all around the area to deter anyone from getting too close.

When he neared her, Audrey squirmed across the floor. She didn't get far hogtied the way she was. It was amusing watching her try though.

"You know, Aud, those fake tits look much more interesting bobbing and jiggling while you struggle for your life than they did while we did the nasty."

Looking down at her with indifference, he said, "I hope the rape is more exciting than when we fucked the other day. Forced sex should be more pleasurable, for me anyway," he gazed thoughtfully down at her.

His sigh irritated and heavy, he yawned. "It's hard to make any impact on assaulting a woman who just gives it away for free to any guy with a dick. I think the only one you steered clear of is doughboy Chester Cash. Don't blame ya there. Boy is creepy."

He smirked as Audrey continued her attempts to squirm away from him.

"Anyway," he said, "it has to be done. The rape is part of the process. Maybe tied up the way you are will make it more interesting. At least I'll get off when I slaughter you. It'll be good for you though, sort of," he snickered.

"I mean, asphyxiated orgasm. Being choked while you come, it's supposed to be the biggest high. I'll never know, but you will."

He gave her a wink then turned away, his lip curled in detestation. Her muffled shrieks continued from the floor while she jerked and flopped like a fish out of water.

He stepped over Audrey, already bored with her, and deliberately dragged Michael's inert body right over her thrashing body then he wrestled him onto the bed, chuckling at the muffled moans and squeals from Audrey getting rolled and stepped on.

Michael was still out, he had given him a double dose of the Taser. Michael was strong enough to put up a good fight, therefore he'd had to make sure he was completely out and for a while.

After stripping him, the man placed two pillows in the center of the mattress and rolled Michael over making sure the pillows were under his hips.

Humming while binding his victim's wrists and ankles, splaying him like a starfish on his belly, he grinned at the swishing sound of Audrey trying to wriggle her naked ass across the wood planked floor to the door. Hog-tied, she could only squirm on her side.

"Whatcha gonna do, Aud, turn the knob with your teeth and make your getaway rolling like a log through the woods?" He grinned with devilish merriment when he heard her stop struggling. Her sobs were muffled from the gag.

When he was done restraining Michael, he stood back to admire his handiwork. Satisfied, he trod to where Audrey had slithered to near the door.

"Tsk tsk, hon, bad girl. That's not where I want you for Mikey's optimum viewing pleasure. C'mere."

He grasped the rope that bound her wrists to her ankles behind her back and dragged her to a few feet to the bed. The way he pulled her made her body bump and flop over onto her front, her bare skin and face scraped on the wood floor.

"There, that's better. You don't want ol' Mikey there to miss any of the action do ya?"

He lowered and sat beside her on the floor. Her muffled curses ceased now that she fully took in the dire situation, and she started crying.

He grinned broadly at Audrey's hysterical huffing and sobbing, her eyes pleading with him to let her go.

"Alrighty, now we just sit here and relax and wait for Mikey boy to wake up." He gazed down at Audrey, his lips pursed. "Unless you want to start a little action while we're waiting?"

The fright in her wide eyes made him smile.

"Yeah, okay, if that's what you want, Aud, let's get this party started." He reached for her, relishing her screams against the rag he'd stuffed in her mouth.

****

Nigel called Talon to the front of the lodge on his phone. It was the first time Talon had ever heard any sort of cadence in the man's voice. And right now sheer distress came hurtling out of the austere butler.

Talon jogged down the long staircase and made his way to the grand room. He faltered when he saw Dutch Kross standing there with a grim expression.

"Shit, Kross, what is it now?" Talon's own concern matched Nigel's as he approached the sheriff.

Dutch tugged his Stetson off his head, dark blond hair tufted under it, he combed his fingers through the locks. Holding the hat in one hand against his thigh, he said quietly, "We found Michael McShane and Audrey Danvers." The tone of his voice implied they weren't okay.

People started coming out of the hall that led to the dining room. They gathered without speaking seeing the tense look on Dutch's face.

Dutch lowered his voice and said, "Someone needs to get Devis McShane, better grab Patricia too."

"Aw fuck," Talon muttered, and said to Nigel without looking at him, "get the McShanes."

In minutes Devis McShane's howls and Patricia's inconsolable wails reverberated around the stone walls of the grand room.

Chapter Nine

*T*alon and Stone Cash met with Dutch in Talon's office.

Dutch sat on a leather sofa. He clasped his hat with both hands and leaned forward with his wrists set on his thighs and his back hunched.

He said, "It's too much for Diggler's Rock to handle. The police force is too small and we don't have the experience or the means to investigate these murders. I need to call in the State Police, and probably the FBI."

Talon had been sitting in his office chair, he stood up with a terse, "No."

Dutch's brows arched. Stone didn't move an eyelash.

"No?" Dutch repeated. "What do you mean, no? I can't ignore the homicides for fuck's sake, man. We just aren't equipped to handle the magnitude of the investigation. Even the DNA has to be sent out. Getting into bank records and phone dumps, and surveillance cameras, hell DeMar," he got to his feet.

"There's too much open land, businesses and residents spread far and wide. We just don't have the manpower to canvass or the forensics to capture the info we need as quickly as we need it."

Talon moved to stand a few feet from the sheriff. "Okay, calm down, Kross. I hear you, but, there's a..." he paused unsure of how much to say.

Dutch Kross was known as a tough sheriff that brooked no misbehavior from his deputies. He made them work hard and honest. Anti-corruption was his middle name. The man had integrity up his ass.

Brows beetling, Kross snapped, "A what? What could be more important than stopping a killer? We have four homicides, man."

Holding his palm out, Talon, said, "Yes, yes, I know. This town, these people," he took a breath and started again. "There are a lot of people here that have a lot of...secrets. Heavy duty secrets that could ruin a lot of innocent lives if they are exposed."

Dutch exploded, "What do I give a shit about a bunch of lowlife cover-ups?"

"All right, keep your shirt on, Sheriff." Talon palmed both hands through his slicked black hair although it was always as neat as a pin. "You want a bunch of State cops and FBI crawling all over your territory? Taking the credit, overriding you, bulldozing you and your deputies?"

"I don't give a crap about that, DeMar, I only care about protecting the citizens of Diggler's Rock."

Talon crossed his arms. He lowered his head then raised it to gaze intently at the sheriff. "Okay. Listen, the victims are from our inclusive group here. Someone is targeting us. It's too coincidental that the victims are the Duncans' and McShanes' sons and their women. There's a message being sent or something. I think we have a better, quicker chance of uncovering the perpetrator by working from the inside."

Dutch blinked. "What the hell does that mean?"

"I know you worked some sort of Special Ops, you were a Ranger or whatever. You worked with others like you. Can't you bring in someone that you know is capable of discreetly investigating this scene?" Talon eyed Dutch, gaging how much he could control him. For now.

At Dutch's wrinkled brow considering Talon's words, Talon went on quickly, "You do that and we, you, keep control of everything including what secrets you discover you can continue to keep buried, or expose them if you feel it necessary. You have mighty rich and powerful men here, Kross, with big powerful secrets that could destroy a lot of lives while causing immeasurable devastation to the town."

Dutch chewed the inside of his cheek as he pondered DeMar's words. He shook his head. "No, man, that's insane. This is police work. None of the men I dealt with that I think could handle this are cops, in fact," he shook his head with a crooked smile, "somewhat the opposite."

His expression turned serious, eyes tapered incredulous at Talon. "You want me to bring in a- a mercenary to work these crimes?"

Talon shrugged, he shared a glance with Stone Cash who had joined them but remained silent during the conversation. "Yes. Bring in someone dirty to fight dirty." He didn't say out loud, *and keep our dirty laundry to ourselves*.

One hand cupping the back of his neck, Dutch slapped the Stetson against his thigh. "I don't know, man."

Hearing the hesitation in his voice, Talon could see the sheriff was on the edge of falling his way. "Okay, listen. Even if you call in the State Police and/or the FBI, it'll take time for them to show up, catch up, and mobilize. You know this land, they could never get around this open country on their own.

"Bring in someone who has an extraordinary sense of direction and place. Someone tough, daring, skillful, someone who is as dangerous as the killer." He watched Dutch's eyes flick back and forth as he contemplated Talon's idea. Then, Dutch closed his eyes and made a slow nod.

Drawing in a deep breath, Dutch let it out slowly. "Okay. I have someone I can call. I trust him and he is extremely…skillful. Plus he carries a…sort of badge. But," he held a hand up as Talon smiled and opened his mouth. "There'll be a time limit. I will pull the plug and call in the big guns ASAP if we get nowhere."

Talon nodded. "Fine. What kind of time you thinking of?"

Dutch set his hat on his head and murmured, "I'll decide when I think it's time." He strode out the door and down the hall leaving Talon and Stone Cash staring at each other with bemused expressions.

A pall of sorrow stitched with fear hung over the room. Everyone sat morosely around the dining table as the servants cleared the dishes. A pin could be heard dropped on the plush carpet for all the silence.

As soon as dinner was finished, all of the young women except for Keti fled the table. They hurried to the stairs giggling about Sabine's new professional makeup case they couldn't wait to experiment with.

In their thirties, the women were still young enough to think the horror would never touch them. They were immortal. Right now they wanted to distract themselves with something more pleasant than ruminating on the deaths of their friends.

Diana Ansberry let out a fractious sigh of boredom through her thin patrician nose. "Andrew," she said, turning to her husband who was sitting next to her.

"I know we should be in mourning, but the McShanes and the Duncans returned home to deal with the funeral issues and such. The sheriff released them declaring they weren't likely suspects in their own children's murders. Anyway, they need to meet with Annabella's family and Audrey's mother. The poor girl's father ran out on them years ago."

"No father figure, no wonder the girl is such a slut," Jeanie Griggs murmured. A few snickers rounded the table.

"Jeanie!" Talon barked. "That's a shitty thing to say. Audrey is dead, she died in a horribly torturous way that I wouldn't wish on my worst enemy."

"Huh, well maybe I would," Stone Cash drawled, and a few others nodded agreement with gory grins.

Garret Griggs warned, "Be careful what you say, Stone, the police may come after you."

"Oh poof." Jeanie Griggs made a moue with her skinny lips painted scarlet. "They couldn't find their asses if they were bent over right in front of them."

Louder sniggers crackled at the picture she'd drawn.

Jeanie wore a fall under her brunette hair for lift then it fell straight to her shoulders in an up-curl on the ends. She kept the locks tucked behind her ears.

She liked the style but she mainly did it to show off the gigantic diamond earrings her husband Garrett had given her for their 25th wedding anniversary.

Miles Burton groaned, the chandelier above the long cherry wood table shone a halo on his bald head. He wore a blue bowtie and red suspenders. The material of the white shirt gaped at the buttons, the suspenders stretched around the sides of his big stomach. "Not cool, Jeanzer, with the way Ollie and Michael were…ah…assaulted," he trailed off, red rolled up his thick neck to his broad face.

Jeanie's eyes narrowed above her pointy nose raised in the air. "Don't call me Jeanzer. You know I hate that."

"Sure, Jeanz," Miles said, smirking at her haughtiness. "It was okay when we were snot noses running around the playground. Now you think you're some rich bitch celebrity too good for the rest of us."

Her eyes shrunk to angry slits, Jeanie snarled, "Miles you insufferable blowhard. You're just a freakin' retired police chief while Andrew Ansberry was an astronaut, and my Garrett was the mayor of Bryndale-"

Miles sneered sarcastically. "Hello, the key word being *was*. Andrew went up in space once and was done. Garrett *was* the mayor of an itty bitty-"

Jeanie grew louder, "And you *were* the police chief of that same itty bitty-"

Stone broke in with derision, "None of that shit matters, we all get our money from the businesses we're partners in."

"All right, come on, what are we, fourth graders?" Diana fluffed her blonde bob and rolled her eyes. "What I was saying before I was interrupted," she sent an annoyed glare at Jeanie who sent one right back. "We can't do anything about Ollie and the rest of them, poor things, but it doesn't mean we have to sit around and play tiddlywinks. I was thinking we should hit the town."

Alice grinned. "Hey, that's a great idea. Our sons are already out to the bars carousing and skirt chasing. They left their significant others here and you know how those boys are when they're on the loose like that."

Her husband Miles Burton was the complete opposite of the dominant Talon DeMar, and the secretive Stone Cash, and he wasn't like the bawdy Garrett Griggs, or the aristocratic Andrew Ansberry. Miles talked big and blustery but that was all.

Jeanie Griggs was almost birdlike compared to her husband Garrett's husky build. She reminded them, "The sheriff said we can't leave the area."

"Dutch Kross said we couldn't leave town, but he didn't say we had to stay glued to the lodge," Diana responded with a haughty tilt to her blonde head.

His eyes eating up Keti across and down the table from him, Rein reminded the people finishing their after dinner coffee, tea or aperitifs, "What about the danger? I mean, four of us have been butchered and it appears it's not a random attack. They're after our group. It can't be safe for us to go…" he waved a beefy hand at the window, "out there."

The dining room was done in blush and roses, the drapes at the large window ruffled deep crimson. Surrounded by lavish paintings and china cabinets chock full of expensive treasures, the group sat chatting long after dinner was done.

"What are you worried about, van Baer, it's the younger crowd the killer has his or her evil designs on. I think your hefty old booty is safe," Garrett disparaged the large, auburn-haired man.

"Get fucked, Briggs." Rein scowled. His head down, he peered surreptitiously at Keti to see if she heard Garrett's mocking. He hated when anyone mentioned age around him and Keti, it was a reminder of how much older he was than her He was in his fifties, thirty something years older than her. He was the same age as Talon, her father. Stepfather.

It shouldn't matter, though, really. The rumor was, that after Talon caught his first wife, Ava, who was half Talon's age, in bed with the chef of a hoity-toity restaurant, she then dumped the chef, and ditched her family and ran off with another paramour.

After seven years Talon divorced her in absentia for abandonment. Roger and Tommy, to say the least, were devastated their mom ran off and left them.

Soon after, Talon cozied up to Keti's mother, Caralina so he could get his hands on the other half of McMaster Lexington, Inc. But although even when Caralina became ill, she had turned out to have a backbone of steel and fought him at every underhanded enterprise he tried until she died from lung disease.

She was sick for a long time, yet she refused to be badgered into signing something she thought would ultimately harm others.

She started becoming ill when Keti was around seven or eight. Her illness dragged on for years before she finally succumbed. She tried to be a mother to Keti, but she was terribly sick most of the time and often the child had to fend for herself. So Ava deserted Talon, and Caralina croaked on him.

Rein's gaze caressed Keti as he promised himself, she will never leave him once he gets that wedding band on her finger. He has ways to ensure she can't run away. She may not like them, but, a small smile rounded his thick face as his gaze at her turned from affectionate to lustful, it didn't matter what she wanted.

Only what he wanted was important. She was so young and he had so much to teach her. According to Talon, the girl has never been with a man, well, except-

Talon stood up breaking Rein's musings and the others' conversations. "I agree with Diana. We'll go out as a group, stick together, we'll be safe. The younger women will stay here behind locked doors. Nigel will see that no one leaves the house after we go. And our boys know to look out for each other so we don't have to worry about them. Okay?"

"Seriously, Talon," Rein tried again, "you are all taking these horrendous murders on the cuff like they're nothing. We shouldn't be partying and taking this all so lightly, we-"

"Buggar it, Rein, you're a big fucking pussy." Miles sneered his contempt, his chubby lips vibrating with his boorish words.

His wife Alice slapped his arm scolding him, "Miles, honey, potty mouth." He actually flushed all the way up to his bald head at her admonition.

Diana jumped up and grabbed her husband's hand. "Come on, Pops, let's put our dancing shoes on!"

Rein left his chair and started for Keti but Talon cut him off. "No. She stays here. It's bad enough the boys are out catting around where there could be danger, the girls stay put. Let's go." He motioned towards the stairs with his head.

Reluctantly, Rein followed him to change his clothes but kept his eyes on Keti until he was out of sight.

After they left, Keti and Bonnie met in the library.

"Oh, finally, the old farts are gone," Bonnie chortled as she plopped on the floor. She set a large basket containing items on the rug beside her and leaned her back against the couch.

Keti dropped to her knees then sat in front of Bonnie with her legs crossed. "Whatcha got there, Bon?" She leaned over to see inside the basket.

"Well," Bonnie grinned at her and said, "first we have the most important thing." She pulled out a bottle of Crown Royal Whiskey and set it on the coffee table. Next she took a bottle of red apple liqueur, and a bottle of cranberry juice and set them on the table.

She told Keti, "Libbie Burton is bringing the ice, and Sabine has the fresh mint and glasses. We're gonna make red appletinis, Crown Royal red apple martinis. You ever have one?"

Shaking her head with slight trepidation, Keti watched Bonnie remove several bottles of nail polish and nail implements. The other girls, Libbie Burton, and Sabine Shepherd who was Eddie Ansberry's fiancée, along with the now deceased Annabella and Audrey had never been nice to her.

Actually, they had been downright ridiculing and viciously bullying to her. Her brother Tommy had always told her to let it roll off her back like water on a duck, and she tried to do as he suggested. But, she held a bit of trepidation how an evening with the mean girls would go.

As it turned out, the girls all laughed together doing each other's nails, watching chick flick movies while they got rip-roaring drunk. A real corny girlie night. Keti had a good time, for the first time in a long time.

She was asleep the second her head hit the pillow. Most of the night was dreamless, except there was one tiny flare of Stone Cash snarling over her while he pushed her thin thighs apart. Thankfully, the image dissipated quickly and she dreamed of digging in ancient burial grounds and discovering long ago extinct civilizations.

Chapter Ten

A day and a half later, Keti was out by the stables. As usual, she was hiding from Rein's relentless pursuit. She knew in another day or so her father would grab her and literally tie her down to hook her up with Rein.

Then there was also the damned bridge paperwork. She had seen the maid come in from town with a stack of mail and a large manila envelope in her hands.

Her heart beat frantically against her ribs. Her time had run out. She was looking for Ben for one last horse ride before she was irrevocably bound to Rein, and the poor people of Gangspoort will be made poorer and perhaps become a future extinct population.

The temperature was cold but not enough for snow to fall and stick around. Keti realized she'd forgotten her hat and gloves, she shrugged. "Oh well, I'll be moving, that'll keep me warm."

She stepped up to the open stable door and surprisingly Ben was nowhere in sight.

"Well," she mumbled, glancing around, "that's unusual. Ben is always in or around the stables." Other hands worked or walked the horses, Ben groomed and fed them and took care of the insides of the stables.

She called out, "Ben?"

There was no response. Poking her head inside, the barn was musty from the smell of dry hay and horseflesh. She heard a few of the horses stomping their feet and snorting, but no Ben.

She stepped further inside and called out louder, "Ben?" Nothing. Tilting her head to listen, she wondered out loud, "Where on earth could he be? It isn't lunch or dinnertime, he's always here."

A flicker of concern blossomed in the bottom of her belly. There were already four deaths, what if Ben- *oof*!

Something barreled into Keti and slammed her to the ground- as she landed, the wind was knocked out of her lungs.

Just inside the doorway, flat on her back, before she could move a muscle, a big man jumped on top of her. It took her several seconds before she could suck in a breath and let out a terrified scream.

He wrapped his hands around her neck and started squeezing. She hit at him, kicked at his legs as she fought to get him off her or wriggle out from under him. But he was big and heavy and strong, and her punches didn't faze him a bit.

Keti opened her mouth to scream again. She got one out and tried for another but he squeezed harder cutting off her breath. White dots floated in her eyes, her ears buzzed, she couldn't draw a breath.

She clawed savagely at his face, her nails raking his rough skin drawing blood. He yelped and slapped her. Then he wrapped his beefy hands around her neck and started relentlessly squeezing again.

Her ear ringing, cheek stinging, Keti blindly reached out and scrabbled all over the ground beside her, feeling for something, anything that could be used as a weapon. She'd seen a metal bucket near the door when she'd come in.

Muttering curses, he held her down with his weight, and Keti reached her arm out, her fingertips touched the bucket.

Stretching further, further- blackness started rolling over her and she lurched to the side and grabbed the handle of the bucket and slammed it into his temple.

His hands went to his head with a wounded bark and he toppled off her to the side. Keti scrambled up and ran.

Lying on the ground, he reached out blindly and grabbed a hold of her jacket, "*Bitch*," he snarled. Keti slid out of the jacket and fled.

Thankfully he wasn't blocking the doorway. Coughing and gasping, she rushed through it and started running towards the lodge, but the stables were tucked a distance back with the spreading green pastures separating them from the main house as well as the other cabins. She heard his feet stomping and his curses right behind her.

She put everything she had into making her feet move- he grabbed her hair and she was yanked backwards. She hit the ground with a bone-breaking crash and a scream pealed from her just before the man leapt on top of her again.

He strung his fingers around her neck and ground enraged, "You little bitch, this time I'll just break your fucking neck and be done with it. Supposed to make it look like a hangin' suicide, but screw it." Blood dripped from a cut at his temple where she'd hit him with the bucket.

Keti didn't recognize him, she'd never seen him before. She thrashed her legs and hit and clawed at his hands but he lifted a hand to put on the side of her head so he could snap her neck in half.

This was it, she was dead. It was ironic, Keti had thought about dying being the only way to get out of marrying Rein and signing the bridge papers, and here it was actually happening. His fingers dug into her head- and he was suddenly gone.

Another body tackled him, knocking him off her. Catching her breath, Keti pushed up to lean back on her elbows and saw the two men rolling on the ground throwing punches.

In a matter of seconds it was over. The man who had attacked her lay prone, his huge chest no longer rising drawing in air, his eyes open and staring blankly. She looked up at the man who had killed him, and felt her insides scream.

He...looked...dark. Not his skin color, no, it was darkness inside of him that oozed out of his pores and rained in his eyes. He looked like a killer...and apparently he was.

The shaking started in her limbs and travelled all the way through her body and into her brain, flooding her senses with a terror she'd never known. Terror even beyond the fear the violent tempest that Talon DeMar, or Stone Cash inflicted on her, or even the present attempted murder.

This...male, he almost looked like...an animal. When he speared her with his dark penetrating stare he appeared to be almost...a wild animal, a vicious creature that could tear her apart with razor teeth and slashing claws. She shook her head to clear the weird vision.

No, he was a man, a male, still...he looked damned scary. She started to scoot away before he could grab her too, and murder her as easily, easier, than he had that dead guy. But, he stalked to her in a few long-legged strides and was upon her.

He stood over Keti, fencing her in, making it impossible for her to get up and flee. Then he spoke. His voice deep as a cavern and dark as the black night. He had an accent that she had never heard before.

"You are Ketherine DeMar?" His strange accent pronounced her name Ketereen Daymar, rolling all the r's.

Her eyelashes flapped straight up over her wide green eyes. She just stared dumbly at him.

Something like a growl abraded from his huge chest, his voice a low rumble, the sound held a tangible threat that shot tingles of alarm right to the roots of her hair. "I asked you a question. Do not make me ask it again." Power and brutal aggression resounded in that deep dark voice.

But Keti couldn't make herself speak, words bottled up in her quaking throat. She leaned back on her palms, her shoulders hunched, she instinctively tried to scuttle away from him.

He suddenly bent, grasped her upper arms and lifted her up, with a small yelp she was completely off the ground then he set her on her feet.

He kept hold of one of her arms and let the other go. Keti could feel her skin blanching white with fright. Her lips parted so she could suck in a breath, her chest rose and fell rapidly, and his panther's gaze lowered to it, and stayed there.

What, she thought, was he some rutting beast that was going to just shove her back down and-

"You were described to me. I will take it that you are Ketherine DeMar. Come with me. Johnnie Frog is in town."

Her chin trembled, she looked sideways at the dead man lying a few feet away. Her stomach retched and she yanked her gaze back to the male holding her, then quickly lowered it, he was too frightful to bear.

"No," he said, "that is not Rana. Tis muscle he sent to take you out."

Her head shot up, eyes flashed shock and confusion at him. She unconsciously turned to look at the dead man again, but the...animal jerked her to face away.

"Do not look at him. Tis over. Well, he is over, Rana will be sending more after you, or he will come himself. He normally likes to do the females himself," he said that with a twitch of contempt to his lips.

"He enjoys overpowering them and making the scream. Come." He started walking and she had to go with him or she would fall on her face. His strength was immeasurable, she didn't doubt he would drag her.

His pace was fast. When he heard her huffing, he glanced at her in mockery and slowed his steps.

Most everyone staying at the retreat was huddled on the patio at the back of the mansion. They all gaped at her and the monster that held her in his steel grip. She couldn't help but sneak another glimpse of him.

He was actually wearing a suit and tie. A wild animal that murders a man as big as the guy who attacked her with tremendous ease was dressed in a suit. The white shirt stretched tight over his thick chest, powerful thighs bunched the material of his slacks as his legs ate up the space to the mansion.

Keti imagined she was floating off to the Emerald City. Any minute now the flying monkeys would come swooping in and- a frantic giggle gurgled out of her.

She felt his sudden attention on her. Really, who giggles at an attempted murder on oneself and witnessing the subsequent brutal slaughter of that villain? Hysteria was apparently nipping at her heels. Keti sobered at the sight of the group watching her and the animal approaching them.

He brought her straight to Talon who had been hastening towards them but now stopped a few dozen yards in front of the crowd. His brows hooked up as he looked to the man holding Keti.

Sheriff Dutch Kross caught up with Talon and stood waiting with him, leaving the people gathered behind on the patio chattering and wondering.

"She okay, Valdimar?" Talon nodded his head at Keti but his eyes were on the animal that still had his big hand wrapped around her slender arm.

The male Talon called Valdimar held her in an iron grip, which she was ineffectively struggling to break from. He didn't even spare her a glance, his gaze flicked to Sheriff Kross, the two men exchanged a look.

Valdimar said to Talon, "She is fine. Another second and there would have been another funeral."

Keti gasped, the color that had suffused due to the brisk walk drained from her face.

The animal said calmly to Talon, "After our meeting earlier, I was surveying the perimeter and found your stableman. You need to send someone to free him. He does not appear to be seriously injured, perhaps clocked in the head from behind. He is unconscious and tied up behind the stables."

The gawking crowd behind them still chattered with curious stupefaction.

Talon turned around and called out, "Griggs, go to the meadows and grab a couple of hands to help release Ben. See if he needs medical care." Garret Griggs looked confused but he did as Talon ordered.

Talon said to Valdimar, "How did you come upon my daughter? How did you know she was in danger? We thought we heard a scream. Kross and I came outside and we saw the fight."

His hand still tight around Keti's arm as if he thought she'd bolt, he answered him, "As soon as I came upon the stableman I heard her scream. Rana's man was throttling her. He will not be harming anyone else."

The sheriff held his cell in his hand, he uttered orders into it, "I need deputies, the ME and forensic techs out to Caesar Peak Lodge, pronto."

Rein van Baer started to come forward but Talon shook his head. Rein's displeased frown gritted further when he saw the strange man holding his fiancée, and Keti's father didn't want him to go to her.

"Is that guy laying out there in the field the one who killed Ollie and Michael?" Stone Cash asked as he joined them. His son, Chester stumbled along beside him.

Chester resembled a cherub one would find in a church's stained glass window. A cherub with a pug nose and light orangish hair. He had his father's blue eyes but not his blond hair.

Stone, a fierce, dangerous man was deeply chagrined over the pasty blob he'd spawned. He brought him along on the retreats hoping he could toughen the young man up with some hunting, hiking, fishing, unfortunately, Stone was always inevitably disappointed.

Stone's wife Raquel had long fled the domestic abuse leaving her wimpy, chubby son in her husband's dispassionate cruel care.

"No," Valdimar replied. His voice was as cold and hard as his face.

Keti kept her head averted from him, just looking at him sent chills prickling through her body and made her heart race with apprehension.

She lifted a hand to her face where the thug had struck her, her cheek still stung. She couldn't move her other arm, the man held her so tightly, yet not enough to bruise her.

At her movement he slanted his head and looked at her. His gaze bee-lined to the red imprint of a hand on her pale face.

He suddenly cupped her jaw and lifted her head up so he could see. Dark brown brows lowered over dark inscrutable eyes. His thumb brushed over the print. Keti sucked in a breath and turned her face away. He dropped his hand and turned back to Talon.

Stone Cash asked him, "How do you know that's not our killer?"

"He is one of Johnny Frog's muscle. He came explicitly for the girl, to kill her." At Keti's gasp and her legs wobbling, Valdimar tightened his grip to hold her steady.

Giving him a dirty look, Stone asked, "You recognize him? You hang with that mobster?" He was one to talk, he had many dealings with the criminal. But they weren't exactly bosom buddies.

Valdimar didn't reply to his question, just shifted his cold eyes to Talon then to Dutch. "Rana will send more. If they don't take her out, he will come and do the job himself. Those papers," he turned his attention back to Talon, "that you told us about that you want her to sign," he tipped his head in Keti's direction.

His head cocked, Talon's eyes narrowed but he nodded.

Valdimar said, "The same ones Johnny Frog does not want her to sign, they are important enough he will make sure she is not able to sign anything ever again." His guttural accent collided oddly with his stiff English. He meshed contractions with formal words as if he was still learning the language.

"What about DeMar, Wolf?" Dutch asked. "Why doesn't Rana just take him out?"

Valdimar shifted one of the sides of his suit coat back and set his hand on his hip. The movement briefly exposed a shoulder holster. He totally ignored Keti's struggle to break from his grasp.

Dutch's gaze lowered to her then rose to the man with an arched brow. The edge of Valdimar's mouth nicked up making Dutch frown.

"We have other...business together. He needs me," Talon answered Dutch's question. "Swatting Keti out of the way like a moth will be like drawing a simple breath to him. Life in his business has little value." He chuckled and added, "Make that zero value."

"All right." Dutch turned to Talon, his eyes shifted to Keti before settling back on DeMar. "I spoke with the ME earlier. He found some hairs on Michael McShane's shirt that was piled with their other clothing beside their car. I got a warrant and had a deputy remove strands from her hairbrush," he jutted his chin at Keti. "They're a match."

"What?" Keti blurted aghast. "That can't be true!"

"You have remarkable, unforgettable colored hair, Miss DeMar. I recognized the long wavy strands at the autopsy. How close were you with Michael McShane?" Dutch inquired with one sandy brow low over an eye studying her reaction as he waited for her to answer him.

She blinked in confusion.

"Were you two having an affair?" His disapproval of the possibility tugged his mouth down.

"What?" she repeated, feeling like a parrot. "We're not-not close. Not at all. We've barely said two words together over the years. He's at least twelve or more years older than me."

"Uh huh," Dutch grunted. "And your father says you're to marry Rein van Baer who is more than double your age."

As she opened her mouth to respond he went on, "I heard you had an argument with Michael McShane at dinner the other night," Dutch's inquisition wasn't over.

"No, I didn-" her eyes fell to the ground, pink submerged her cheeks making her look guilty as sin.

"She doesn't have to answer your questions, Sheriff." Talon pulled his phone from his pocket.

"No, wait-" Keti floundered. "It's okay, I don't want any misunderstanding. I want to cooperate, Sheriff." Clearing her throat she forced herself to make eye contact with Dutch although her knees were shaking.

Her voice slightly trembly she explained, "He was disparaging my brother. He has always bullied the younger men like Tommy. Tommy doesn't back down, but I was afraid they were going to go outside and brawl. I got involved to prevent a fight. That's all."

Dutch studied her silently for a few beats then said to Talon, "I have to take her in, DeMar. I have evidence of her at both crime scenes and she was witnessed having a heated argument with Michael McShane shortly before he was found murdered. Her brooch was found with Ollie Duncan's remains." He pulled cuffs from the back of his belt and ordered, "Please turn around, Miss DeMar."

"Come on, Sheriff." Talon held a hand out to Dutch. "Anyone could have stolen her brooch and hair and planted them. That's not enough evidence to arrest her."

Dutch reached for Keti. "It's enough to hold her while I investigate further. I can't have her fleeing the jurisdiction."

"No," the man holding Keti said flatly. "I am taking her with me. Rana and his men can get to her in jail or here. She would not stand a chance of surviving out the day. I will ensure her safety in my sole custody."

Chapter Eleven

Astounded at the stranger's proposal of her staying with him alone at God knows where, Keti's face blanched white as a sheet. Wrenching at her arm, she exclaimed, "No! I don't know you! Let go of me right now!"

She felt like a tiny fragile doll standing amongst the huge powerful men. She should have felt safe, protected by them, but she knew better.

Keti was an adult, but that meant nothing in these men's world, women were considered property to dispose of as they saw fit. And she was completely powerless to fight for her freedom, Talon had seen to that. He had total control over her. Nonetheless, she was not going to just go along with some strange man's proposition.

Steadying her voice, Keti strove to stay and sound calm. "I am perfectly capable of seeing to my own safety."

She glared at his hand wrapped around her arm and then up at those animalistic eyes. Repressing a chilling shiver of fright at his beastly mien, as coolly as possible, she said, "Now, release me and I will be on my way. I have things to do."

"While you are with me I will teach you how to do as you are told," Valdimar chastened her with his unveiled threat.

"What? Are you kidding me? That is not happening." She tugged at his fingers circling her arm but they were like latched iron pegs. "Let go of me, you have no right-"

He gave her a commanding shake and ordered tersely, "Stop acting like a child, Ketherine, you are coming with me."

"No! Father!" She turned in a panic to Talon, her long hair swinging around to wave over her shoulder. "He can't make me, Father, please don't let him take me!"

Talon stood still, the side of his finger and thumb tugging at his lower lip as he considered everything. His brows lifted, he said to Dutch, "Sheriff?"

Dutch shrugged. "I know Wolf won't let her get away, and he'll keep her alive long enough if there's a trial. I'm good with it."

"Fine. Let's go," the man called Wolf stated and started to pull her towards the house.

"What!" Keti shrieked. "No! I am not going anywhere with him! Let go of me!" She kicked out at Valdimar and in a blink he swung her around, her back smacked into his chest.

With one hand he caught and held her wrists behind her back, the other curled around the front of her neck like a dog's canines at her jugular. She stilled immediately.

His voice gruff and stern, he said to the back of her head, "You will come with me Ketherine, without a fight, and you will obey my every directive. You would not last an hour in a jail cell. I guarantee Giovanni Rana will make sure you are dead before the cell door locks."

85

He lowered his head and put his mouth near her ear, whispered, "I will keep you safe. You only have to give me what I want and I will not let anyone get near you." His harsh accent with the innuendo of his words abraded her ear.

Her legs trembling, tears of disbelief welling, she croaked, "G- give you what?" She was positive she felt him smile against her hair.

He moved her hair back with his chin. The others couldn't hear his whisper, but it growled in her ear. "What do you think I want, Ketherine? What would a red-blooded male want with a gorgeous woman and her hot body?"

He paused as she shuddered in his grip. "I want it all, Ketherine," the growl lowered to a husky rumble. "You willingly in my bed, doing as I command."

Aghast at his outrageous proposition, she adamantly shook her head, it brushed against his still lowered chin. "Are you out of your mind? Let go of me! Father, help me!"

"Hush, Ketherine, calm down or I will take measures to calm you down." Valdimar sounded dangerously brutal with his threat. "Now, stop fussing and come with me."

"No, I won't." Jerking her jaw from his grasp, she adjusted her head so her face was away from his mouth. "I don't know you, I don't want to know you, and I sure don't want your hands on me."

An obvious quiver of loathing roiled through her. He couldn't be more deadly disturbing if he had red horns, claws and a pointed tail.

Chester Cash stood beside his father and just a few inches behind him. His eyes like blue quarters rounded in avid interest at Keti. His lizard tongue slipped out and trailed around his parted lips as his gaze stroked like a sweaty palm up and down her restrained body.

The way the man held her caused her breasts to thrust up and out at the thin pink sweater she wore, making her exceedingly vulnerable. Eyes bulging in brainless lust, drool gathered in a corner of Chester's slack mouth.

Stone jabbed him hard in the ribs and barked a whispered, "Control yourself, boy."

Swallowing, Chester's gaze dropped to his feet then slowly slunk back up to continue groping Keti's body with his eyes.

Valdimar released her wrists but kept his hand around her neck. Since she deliberately kept her attention diverted from him, he pushed his thumb under her jaw raising it again so she had to look up and back at him.

"Listen to me, my beautiful kitten. If you go with the sheriff, he is going to lock you up with hard-core criminals. Any one of them would kill you for ten bucks. Some would do it for free, just to get on Johnny Frog's good side."

The other men silently watched their exchange. Talon and Stone Cash's expressions were impassive, beside them Dutch was staring at the ground.

Valdimar let go of her neck but stood so close to her she could feel his brute energy. It was as if he expected her to bolt, like he wanted her to run so he could give chase and take her down. Then tear her body apart and devour her, leaving her bones to blanch in the hot sun.

Keti knew she was being fanciful but she felt, and saw his barely leashed violence.

Talon asked Dutch, "Can he do that? Can you do that? Let her leave in this man, ah, Valdimar's custody?"

Dutch shrugged. "It's uncommon, not quite kosher, but yes, I can let her leave with him. I know Wolfgang Valdimar. He won't let her escape, and he won't let any harm come to her. He has official credentials so he can legally do it." He mumbled under his breath, "May not be American credentials, but still technically legal."

"That is that then." Valdimar grasped her arm again.

"No! Wait!" Keti cried. "He- he wants me to- to trade sex for his protection! That's- that's illegal! Father," she looked beseechingly at Talon who only coolly stared back at her. "This is crazy, he can't do this! Father, stop him!"

Talon negligently bumped one shoulder. "You got yourself in this mess, Keti. You sign the papers right now, accept Rein's proposal and I'll bond you out of jail after you're booked and you can stay here."

"She stays here she will be dead within the hour," the man Wolf commented. "And, as I said, she will not last the day in jail. You will not have the opportunity to bond her out."

Talon nodded. "Then she goes with you, Valdimar."

Keti's eyes jumped from one man to another with increasing horror. "You can't be serious, you'd let this- this...*person* just- just take me and let him do what he wants with me?"

Talon's mouth turned down, then a corner shifted up. "Whatever, Keti. Rein ain't gonna be happy, but you're a grown woman. Young, yes, but it's not like it's not natural for men and women to fuck. Don't be such a dramatic prude. That's all he wants, it's not like he's going to nail you naked to the floor and let all his men gangbang your ass." His glanced flicked to Wolf.

Wolf gazed back at him. Most of his dark eyes hidden under a low brow and hooded lids presented zero indication of any human warmth or mercy.

Back to Keti, Talon said, "It'll keep you out of jail, out of Rana's reach, and, well, for now, mine as well. But it'll keep you safe until I regain the papers." His lips bunched in irritation. "Somehow the originals have been…lost. Or taken." He squinted an eye of suspicion at Keti.

"No! This is outrageous! It's- it's kidnapping! Father, I don't want to go with him!" She twisted wildly to break free but the man held her as if she were a ragdoll. Keti knew Talon wanted her alive, for now anyway, otherwise the company could be up for grabs.

"You don't have a lot of choices. I'd say he is the least of the evils, right Stone?" He smirked at his friend.

Stone Cash's expression remained inscrutable, his lips tight.

Keti gawked in disbelief at her stepfather. How could she mean so little to him? He stared back at her with a blank face.

"Dad," Chester whined beside his father, "why can't we take her? If that shithead can have her then we could too, right?" It was like he had no control over his erection or his eyes that bounced from Keti's breasts to between her thighs to her breasts, or the tongue that swirled in the drool at the corner of his chubby mouth.

"Shut the fuck up, boy," Stone slapped the side of his son's head so hard Chester's eyes crossed.

Valdimar turned his cold lethal glare to Chester.

Chester blinked. He may have the IQ of a horny squash but he recognized a deadly threat when he saw it. Gulping, he grabbed a hold of his family jewels as if trying to hold back the terrified piss that Valdimar forced out of him by just his glare- as if he could rip Chester's balls from his body with just a look.

An immature thirty-year-old coward, Chester darted behind his father, missing Stone's exasperated eye-roll and muttered, "Pussy."

Keti turned her head so the men couldn't see the tears in her eyes. "Take me to jail, Sheriff," her voice caught. She turned so her back was to Dutch and held her hands behind her back. She didn't see the men's look of surprise. No one moved for a second.

Chester's eyeballs goggled out of his head watching Keti about to be restrained with her hands cuffed behind her back.

The cool air turned her nipples hard, he could see them through the thin sweater. His tongue poked out the side of his mouth, he palmed his crotch again but this time with a licentious groan.

Dutch gave him a dirty look then wound his fingers around Keti's arm. "I don't think we need the cuffs. I'm not worried you're going to overpower me." He glanced at Wolf.

Wolf Valdimar didn't say anything, but a look crossed between him and the sheriff.

Bonnie bounded across the trim grass to the small group, wearing an alarmed expression. She stopped in front of Keti. Panting breaths rushed her words, "Shit, girl, what's going on here?" She looked from male to male.

"They're taking me to jail, Bonnie," Keti replied, anxiety coating her soft voice, "they think I killed Ollie and the others."

Strawberry blonde brows shot straight up with incomprehension. Her hands on her hips Bonnie scolded the men, "Are you out of your ever-loving minds? What on earth is the matter with you guys? You think little Keti could abduct four grown adults, sexually assault them and then kill them? I mean, the news said they were strangled. For Pete's sake, look at her tiny delicate hands, are you kidding me right now?" She glared at them in exasperation.

"You mind your P's and Q's, missy." Talon's face was a granite block of censure. "You just go keep Kyle Griggs satisfied and stay the hell out of our business."

Bonnie's mouth dropped open. "What? How dare you talk to me like-" Her words died in her mouth at the look he gave her, as if he was about to choke her like the deceased victims had been.

Her lips snapped shut, she lowered her head and stepped back. Talon DeMar was king of this land, speaking out against him would entertain certain…pain.

Rein van Baer had marched halfway across the lawn to them when he saw Talon shoot Bonnie down with just a look. He slowed, then stopped and stood still, watching it play out.

"All right, enough of this, come on, Keti." Dutch gently tugged her to start walking.

Wolf set a hand on Keti's shoulder before they could leave. He turned her to face him. "When you get a taste of the jail, you tell Dutch when you have had enough and he will bring you to me."

She stared at the ground. He grasped her jaw more roughly than before and raised it with ire. "Trust me, little kitten, you will be at my place by the end of the day. And," the side of his lips curved in a cold smile, "you remember my conditions." He glanced at Dutch and said, "I will call you in a few."

Keti blinked at Valdimar but said nothing. He dropped his hand and nodded at Dutch, and the sheriff started walking. She stumbled along with him. The rest followed behind.

As they reached Rein, Keti heard Rein say to the wolfman, "Are you the international assassin, that government merc Dutch said he was bringing in to help him catch the killer? The real killer?"

She didn't hear the wolfman's response. Dutch brought her to his cruiser and helped her climb into the back seat and he drove off to the Diggler's Rock south satellite jail.

Chapter Twelve

*D*utch ended his call with Valdimar as he parked the cruiser near the jail. Keti hadn't heard much, just Dutch nodding and muttering periodic, "Uh huhs."

Exiting the car, he went around to open Keti's door in the backseat. She sat stiff as a poker, her fingers tearing at each other. His voice soft with compassion, he said to her, "Come on, honey, this was your choice."

She tipped her head back and looked up with frightened bleakness at him. "Really? What choices did I really have, Sheriff? Get murdered by Johnny Frog, or raped by that- that wolfman, or go to jail."

Dutch's lips pushed out. "It's Wolfgang, not Wolfman. Listen, Ketherine, I know Wolfgang Valdimar very well. We've fought side-by-side in the military. He and I of course come from opposite sides of the world. His origin of birth I believe was Estonia, not sure, he's very closed about his childhood.

"Yeah, he's a...rough man. And yes, a dangerous one as you witnessed today. But, you will be safe with him, he would never let anyone get near enough to harm you."

Tears welled in her green eyes. "Sure, but what about him? Who would protect me from him? He made it clear,

Sheriff, that if I went under his protection I would have to sleep with him. That's coercion, another form of rape."

Dutch couldn't deny what she said. He'd seen the way Wolf had looked at her when they were out in the field standing by Rana's dead enforcer.

Wolf wanted her bad, so badly he'd do whatever it took to have her. And he wasn't the sort to court a woman, likely never had. Didn't know how even if he was inclined to, which he never had been. That's not the kind of world Wolf came from.

Dutch told her, "He knows nothing of his family. He lived in the streets when still practically a toddler until a couple of soldiers in town grabbed him up and stuck him in the military."

"So you're saying he's a heathenish, rapacious warrior, Sheriff? And because of his upbringing that makes it okay?"

What she said was basically true, no point in arguing about it. Wolfgang Valdimar knew nothing but guns, fighting, killing. The women he had contact with were rough and raunchy tramps that groupied barbaric soldiers. Prostitutes and whores, they were there for the taking, and leaving.

Keti was going to be a whole different kettle of fish for Wolf. The girl was soft, dainty, ladylike, but unremittingly cold. She urgently kept herself from people, especially men. Only a serious hurting would have caused that.

Talon DeMar was tight-lipped when it came to Keti's childhood.

Dutch had wanted her for himself. He sighed, but he knew he couldn't, and wouldn't fight Wolfgang Valdimar. He owed him too much to try to fight him for her. Even if he didn't owe Wolf, Wolf had clearly put his claim on the girl, and he wasn't the kind of man to let anyone try to take what he considered his.

His smile rueful, Dutch thought, *it's going to be damned interesting to see how it all plays out, because Ketherine DeMar will be in Wolf's bed by the end of tonight.*

He had spoken with Wolf on the way, well, actually listened to him as he told Dutch what he wanted him to do with Keti at the jail to ensure she begged to not be left there and thereby forced to have to choose to go under Wolf's protection.

"Come on, let's get this over with." He reached in and caught her arm and helped her out. He could feel her shaking in his hand.

Dutch hadn't been to this jail in a long time. It was on the outskirts of town. It's where they housed the most violent criminals while they awaited trial. This little girl was going to be in for the shock of her life when she steps into the building.

He should book her, fingerprint her, but he decided to skip it for now. Sure, she was a suspect, but he didn't truly believe she was the guilty culprit. But the evidence against her made it procedure for him to lock her up while considering filing murder charges against her. He could hold her for 48 hours without charging her.

Of course that was all moot, because she wasn't going to be there for even thirty minutes. They had a plan to frighten her right into Wolf's arms.

At least once she was behind Wolf Valdimar's iron doors, the DA couldn't get to her, neither could Rana.

Dutch ushered her past the guards lounging in the front area. His lips firmed with ire. The guards were sprawled about playing cards and watching porn on their computers.

Hell, he needed to send Sergeant Falk to come and clean up the fucking dirty, corrupted mess.

They heard the noise the second they stepped through the second doorway.

Dutch led Keti down a corridor tiled in yellowed flooring, the off-white walls were scraped and scuffed. Their footsteps couldn't even be heard over the squalling racket coming from the hall at the end of the corridor.

The closer they got, the louder the bedlam. Keti tried to stop walking but Dutch pulled her forward.

They stepped into a room and Dutch almost gasped in shock right along with Keti.

The cells were not occupied the way they were supposed to be. Only two cells were being utilized. Dutch could see the other unoccupied cells were filthy with rotten food and feces smeared on the floors and walls. The stink of the place was gagging.

"What the hell?" he muttered under his breath.

Keti couldn't hear him, but she stuck her feet to the floor trying to keep him from pulling her forward.

In one cell there were only males crammed into it, and only females in the cell adjacent to it. Problem was, the two cells shared the set of vertical bars that separated them.

The men were shouting and cursing and raising their fists as if they were at a rowdy football game. They were all crowding the bars that separated them from the females.

The females were also crowded in a bunch, but they were huddled to the far side of their barred chamber, as far away from the males as they could get.

The roaring men were reaching their arms through the bars as if they could grab a woman and pull her right through to their side. And it appeared that was already happening.

A woman with her open shirt hanging off her back was up against the bars. A male had his arm wound around her waist holding her up off her feet and against the bars.

Her naked breasts were actually protruding through the bars, and the men on the other side were helping themselves to them. Half a dozen hands were groping, pinching the meat of her breasts, pulling, twisting her nipples.

She had bright pink hair and had been wearing shorts, they were now hanging from one ankle as her legs were bent and spread like a frog's and her bare vagina was pressed to the bars. Men had their fingers in both her holes and they were howling with lewd glee.

The woman, her head draped back, was laughing maniacally as the men mauled her captive body.

The males that couldn't get through the crowd to her were reaching through the bars, beckoning the other females to come and join the fun.

Guards stood around as if watching a randy show, they cheered the men on, goaded them to do more to the hapless female. One actually mirrored the many convicts who had their penises out in their fists stroking them hard. They were acting like wild primates hanging from trees and pulling their puds.

Dutch could not believe what he was seeing. He would have stopped the assault on the woman but she appeared to be really enjoying all those hands on and inside her. Even two prisoners on either side of her, each gripped a handful of her ass and was squeezing and pulling so hard Dutch feared they'd tear her butt cheeks right off her body.

After he took care of Keti he would be getting on the horn to his captains and getting this shit cleaned the fuck up, quick. In the meantime, he had a mission to complete.

Wolf wanted him to frighten Keti so much she'd run to him with open arms and agree to anything he wanted. Dutch wasn't happy about it, but Wolf had saved his life so many times overseas in some godforsaken, guerilla-soldier infested jungle he owed him ten times over. Besides, ultimately, she would be the safest in Wolf's protection.

With this horrendous display going on, they wouldn't need to implement his and Wolf's plan to scare Keti into his arms. She would likely run screaming from this scene at the station and directly to Wolf's compound.

"Come on, Keti, let's go. Which side should I put you in?" Dutch couldn't believe how malicious he sounded, but he had a job to do.

It was shockingly outrageous that the guards had stuffed the females in one cell, and all the males in one cell out of pure laziness. Heads were gonna roll.

Hell, the guards had put the women at such risk, he'd make sure charges were filed against them. If the females grew angry at one of their own they could just toss her in reach of the rampaging men and that would be it for her.

Keti froze and dug her shoes into the floor. "N- n- no, Sheriff, no, please," she cried, trying to turn and run but Dutch was behind her and gripped her arms.

He held her so her back was flush against his chest. She quivered like a flag in the rippling wind. It was wicked to scare her this way, but she really would be safest with Wolf, and Dutch couldn't force her to go to him. He had to let it be her decision. Not that they were leaving her much option.

"I have to lock you up, Ketherine, you're a main suspect in the homicides. Your choice was either going in Mr. Valdimar's custody or here. You chose here." It was so hard to hold her quivering body knowing she was scared to death and he was forcing this shit on her.

Dutch felt like such an asshole, but it had to be done. She would certainly be murdered if he left her here or sent her home. Rana could easily pay off one of the crooked guards lounging around the jail or a con to kill her.

Dutch needed to find out who was corrupt, and clean them the hell out of the service. But that will take time that he didn't have at the moment.

"Please, Sheriff, why can't I post a bond and go home?" Tears streaked like bullets down her face.

"First of all, a judge isn't likely to set a bond for the grisly quadruple homicides. And if he did, you couldn't afford it, and although he said he would, you can't count on that bastard Talon to pay it. Besides, the judge won't be presiding over Magistrate Court until tomorrow morning." He spoke in her ear so she could hear him over the shrieking and roaring in the room.

"Plus, we made it pretty clear you wouldn't last an hour at home with Johnnie Frog after you. Hell, this is not make believe, girl, you were already attacked. If not for Wolf Valdimar's quick action you would be dead right now. We were all too far away and not wary enough to help you."

The quivering in her body turned into full body shaking.

"So," he said, "I shouldn't put you in with the males, they'd tear you apart." Not that he would but she didn't know that. Keti fought to get away from him, gasping, crying, she twisted and jerked her body but she was no match to the brawny sheriff.

The women noticed them. Several sauntered to the front of their cell making sure to keep clear of the reach of the men housed next to them. They were big, rough looking females. Tattooed and muscled.

One of them spoke looking and sounding more like a man than some of the men, "What do we have here, Officer?

You've brought us a little dollie to play with?" She moved closer to the front.

Keti pressed her body into Dutch as if she could move through him.

Dutch grinned, playing his part. "Yeah. I heard y'all were bored, I brought you some fun." He forced the cheerful look to stay plastered on his face. God, he hated himself so much right now.

Two other harsh looking women approached and grinned wickedly at Keti. "Ah," one of them said, licking her chops, "young and fucking fresh. Let's have at her. After we've had our fill, we'll toss her to the bars for the men to play with, like Sheena there. Who knew that freak chick liked gangbangs?"

The pink-haired girl hooked to the bars was still laughing as more men got their hands on every part of her.

"Yeah." The first woman's smile was unpleasant and sent new rolls of fright up Keti's spine. "We give the guys something to play with and for a while they'll stop spitting at and throwing their shit at us."

That's when Keti saw from the bars separating the cells to about five feet in, the floor was awash with spit and feces. "*Oh God,*" her stomach turned over in revulsion.

"Hey!" one of the men called out now they were becoming aware of Dutch and Keti's presence.

Moving to the front of the cell, he told them, "We got it figured out now. We can't get our peckers through the bars enough to fuck Sheena, and we can't make the guys that have her now let her go so we can try our idea, but," he was smiling, his eyes slits of lecherous malice aimed straight at Keti.

"We can bend that one over and pull her ass to the bars. With her pressed tight against the bars and dudes holding her butt cheeks apart, we can reach her with our dicks and fuck whichever hole we can get into the easiest."

Keti was so afraid it felt every hair on her head was standing on end, any second she was going to puke with her fright. Her body shaking like palm fronds in a hurricane, she was growing lightheaded with the terror.

She whispered, "No, please, Sheriff, you can't do this." She struggled to break from his hold and run for her life. Her panicked breathing came in rapid, frantic gasps.

Dutch lowered his head again to speak in her ear, "Well, it seems I can. You ready to go in now?" He wanted this repulsive farce freakin' over with.

Still gripping her arms tightly, he gave her a little nudge forward and the prisoners in both cells shrieked and shouted with delight.

Hollering and cursing and laughing, males and females alike were now thrusting their arms through the bars as if to reach out and grab Keti and yank her inside.

A nightmare, she was awake in a horrific nightmare. Tears poured down Keti's face, her breaths tumbled out faster in shallow hysterical rasps.

"Please, Sheriff, please don't!" she cried. "This is crazy, you can't do this to me, I didn't do anything wrong! I can't believe you're arresting me, this just can't be happening!"

Dutch paused. "Well, you had two options. Here, or go and be Wolfgang Valdimar's plaything, put yourself in his custody and under his protection. You changing your mind about the choice you made?"

He felt her shaking body and knew the second she caved. The breath rushed out of her, her head fell forward, the long mahogany hair draped over her sobbing face.

The words stammered out brokenly, "Y- yes, yes, please take me out of here."

The screeching and cursing roiled around the room like a savage whirling dervish. Keti tried to leave again but Dutch swiveled her to face him and held her fast.

"I want to make sure, Ketherine, that you are sure what you are agreeing to. Wolf said if I take you to him you have to submit to him without a fight. Stay at his place and do as he orders. Is that clear?"

She nodded wordlessly, the tears rolling over her cheeks and falling to splat on her blouse.

"Out loud, Ketherine," he prodded.

Her barely audible, "*Yes*," hitched out with a sob. Then she practically snarled, "This is coercion. It has to be against the law. This is wrong."

Well, she was right. Unfortunately, to keep her alive, Dutch was forced to use coercion. But to make her agree to be a man's sexual toy to keep her safe, yeah, that was wrong. Dutch was caught in the middle. At least he knew Wolf well enough the man would never seriously injure a woman.

"Okay." He was relieved she gave in. He couldn't have left her here, and Wolf would have been royally pissed if he brought her to him with her still being adamantly unwilling.

Wolf would full on coerce, but he wasn't partial to rape that Dutch knew of. Not that he'd ever had to before, women dug his frightening animal magnetism. Until Keti.

As Dutch had thought before, Ketherine DeMar was different. A small smile crept up the side of his face. That little girl was going to give the big bad wolf a run for his money, he just didn't know it yet. And it was gonna be fun to watch.

The girl was a total knockout and a heartbreaker for sure. She was nothing Wolf was used to, and he wasn't going to know how to deal with her. Keti wasn't a girl you used and discarded, she was a woman you cherished and kept for a lifetime.

"All right. As soon as I get you outside I'll call Wolf and tell him that you acquiesced to being in his custody and under his control and terms."

Curling his arm around her shoulders, he turned her around and they walked out of the room leaving the sick, maniacal shrieking and roaring cheers behind.

When they reached the bullpen area, Dutch moved Keti near the door than trod back to the guards playing cards.

Rage shaking his voice, he told them, "You get your asses in there and get that female away from the males and put everyone in individual cells like you're supposed to. Sergeant Falk will be here in thirty minutes to check on things," *and fire your lazy asses.*

Dutch helped the boneless Keti into his car, putting her in the front seat since he didn't expect any more trouble from her. She was so overcome with shock and despair and terror he had to buckle her in.

Dutch felt like shit for his part in the scheme, but the girl wouldn't be safe at home, and he was honor bound to arrest her. But, she'd be in just as much danger from Johnnie Frog's assassins if he locked her up in jail.

However, he could legally put her in Wolfgang Valdimar's custody. As soon as he got her settled in and her door closed he called Sergeant Falk. He didn't want Keti to hear him blister Falk's ass.

Chapter Thirteen

They didn't speak on the ride to the estate Wolf was renting while he was in Diggler's Rock.

The guard at the gate waved them through and Dutch drove right up and parked close to the house. Mansion. It was built of stone like the lodge, three stories, surrounded by a green pool of grass, and beyond the lawn, dense forests sheathed the vast perimeter.

Dutch counted six chimneys. Wolf had no family, no wife, no children, but he rented a home that took up a city block. Well, he did have friends, servants, and soldiers staying with him.

His friends, who were basically legionnaires like him, would help with the manhunt for the deranged killer targeting Talon DeMar's people.

One of the double doors opened before they were halfway up the broad steps. A man in a black suit stood to the side of the door, he shared a nod with Dutch.

Keti walked with her head down. The horror of what she'd been through, and what she was expecting now, was written in the icy skin stretched taut across her beautiful face.

Dutch felt sorry for her, but he knew Wolf wouldn't really harm her. Much. But he would do what he had to, to keep her fine little behind in line. Anything above that Dutch didn't want to know about since he'd had designs on the girl himself.

"Absolom," he greeted the tall austere man at the door that bowed briefly as Dutch ushered Keti into the house. They stopped in the foyer that was tiled in shimmering blue and silver.

The walls were white brick. A marble table sat in the center of the space, in the middle of the table was a vase with an enormous spray of colorful flowers. That wasn't there before, Wolf must have had it brought in for Keti. Who knew the governmental assassin was a romantic?

His hand anchoring Keti's small shoulder, Dutch smiled and finally relaxed. Apparently Wolf was enamored with Keti, and it wasn't all about the sex. Dutch wondered if Wolf realized that about himself.

Dutch grinned as his friend entered the foyer, it was going to be interesting to see how Wolf gets the lovely Keti on board. Although cold and standoffish, the girl was pure feminine daintiness, her mannerisms innocent, ladylike and elegant.

Her body, small with delicate bone structure held surprising abundant curves quite nicely. And her face, soft and gorgeous, huge, luminous green eyes that were at once shy, wary, frightened. She looked that way every time Dutch had seen her.

The girl made a man want to protect her from all the evils of the world and fuck her brains out at the same time.

His eyes on Keti, Wolf came forward. He nodded at Dutch.

Dutch had called him after he'd ripped Falk a new one and told him what had transpired with the wild carnal abandon at the station. He had warned Wolf that Keti was brittle, terrified and in shock. And very unhappy to be there, but she had agreed to Wolf's terms.

"Thank you, Dutch," Wolf said, his gaze fell to the hand Dutch had on Keti's shoulder. "I have heard from Johan."

Dutch's brows rose. "Yeah? Anything substantial?"

Wolf frowned. "No. They dumped all the phones from the residents of the lodge as well as the family members that hadn't come for the retreat. They found nothing that they were not able to match to a person or a business. Nothing, no one strange, no untraceable burners leading to the killer."

Wolf wore a dark blue suit, white shirt and tie. A wolfman in human clothing.

Dutch's eyes shifted to Keti and back to Wolf.

Wolf lowered his brows at him and glowered at the hand still on her shoulder.

Dutch bit back his grin, Wolf was already showing proprietary ownership of Keti. He patted her shoulder then removed his hand and said, "Uh, yeah, well, I guess I'd better get back to work. Your guys will update me on the canvassing. Wilhelm has men taking the victims' cars apart, and more are up studying the highways to trace what happened, what caused the crashes. Uh…well," he looked at Keti, her head was down.

Wolf spoke, "Ketherine, you-"

Whack!

Keti slapped him.

Wolf had seen it coming a mile away. He hadn't bothered dodging it, or even stopping her. It hadn't hurt him at all, but she struggled not to grasp her pained hand and hold it to her chest.

Her enraged eyes flung wide, shocked at her own abnormal action. She'd never struck someone before in her life. It proved that he wasn't a real man, he didn't even flinch when her palm hit him.

Definitely an animal, a bull, a gorilla, a wolverine, whatever, he wasn't human. She knew she was being imaginary, but, he truly did frighten her to death. Nonetheless, she still burned with fury at being forced into this untenable position.

As if she hadn't slapped him, Wolf said calmly, "I will take you upstairs, Ketherine, to our suite." Her eyes rounded more at the word *our*.

Wolf turned to Dutch. "Let me get her settled and I will be back down. We need to compare notes and information."

"Uh," nodding, Dutch mumbled with his lips pulled in. "Of course." He gently touched Keti's arm, said softly, "Keti, it'll all work out for the best, you'll see."

Her big eyes turned up in desperation to the sheriff.

He sighed. "Honey, this is the safest place you could be. Nothing can get to you here. Wolf's men have been with him for ages, as have his servants. You'll stay protected behind these walls, and it'll soon be over and you can go home."

Her mouth twisted. The ludicrous unfairness of it all astounded her, and it was all in her voice as she said wryly, "Oh goodie. Once he's done assaulting me here, I can go back home and get beaten into signing the bridge papers before I walk down the aisle as Rein van Baer's bride and he gets to assault me too. It only gets better, Sheriff. Thanks so much for your caring help."

Both men surprised at the way she spoke up, watched her fight her anger and the terror that gripped her from the predicament she was forced into. Wolf's lids flattened over his dark eyes at her mention of Rein.

Keti's eyes narrowed at Dutch, she derided, "I wish you men could experience what it's like to be a woman controlled by men who don't give a damn about her well-being, the only important thing is them.

"Their egos, their power, their money," she jerked a glare at Wolf, "their lusts. Try seeing what it feels like to be helpless, defenseless, vulnerable, basically a slave with no rights. To be a virtual prisoner. Not able to do what you desire to do, go to work, school, have the freedom to do as you please."

Her lips curved down forlornly, she said with bitter sadness, "Marry whom you please."

Dutch shifted his feet, he looked down then at her. "I'm sorry, Keti. I'm sorry the coins tossed in your life made you Talon DeMar's stepdaughter, and so breathtakingly beautiful that men will want to possess you. You are so enchanting males will think they need to imprison you so another man doesn't steal you from them."

She blinked, taken aback at his words. A rusty swallow rolled down her dry throat. In a soft tremulous voice she groused, "I am not a possession to be owned, Sheriff. I am a free adult woman, a citizen of America. It isn't right what you men, my father, Rein are doing to me. Don't you stupid men see that a person can be held by love instead of chains?"

Dutch replied, "But there are too many men that feel they are entitled to have what they want, men that haven't the patience to wait until they earn love." He slew an accusatory side-glance at Wolf.

"All right, enough platitudes, Dutch." Wolf held his hand to her to take. "Katherine, come, I will take you to our room where you can settle in. Margot will bring you a drink and something to eat. It has been a rough day for you, I am sure you are weary and hungry."

She ignored his hand and looked away from him.

His expression remaining blank, Wolf lowered his hand and said, "Okay, Ketherine, I need to speak with Dutch for a minute. Stay here," he nodded his head that he didn't want her to move from where she stood.

Pretending he didn't see her frown of irritation at being told what to do, he tapped Dutch's arm and motioned for him to follow him.

The two men strode through a hall and into the first door they came to. It was used as a study.

Dark brown and warm creams, a handsome stone fireplace with a dancing orange glow and two walls of bookshelves, sturdy masculine furniture, it was clearly a man's room.

Wolf told him, "I will be a few minutes taking Ketherine to our suite, Dutch, have Absolom fetch you a drink and food if you would like."

Dutch grinned at him. "I think you're gonna want more than a few minutes with her, Wolf."

Wolf's lips lifted crookedly, he shrugged slightly. "True. But tonight I just want her to settle in, feel safe for probably the first time in her life."

Dutch's expression turned serious. "That is so not likely to happen. She was quite clear in her shouted statements that she didn't want to be with you, didn't want you touching her. But I know what you're saying. My understanding is that something traumatic happened when she was around 13 or so and then she was sent away."

At Wolf's short nod of agreement, Dutch said, "My guess is one of them," the side of his mouth lifted in anger seeing Wolf knew what he was referring to. "Or more than one of them went after her. Talon refused to discuss it with me, and I never met her mother who died almost two years ago now."

"*Jah*, I get the same vibe."

"So," Dutch spoke slowly, "then perhaps you should think twice about forcing, ah, expecting her to submit to you. She's obviously frightened of you, not that I don't blame her," his lip quirked in humor.

Wolf moved to stand near the door. "She is one thousand percent shut down, closed off. She would never come to me willingly, I have to push the issue."

Crossing his arms, Dutch cocked his head. He argued, "Why push it? If she doesn't want to fuck you then why force it?" A short smirk on his handsome face, he said, "Get over being refused by a woman for the first time in your life, bro. I'm sure you can find one as beautiful, or near to, that will salve your crushed ego."

One shoulder bumped, Wolf replied, "I have no desire to choose another woman. Besides, she will not be safe anywhere but here." One brow arched satirically. "You think I can have her in my house and not take her?"

"So, keep your greedy hands to yourself, Wolf, leave the girl be. Stick her in a room where you don't have to lay eyes on her until this whole mess is over with."

Wolf unknotted his tie and moved it to sling loose under his collar and down the front of his shirt. He pried the top few buttons open exposing dark chest hair. "You think you could stick that woman, to use your pretty words, in a room and forget she is here?"

Dutch smirked. "Of course not. But that doesn't mean you have the right to force her, coerce her into having sex with you."

"Dutch," Wolf sighed. "If I had the time, if I thought with time I could bring her around to accept me as her...mate, to use an animalistic word since I have heard her refer to me as the wolfman, I would have set out to, what do you call it? Woo her?" He shook his head.

"Even with time, she has been too…traumatized, and she is too afraid of me, she would never let me near her, never let me in. She is never going to let any male in. I have to force the matter."

He paused, pushed the sides of his suitcoat back and set his hands on his hips. "Dutch, I am not just planning on screwing her until this whole issue is over then sending her home. I plan to make her my wife."

Dutch's brows shot up. "Whoa, bro, what? You don't even know her." He squinted at Wolf. "I never thought of you as having…wanting any kind of serious relationship with a woman. Talk about closed off…"

A small grin gracing the side of his harsh face, Wolf said, "I had never met Ketherine DeMar before. She is not just a pretty face with a rocking body, there is…substance to her. You saw it earlier, she's a sexy bundle of soft womanly granite. Shy as hell but she has a backbone, and, there is a spark that lights her, the world, up. It was like I was struck by lightning the second I laid eyes on her. And it is not going to change."

Dutch smiled slightly. "Yeah, I know. I wanted that light for myself, bro."

Wolf grinned wryly at his old friend. "Next time, move quicker."

"Sure," Dutch chuckled, "with you anywhere near the picture I had snowball's chance in hell. You were on the money to go look for her and check the perimeter. Put you in the right place at the right time, my friend."

Wolf's grin widened then he sobered. "Now, the longer I leave her the more anxious she will become. I will get her established in our room and come back down and we can update our notes. I will send Absolom in to see to your refreshment needs."

Wolf started to turn to walk through the door, but Dutch spoke. A sly intonation oozed like sensual silk with his grin. "Wolf, that slap, shit man, that was hot. Girl had the balls, or whatever it is that ladies have, to strike you. There is fiery passion hidden there. Turned me on, wish it had been me."

His smile wily and erotic, Wolf responded, "Oh *jah* it was hot. See, sparky, but too, how do you call it, dainty? To do any harm." His smile stalled.

"However, she hurt herself. I regret that part. But, I had wanted to let her do it because, hell, I damned deserved it for putting her in this position. Still," he grinned, "hell yeah it was hot. And," he started out the door, said over his shoulder, "I am damned glad it was me."

Wolf left with Dutch's chuckles ringing in his ears. As he figured, Keti wasn't where he told her to wait. She chafed at his ordering her around and was going to see how far she could push him.

Seeing Wolf had left Absolom to guard her, standing in front of the door they had come in, she had meandered over to a narrow window off to the side of the foyer.

Wolf could move as silent as a sailboat on the high sea, but he purposefully let his footsteps make a sound so as not to frighten the already skittish woman.

He knew she heard him coming by the stiffening of her shoulders, but the fierce little kitten wouldn't give him the satisfaction of turning around at his approach.

Wolf wanted to get right to teaching her how to submit to him, give her a tiny punishment for her not obeying his instructions, her rudeness at showing him he didn't matter one whit to her.

Then, he caught her reflection in the window. Her eyes were shiny with unshed tears, she bit the bottom of her lip to still the trembling. She was staring blankly off into nothingness, her abject fear and loneliness reflected back at him.

He stopped beside her. Waited. She didn't make any move to look at him or say something.

Swallowing his sigh of frustration, Wolf said, "Let's go, I will take you upstairs, I have business to go over with Dutch."

Keti didn't respond, as he assumed she wouldn't. Her cloak of self-protection has always been avoidance, silence, hiding. Well, she can do that with everyone else except him.

He motioned to Absolom to see to Dutch then he gently clasped her arm and ushered her through the large foyer then to the wide staircase covered in a rich burgundy carpet that rippled up to the upper floors.

Chapter Fourteen

When they reached the steps, Keti faltered, her knees turned to rubber.

Wolf tightened his grip. "Are you terribly fatigued, Ketherine? That man at the lodge brutalized you before I got there. Here, I will carry you-" He bent to slip his arms beneath her back and legs. She pushed away from him.

"No." Although Keti felt drained, as if she were hanging on by a thread, she didn't want his hands on her. She reached out and gripped the polished bannister. "I'm fine." Using the railing for support, Keti started up the stairs.

Nonetheless, Wolf moved beside her and slid his arm around her back to help brace her. She tried to lean away from his big hulking body, but he tightened his hold and she was forced to press against his hard form. So hard he felt like one huge, unbreakable diamond beast in a suit.

Wolf led her down a hallway passing many doors, she was relieved no one else seemed to be around. Her humiliation was demoralizing as it was.

He stopped at a door, all of the doors were ten feet high.

Turning the knob, he opened the door. His hand moved to the small of her back and he ushered her inside. The warmth of his large palm leaked through her thin sweater, she tried to push back, stop from having to move further inside, but he just pressed her along.

Feeling her shivering against his hand, he murmured, "None of us idiot males thought to grab your jacket. I will turn the heat up."

They entered another foyer, smaller than downstairs, and he drew her through, their shoes tapping on the glistening, pale blue tiles. They moved through a short but extra wide hallway then came to a large room.

It was warm due to the huge brick fireplace that was blazing against one wall. The furniture was also large and masculine, brown leather mixed with chairs that were thickly cushioned.

An entertainment center took up another wall that most of the furniture was arranged in front of in a semi-circle. Keti's shoes squashed the thick carpet as he kept her moving.

As Wolf led her past the living area he said, "We have a kitchenette, but the chef and his assistants prepare most of the meals. Dinner is generally served family style down in the dining room, and breakfast is a buffet. For lunch, people are welcome to go into the main kitchen and fix themselves sandwiches, select leftovers or salads or whatever."

Keti didn't say a word as he kept going. She didn't care a whit about anything to do with his house and she wished he'd stop using the plural terms: our, we.

The next room was the bedroom. Also huge with heavy masculine furniture. Wide windows stretched across most of one wall, the bed of course was immense. Keti shrunk back as he pulled her inside.

Feeling her reluctance, Wolf frowned. He curved his hands around her upper arms and turned her to face him.

Scolding her gently, he said, "I will have none of that resistance, Ketherine. When you agreed to have Dutch bring you here, you agreed to my terms. I was quite clear about what I expected. Complete willingness, no averseness whatsoever on your part. Do we have that understanding?"

Keti pulled her head back and looked up at him.

He was still a frightening male to view. His face was glacially sharp but blunt as well, hard, his mouth harsh, nothing but darkness emanated from his enigmatic eyes. She took a deep bolstering breath, let it out.

Her voice soft and trembling, she said, "You know I don't want to be here, Mr. Valdimar. I don't understand why- why you insist that I'm to stay with you. Why would you want someone who does not want you?"

His expression didn't alter, but his brows lowered slightly. "Ah, a question asked by a very young woman in her innocence of the ways of men. The thing is, Ketherine, that some men, men like me that were raised deep in the jungles of war, living mostly with savage men just like them, these men are used to taking what they want. I want you."

"But, I don't want you. I have rights." She stood stiffly, her fingers wringing each other. "You are using the mask of protecting me to snatch away my rights, to take what you want. It's against the law, what you are doing to me."

His hot gaze roamed her face, down her figure and back up. "The way I was raised, women had no rights. They were brought to us for our pleasure, for us to do with as we desired.

"Most of the women were thrilled about it. They received money or gifts. Some just wanted the savage sex. But, those that refused, ah," he drew a breath, "they were punished until they complied. Or, mostly, they were just…forced. Humans were a low commodity in the jungles I fought in."

She found it hard to maintain eye contact with him. He was so…brutal looking, scars etched in parts of his face. It wasn't that he wasn't good-looking in a fearsome coarse way, it was the animal fierceness that hovered like a cloak around his strapping physique. Keti found him so bone-chillingly terrifying.

She felt a quiver that he had a look like he wanted to chew her up, literally. Like the wolf in the cartoons that filed his canines into sharp points about to go out and catch his dinner.

Keti couldn't believe the abhorrent way he described the poor women brought to the soldiers in the camps, forced or punished to do their will.

With an ugly shiver of recoil, she pushed aside the pictures that wrought and whispered, "You don't care that I don't want you? That my skin crawls at the thought of you touching me much less doing anything…else?"

He stared at her with zero inflection. "No. I wanted you the second I saw you hovering in fright on the ground. At that moment I knew I would do anything to have you. And, here you are. Now," he chatted as if they were having a calm friendly conversation.

"One of my men will stop by your father's house in the morning to pack you some clothes, although," he frowned with displeasure as he took in the sweater and baggy pants. "I cannot say I like seeing you dressed like an old schoolmarm. You have a figure under all that loose shit, and I want to see it."

Keti took a step back from him at his pronouncement. She wrapped her arms around her front, grasped her sides. "This is what I wear. I don't want to dress like a- a floozy. Just because you are making me your whore doesn't mean I have to look like one."

117

His brows arched, the side of his mouth hitched up. He didn't comment on what she said.

At not disputing that she was his whore, Keti's voice tight, her words shook out bleakly, "Mister, um, Val-Valdimar, I don't wish to go back to the jail, nor do I want to stay here with you. I would like to return to my home."

She didn't really, but she'd find some way to hide from all of them, somehow. "Uh, if I may use the phone, I'm sure someone at the lodge would come and get me, or I could take a taxi…a bus would do if I-"

"*Enough*," he huffed in exasperation and took a step closer to her. He held up a hand but she half-turned her head and stepped back from him as if she thought he was going to hit her. He dropped his hand.

"Ketherine." He waited for her to look at him. She didn't, just kept her head averted like she'd done before.

Anger was wrapping around his throat, he had to hold onto his rising temper. He said slowly, his words stunted with boiling pique, "Look. At. Me."

His tone forceful and harsh made her jump. Her head turned, she swung frightened eyes up at him.

"When I speak to you, I expect you to acknowledge it. Look at me when I am talking to you. I do not want to…ah discipline you so early in our, ah," he broke off at the color shedding from her normally rosy cheeks.

"Just, anyway," his voice hardened, "you heard the sheriff. You are a suspect in homicides, it is either jail, or here under my custody. You saw how it was at the jail. You told Dutch you wanted to come here instead, and that you would accept my terms, obey my…orders."

He waited for her to say something, but although she faced him, she kept her eyes lowered, aimed at his chest, so there was no eye contact between them.

Letting out a frustrated breath, nodding towards a door, he said, "Anyway, for now, you can take a shower."

When she didn't comment, he went on, "Margot rustled up a blow-dryer and laid out towels and grooming items for you. New soap and shampoo and such. I am sure your poor skin would shrivel in disgust if you shared anything of mine on your body."

Her face pinked at his flip words, but she said nothing.

"All right. You shower, then you will put this on…" he walked to the bed and lifted up a blue shirt. It was a long-sleeved button down, and apparently his.

"Normally I detest when women try to wear my clothes, however, in this case," his heated gaze traveled from her head to toe and back. He laid the shirt back on the bed.

His ebony eyes burned so hotly with desire like lit charcoal, he looked like he was barely restraining himself from pouncing on her. Keti's heart thumped like a racehorse.

He went on, "I actually look forward to seeing you swathed in my clothing. I have thought about it all evening while I waited for Dutch to bring you."

That made her mad, he was so sure that she would come to him. But what choice did she really have? Raped and beaten by many, or by only one man. She kept her eyes lowered, she refused to give him the satisfaction of her attention. His belabored sigh told her it worked.

"Anyway," he said, "I will allow you to wear panties under it just for tonight, to make you feel somewhat…covered. I see you are shy, self-conscious, but only for tonight. Later on I will expect you to be completely nude under my sheets. Our sheets. Margot has provided a pair of underwear, do not worry my little hissing kitten, they are clean. But that is all you may wear for now, my shirt and the panties. No bra."

Her eyes flit back and forth as she tried to contain the alarm triggering like a gunshot in her brain at his words. Naked, in a man's bed. The last thing in the world she wanted, and especially with the wolfman.

Her cheeks heated in embarrassment at his cavalier speaking about her lingerie.

Keti hadn't really been around men much. School had been all females, She stayed tucked in her room at Blackslade, and at work Talon made sure she was mostly confined in the connecting offices they shared. She was basically alone 95% of the time, and she liked it that way.

It was too bold of this maddening creature to mention her undergarments to her. But then he probably had boatloads of women, being the arrogant, powerful scoundrel that he was. He was probably used to stripping women, or more likely ordering them to strip for his lazy pleasure.

If only she'd been born a male. She could become the anthropologist or archeologist she'd always dreamed of, run her life as she pleased instead of being held against her will by a devouring beast and forced to do what he desired.

It was so unfair. She was going to leave the first opportunity she got, she'd take her chances out on her own. Her eyes flit to the door.

Reading her mind, a cold smile lifted the side of his mouth. His gaze pinned her in place. "You will not leave this house, Ketherine. Not without me with you. And until I have Johnny Frog dealt with, that will not happen. He has plenty of snipers and bomb experts in his employ."

Keti felt the breath leave her lungs. If he wanted to frighten her, he succeeded. Nevertheless, she was still making a run for it at her first chance. She didn't need a man to protect her. These medieval men seemed to think a woman couldn't take care of herself. Well, she can, and she will.

Wolf stepped closer to her, bent to bring their faces more even, he reminded her, "You agreed. You cannot take it back. You will not disappoint me by not being a woman of your word. If you try to flee, you will find it hard to get out of the house, and impossible to leave the premises. And if you try, you will face my wrath, and my discipline."

Her lids flapped up at his threat. "You- you would beat me?"

His mouth shut, he leaned back from her and stood straight. "I will punish that little round ass of yours until you cannot sit for a week. You try it again, and the punishment will increase."

His eyes turned shark sinister, they glittered with black threat. "You do not want to cross me, Ketherine. You will regret it if you try. You chose me over the jail, you accepted my deal. I am expecting you to be an honorable woman and not try to back out." He exhaled and tugged at the collar of his shirt in annoyance.

"Now, do as I say. Take a shower, the warmth will help you relax. Margot will bring you a tray. Then when I come back up here I expect you to be in that shirt," he nodded to the offending garment lying on the side of the bed, "and you will be in the bed," he motioned to the massive thing. "Do you have any questions, Ketherine?" He crossed his arms, stood back and stared down at her, his expression blank.

She blinked back the tears and shook her head. Words wouldn't choke out her constricted throat. He was a vile, threatening beast, there was nothing she could say to change anything.

He stared at her for a moment, then turned on his heel and left the room. He closed the door behind him, she heard the lock click.

It was hours later when he returned. Keti was heavily drowsy with sleep when she heard him unlock the door and his footsteps on the carpet.

In the back of her woozy brain, she realized he had deliberately made noise so she would hear him coming. She'd seen the stealthy way he always moved, if he hadn't wanted her to know he was in the room, she wouldn't.

He moved to the bed. Feeling him watching her, she held her breath. What would he do if he knew she'd thoroughly explored the room and bathroom seeking a way out? Surely he would have expected her to search his room.

Keti hadn't rummaged through his things, she had no desire to touch anything of his, and she was not curious about him at all.

Since he had assumed she was coming there, he certainly wouldn't leave anything that could be used as a weapon lying around, or something like a credit card, phone, etc., anything else she could have used as a way out.

The bad news was, she discovered there would be no escaping the suite from the windows. On the second floor, the drop down would be too steep to try, but she had spent a long time considering it.

Now, Keti tried to fight her way out of the thick fog of sleep, but she'd been so tired, so weary from fear and the day's tolls, sleep pulled her under.

His footsteps retreated and she heard the bathroom door open and a few minutes later the shower turned on. A small lamp next to the bed lent a bit of dim lighting.

Keti was drifting back to a labor heavy sleep when she heard the shower shut off.

A few more moments passed and he came back into the bedroom.

A dresser drawer opened and closed, clothes rustled. He neared the bed, then the sound of something clicking and re-clicking. Keti assumed he was locking his weapon up. At least one of them, she knew he carried many.

The light went out then she felt the mattress sink under his weight. The smell of masculine shampoo and soap wafted over her. Frozen into stillness, filled with fright, Keti tried to prepare herself for his assault.

She knew it would hurt. It had before and the wolfman was a very big male. He wouldn't be gentle, he had described his years in the jungle, it would go way past just hurt.

A shiver spiraled through her as she pictured him pounding between her legs, his fanged teeth stabbing deep in her neck holding her immobile for his onslaught.

Wearing boxers and a t-shirt, Wolf pulled the sheet and blanket back and slid inside. He reached for her. His strong hand curved around her waist and he pulled her back against his wide chest.

He nestled his thick erection against her bottom. His hand still at her waist, he pushed it under the shirt and up and covered her breast with his big palm.

Keti waited. He did nothing else. The evidence, a thick hard ridge against her butt told her he wanted to have sex with her, but he didn't move.

He was an assassinating mercenary animal. She expected him to pounce on her, shove himself viciously inside her, brutally take her. But, the clasp of his hard hand on her breast was gentle, albeit firmly possessive. She knew it would be futile to try to push his hand off her.

He didn't squeeze his big fingers, didn't pinch her, didn't hurt her at all, just, held her. She felt the calm breaths rising and falling with his muscular chest so tight against her back. His exhales stirring her hair. She almost felt…comfortable, safe, cared for?

Unconsciously, Keti nestled into his strength, his warmth, his protection. His hand on her breast stayed just gently possessive, nothing like when- she jumped, her body instantly rigid with fright.

"Shh," Wolf whispered against the top of her head, "settle, little kitten."

His voice, different, deep, accented, didn't sound like the voice from her nightmares, still…she struggled to be released from his hold, he tightened his arm around her.

"Tis okay, the bogeyman got you when you were a child, he hurt you, he broke your soul."

Her breath caught in her throat, rapid, shallow inhalations betrayed her fear. How could he know what had happened so long ago?

Wolf spoke softly, "He will never harm you again, my Ketherine, I will never allow anyone to ever hurt you again. Your soul will knit whole once more over time."

He tucked his knees up more tightly under her knees, enfolding her safely within the cushioned cage of his secure body.

His breathing remained slow, even, calm, stirring her hair beneath his lips he gently kneaded her breast. "Sleep little one, no bogeyman will come for you tonight. If he tried, I would kill him." His voice a bare whisper, "When I find out who it was that hurt you so badly, I will destroy him."

His dangerous words should have made her more anxious, but they oddly comforted her, calmed her. She waited, but he only cupped her breast, his chest moving hypnotically in and out.

Keti felt at peace for the first time in her life. It wouldn't last, she was sure of that, but for now, she actually snuggled into his strong embrace and quickly dropped off.

Chapter Fifteen

Wolf woke slowly, he was lying on his back and he wasn't alone. That was strange, he never slept with any woman he fucked. Still, a soft, warm body was curled up against him, or more accurately half over him, her face rested on his furry chest, an arm flung across his abs.

He inhaled deeply, oh yeah, no one could smell that femininely fresh naturally. No one that is, except for Katherine DeMar. He realized his big hand was cupping half her ass.

She smelled amazing, she felt like a million bucks, and she fit perfectly in his arms and sprawled over his body. She still wore his shirt, but she was naked under it except for a tiny wisp of panties. His hard-on was so painful it brought him fully awake.

Nothing in the world he'd rather do right now was to roll that girl over onto her back and screw her brains out until she begged him for more. "Huh," he snorted, and pigs will fly.

As soon as she wakes and realizes she is sprawled over him and he is clutching her ass, she'll hurtle herself off him with a scream of fright.

A sigh rippled from his chest, she needs time. He'll do the best he can, but Wolf wants her as badly as he wants food for his stomach or air for his lungs.

He carefully lifted Keti and gently arranged her beside him then he slipped out of the bed and covered her with the sheet and blanket.

Her glorious mahogany waves spun over the white pillow like ribbons of autumn leaves. Long mahogany lashes curled on her rosy cheeks.

Wolf was loath to leave his sexy little kitten, but he couldn't look at her much longer without taking her.

After dressing, he sought out Margot.

Finding her in the kitchen, he told her, "Miss Ketherine still slumbers. Prepare a dish for her and bring it up before she wakens. I do not want her leaving my room without me, be sure to lock the door to the suite when you leave. Don't make a big deal of it in front of her, be discreet."

Ketherine would more than likely have a fit if the door was closed in her face and locked. Yes, she was technically a prisoner, his prisoner, but it wasn't going to make her any more biddable to him shoving it in her face.

He said, "Tell Priscilla to have Jarrod drive her to the Cesar Peak Lodge, and call Talon DeMar, tell him I sent her to pack a bag for Miss Ketherine."

Margot wore her dark hair in a thick swirled bun. She had quiet dark brown eyes and she only ever said, "Yes, sir," to Wolf, never another word.

The entire staff feared him, which he didn't mind. The only one he didn't want afraid of him was Ketherine.

Well, he wanted her to fear his wrath if she doesn't obey him or puts her life in danger, or flirts with other men. But he doesn't want her to fear his bed because he planned on them spending much of their life in it from now on.

In her early forties, tall and sturdy, as expected, Margot nodded slightly and said, "Yes, sir."

Wolf didn't wait for anything else, just ambled over to a plate laden with eggs, sausages and buttered cinnamon toast, and snatched it up. A fork lay beside it. He poured a cup of steaming coffee and brought the plate and coffee down to the study.

Wolf's best friend and fellow childhood soldier, Johan Karlis was already inside waiting for him.

Romet Kurios, another friend from their other life was there as well.

Johan sipped at a mug of coffee, an iPad at his elbow, he was reading a sports magazine.

Slouched in a recliner, Romet was pouring a liberal amount of bourbon from a flask into his mug of coffee.

Wolf's brow arched at the booze. "Not enough libation last night, Romet?"

Romet shrugged a massive shoulder. Closing the lid, he slid the flask in his pocket and took a large gulp of the brew. "This is how I have always taken my coffee, Wolf, yet you always comment on it."

Romet wore his black hair like a messy bowl over his head. Black brows half-moons over equally black eyes were secretively shrewd and intelligent, and carried a glitter of danger the same as Wolf and Johan.

"That is true," Wolf admitted.

Romet had some difficult memories, just like Johan and Wolf did. Romet handled his pain with booze, Johan with broads, Wolf with business. Business that he used his fists, his guns, and his wits with. Wolf fought his tormented memories with brawling, and killing.

"Hey," Johan said with a smirky smile and set the magazine down. "So you got the little chickadee caged in your room. I cannot believe she chose you over prison, eh?" He chuckled and Romet snickered along with him. "You still planning on keeping her for the long haul, my brother?"

"I said I was, did I not?" Wolf muttered, setting his plate and mug on the round maple table in the center of the room. On weekends, the table was covered with cards and money, the room smoke-clogged from cigars, and the chairs around it filled with gambling men.

"What have you found out?" Wolf cut off a hunk of scrambled eggs, speared it and stuffed it in his mouth. Chewing, he washed it down with a slug of hot coffee.

"Geeze," Johan pretended to complain. "Right to work, no good morning, no asking how my night went. It went very well thank you, I reply anyway, the Dardino sisters were ripe for romping all night-"

"Okay, J." Wolf heaved a sigh. "Just get on with the info."

"Sure, bro, before you set your wandering eye on the little girl upstairs you were just as involved with our global sexual exploits as old Romet there was."

Sipping his bourbon laced coffee, Romet's response was to turn his lazy hooded gaze at his friend and raise his middle finger.

"J," Wolf growled.

Grinning like the Cheshire, Johan clicked keys on his iPad. "You are gonna love this, my brother." The pad lit up, his eyes on the screen, Johan said, "Got stuff back on one of the businessmen at the lodge. Ah, Andrew Ansberry."

"The astronaut?" Wolf asked, chomping an entire sausage at once.

"Yep. I was curious that he did the one and done, one rocket ship ride to the stars and then retired at 45. I had to dig deep, shit was buried with NASA, they didn't want smut on their rocket noses."

"Huh," Romet snorted and threw back the rest of his coffee. He got up and trod over to the side table where a heated carafe sat plugged into the wall. He refilled his coffee, removed the flask from his pocket and poured a liberal amount into the mug then returned to his chair.

"Smut?" Wolf was surprised. "What did the tall, angular Mr. Ansberry with the long comb-over do?"

Johan scrolled the screen with a smug smirk. "Fucked one of the other astronauts. One of the other married astronauts. Bad in itself, but it gets worse, the married astronaut had cried rape. I got a hold of the record. Mrs. Ilene Campbell stated they were alone one night working on the simulator-"

"Stimulator?" Romet coughed, almost spitting out his coffee. "No wonder they got in trouble."

"No you dolt, *simulator*. You know, a practice spaceship. You've seen them in movies and shit. Anyway, they were alone, Mrs. Campbell, well, it was Captain Campbell actually, said Ansberry shoved her over the control chair, ripped her pants down and fucked her."

Wolf's eyes enlarged. "Seriously? I did not think that skinny snooty guy could get it up for his snotty aristocratic wife. Hell, I am almost proud of the boy."

"Skinny, but strong." Johan told them, "Captain Campbell's report indicated he had left bruises on her when she tried to fight him off."

"So?" Wolf asked. "Why is the fucker not in prison getting a taste of his own?"

Johan rubbed his thumb and middle fingers together indicating money. "Ansberry paid her off. The records were actually sealed, but you know, with my genius I was able to get my hands on them."

"It's called hacking, J." Romet raised his mug in toast to his friend.

"Yeah. Anyway, apparently she wasn't the first. NASA got tired of trying to bury his antics so they canned him. Gave him early retirement so they wouldn't have to inform the world they had a rapist travelling the friendly skies of Earth."

Johan sat back in his chair with satisfaction. "Yep, ferreted that shit right out man, with my extraordinary skills."

"Oh hell, J, give us a break." Romet rolled up a paper napkin and threw it at his friend. Johan batted it away and looked for something to throw back at him.

"All right, we have work to do, stop playing like four-year-olds," Wolf scolded them absently, his mind was on the information Johan had divulged.

Wolf surmised, "He is a rapist bully, which might mean he could have assaulted the women, but the males, Michael McShane and Ollie Duncan? The children of his frat brothers?"

Johan grunted. "A rapist is a rapist, Wolf. He violated the astronaut, and apparently others, he could just as easily have assaulted the victims and murdered them this time so he didn't have to pay them off."

Wolf scratched his jaw as he pondered. "True, but what about the men? The killer sodomized them. Did you find anything that alluded to Ansberry having any kind of homosexual leanings? Assaults on males, too?"

Shaking his head, Johan answered, "No, nothing popped up like that on Ansberry. Our killer penile raped the women, there was spermicide found in them so he wore a rubber. He used implements on the males, and hacked up their junk."

He gave a little shudder at the remembrance of the pictures they had viewed of the deceased. "That indicates he wanted to do the women, but the assault on the men was different, a message maybe? Revenge?"

The three men sat and thought about the new information. "Okay," Wolf said, getting to his feet, "keep on it. Check out Ansberry's alibi with a fine-tooth comb, leave no rock unchecked."

"Huh, creep slithered out from under one for sure, Wolf." Romet nodded with a grimace. "Unfortunately he has an air tight alibi. He hadn't left the lodge since he had arrived. He was never alone."

Heading for the door, Wolf said, "Yes, but his wife and his best friends are his alibis. One or more could be lying."

He looked at the tall, thick-chested male with his mop of black hair. "Romet, grab Wilhelm and go interrogate the alibis." Dark brows lowered over his eyes narrowed at Romet. "And take the gloves off. I do not care if you have to bloody them. Understand?"

Romet jumped up grinning. "Sure thing, Boss. My pleasure and my forte."

"Johan, keep digging. I do not care for the bunch of shitheads at the lodge. I saw they are pompous and mean the little bit I was with them. They could all be capable of the savage murders. I heard they were cruel and grab-ass to Ketherine as well, so do not feel you have to hold back."

"Okay. I'll do that as long as you work on the English contractions you so deftly avoid learning." Johan grinned at him while folding the newspaper.

Johan went on, "You sound like a heavily accented robot. I know you didn't have the luxury of living with a family like the rest of us did to pick up nuances of the English language we learned along with our Estonian dialect, at least until we were snatched and thrown into the military.

"But you sound blunted and coarse, downright sinister when you speak. It makes people nervous and afraid of you." He tucked the magazine into the back of his pocket and lifted his mug to finish his coffee.

Wolf ignored his friend's advice and left the room. He had to call Dutch and fill him in. What he really wanted to do was take the stairs two at a time and run back to the sultry, dark-haired kitten sleeping in his bed. Their bed.

His lips tugged down recalling the way her lips compressed every time he'd said we or our. Well, kitten has tiny claws, hot as that is, he needs to train her.

But later, he has work to do now.

Chapter Sixteen

*S*everal days passed with no changes.

Ansberry had been hauled down to the station for in-depth questioning. Disappointingly, his alibis were unbreakable.

The only thing they succeeded at was bringing the despicable man's history of assaulting women and buying them off to the attention of the world.

The media jumped on the information with bared teeth, and Wolf allowed his men to feed that hunger. Ansberry couldn't be tried for his crimes, but his lofty name had turned to profane mud.

Due to the shameful fallout, Andrew Ansberry and his prissy wife Diana fought tooth and nail to leave the lodge, yet Dutch Kross ordered them to stay.

Even with alibis, they were all under the umbrella of suspicion. Most of their alibis, male and female alike, were each other. The women claimed shopping and lunch in the town, some trips could be verified through surveillance cameras Johan had hacked, and some not.

Wolf worked all day each day but made sure he was home for dinner to be with Keti. After dinner, Wolf and Keti separated. He back to work, and Keti to her laptop or to read a book.

Tonight, hours later he went in search of her. He had expected her to be in his bed half asleep and was somewhat dismayed to find the suite empty.

She had orders that she was not allowed out of the mansion, and twice he had been called by his guards to come retrieve her as she was making her way to the gate.

She wouldn't be able to get out, but Wolf cringed at the thought of a sniper perched in a tree in the woods putting a bullet between her beautiful green eyes.

One more attempt on her part to flee and he would be forced to take action, punish her so she would realize the danger she really was in. And learn she was to obey his commands.

Ketherine was a young woman that had basically grown up in a convent of sorts, then was kept secluded at Blackslade, she really hadn't been exposed to the real world.

Wolf knew someone had hurt her, but that wouldn't be enough to teach her the rest of the dangers, the treachery that lurked around her.

He was male and older, experienced, it was his duty to teach her, protect her, and yes, discipline her for any reckless peril she placed herself in, to ensure she didn't do it again. Sure, his beliefs were sexist and old fashioned, he didn't care.

Wolf had trackers put in her purse and shoes. He spent every dinner with her, played chess and cards in the evenings, took her for walks in the walled-in courtyard, and slept beside her at night.

All week he had done as the first night. Held her without doing anything sexual. He wanted her to get used to him and not flinch and cringe every time he came near her or touched her.

Every morning he woke with her curvy body curled into him, or even better, draped partially over him. If she woke first, she became instantly distraught at finding herself lying on his body.

She had accused him of putting her there. "Oh!" she squawked one morning when she realized she was poured half naked, lewdly over him.

She scrambled off his body, snatched the blanket to cover herself and scurried to the edge of the bed glaring at him. Lush hair a sultry mess around her head and shoulders, bosom heaving with anger, eyes still hazed with sleep. God the woman was glorious.

Each time this happened, folding his arms behind his head, Wolf gazed with pure innocence at her and blithely stated how he was sound asleep when she crept over and climbed atop him.

Wolf smiled, she'd gotten all red and flustered, so damned gorgeous his body burned for the want of her.

His lust for Ketherine was eating him alive. He could barely keep his mind on the murders. Plus, he had men searching for Johnny Frog. If Wolf could eliminate him, then Ketherine would be safe.

Not that he would let her return home, even after the murders are solved. He didn't know how much time he had to seduce her before everything cleared and she demanded to be released.

Johan had told him that tackling her, forcing her legs apart and shoving himself inside her before he got her willing would only turn her more against him. Yes, he would do it if he had to, but he'd much rather have a fully aroused, wholly willing Ketherine lying in his bed with her arms and legs open in welcome and desire for him.

On Johan's advice, Wolf had been careful in his slow seduction. He didn't grab at her, but held her hand when they strolled, he strove to charm her at dinner, he touched her non-sexually every chance he got. He stroked her arm, sliding his hand lightly around her waist as he took her on walks in the protected courtyard.

While they chatted about their early years, her dream to be an anthropologist with her interests also in archeology, he would occasionally lean in slowly and graze her mouth with his lips. When he did that, Keti would pause, stiffen, then keep talking like he had never touched her. At least now she didn't slap him or run away screaming.

It was tough and unnatural for him to behave like a damned gentleman, but he thought it was working.

Wolf could see her watching him out of the corner of her eye in confusion. She was wondering why he hadn't jumped on her yet. Had his desire for her cooled? Part of his seduction plan was touching her just enough to almost be arousing yet always stopping before he caressed her sexually.

His plan was to bring her own desire, her natural arousal to peak, like a ripe peach about to be plucked. When she was flush with unabridged passion, then he would attack. Just thinking about it gave him a hard-on.

He pushed at his pants to ease it and headed for the library where he knew she liked to hang the most. He knew she hadn't left the mansion, a guard would have immediately contacted him if she had.

Just as he thought as he entered the library, Ketherine was curled up on the cushiony divan by the large window. The curtain should have been pulled closed as night had fallen. It stirred unease in his belly to see her sitting exposed to anyone that could pass by the window.

Granted, it would only be one of his people, the estate was too heavily guarded, still, he didn't like her being so vulnerable. His thought was proven correct when she didn't look up at his approach, she was so deep into her reading.

Even the fire in the fireplace had dwindled to mere sparks giving off little heat. He would have a word with Absolom about seeing to her comfort, and her safety when she was not in their suite. Keti hadn't a clue how to build a fire or keep it going, and she shouldn't have to.

Problem was she hated asking anyone for their help, fearing she was intruding on them, using them. They'd had arguments about it. She was a lady, his lady, and he wanted her doted upon.

Wolf trod across the room over the beige carpet, his boots sinking deep into the thick rug to the divan. He stopped right in front of her and frowned when she still wasn't aware she was no longer alone.

"Ketherine," his frustration came out in his abrupt low voice.

She jumped, the book clattered to the floor, her hand went to her chest. "Oh! Mr. Valdimar, I didn't hear you come in." Her breathing panted out in a startled rush.

His teeth ground at her words. He had meant to speak calmly, sensuously, but his anger thrust out.

"Goddammit, Ketherine, I have told you to stop calling me by my surname. We sleep in the same damned bed for cripe's sake. I have had my mouth on yours and my hands on your bare body, enough with that shit, it is really pissing me off." She made him feel like a dirty old man when she did that crap, she was trying to keep walls up between them.

Exactly what he didn't want to happen, did. An embarrassed blush colored her cheeks, she lowered her head and demurred, "I…am sorry, um, Wolfgang."

He preferred Wolf. Wolfgang was too close to the moniker wolfman she used when referring to him when she spoke to anyone that contacted her from the lodge. It meant she still kept him in the feral animal category in her head.

Usually her friend Bonnie called to check on her. But he'd take what he could get as long as she didn't call him by his surname, or sir as she's done. He wanted her to see him as her lover, not her boss, or her keeper.

He took a step closer and she bent and picked up the book, then clutched it to her chest as if it would block him from nearing her.

Sighing his vexation at her continued fear of him, Wolf moved to the side and pulled the rope closing the dark blue drapes. The night extinguished behind them.

Softening his voice yet keeping an underlying command in it he said, "Ketherine, I have told you to draw the curtains when night falls."

Her lips tightened, he went on, "And it is cold as shit in here. I do not want you ill. I must insist you contact me or Absolom or any of my people to restart the fire in the fireplace when it diminishes."

She still didn't look up at him. With another sigh, he sat down beside her and bit his tongue to keep from cursing when she shifted away from him. It appeared he wasn't making any headway with her after all.

Wolf reached out and picked up her hand. He strung their fingers together. Watching the way his long thick fingers overwhelmed her dainty hand, a rush of protectiveness rose in his throat making his voice husky. "Ketherine," he started then paused. When she didn't look at him he said firmly, "Ketherine, you know I want you to look at me when I am speaking to you. Please."

She raised her green eyes up to peer at him and his heart clinched. "Ah, thank you." He squeezed her hand gently. "It is late, I expected to find you in our bed. Why are you down here?"

Still holding the book to her chest, she bumped one slender shoulder. "I wasn't, um, sleepy." Her eyes slid away from him and he knew what that meant.

It meant that she could feel his patience withering, his lust building out of control, his energy, his desire for her circling, hovering, looming, she was running out of time and she could feel it.

Like the bunny taking a respite while the lion dallied, his mighty jaw opening wide in tasty anticipation, sharp teeth glistening as he smacked his lips about to seize his dinner.

Wolf released her hand and swept his under her hair to palm her nape. As he pulled her close, he plucked the book out of her clenched hand and tossed it to the end of the divan. He lifted his hand to curl it around her jaw, his thumb pressed under her chin, raising it.

Seeing the fear darken her emerald eyes, he stroked his thumb over her bottom lip. "Ketherine..." he drew a breath, damn he wanted this girl so freaking badly and she stared at him like he was the serial killer wrapping a noose around her neck.

His phone rang, he recognized the tune was Johan. He pulled the phone out and said in Estonian, "*Tere, oodake sekund, Johan.*" In English it translated to: 'Hello, hold a second, Johan.'

Wolf pressed a soft kiss to Keti's parted lips then told her, "Baby, go upstairs, get ready for bed. I will be right up."

A smile tinged his rugged face at the flash of ire that crossed her expression at his order. She did not like to be told what to do. Nonetheless, she had learned to do as he said, or he would just make her.

She had refused to return to the mansion the last time the guard called him to come fetch her, and Wolf had tossed her over his shoulder and carried her back. She liked that less than having to obey him.

"Go on," he prodded.

With a small 'humph' she got up, muttered under her breath, "Of course, Mr. Valdimar," retrieved the book and placed it on the bookcase.

She traipsed back and bent to scoop up her shoes and Wolf swatted her, hard, on her butt. "Oh!" She jumped, her hand to her bottom. She glared at him.

His hand over his phone he said, "You call me Mr. Valdimar again and you will receive many more of those, sweetheart, and it will be hand to bare skin."

Moving out of his reach she set her hands on her hips in an angry stance and opened her mouth, then seeing the rise of his jaw she thought better of it and stomped towards the door.

Wolf turned his grin to his phone and started talking to Johan deliberately in Estonian so she couldn't understand him. With another affronted 'humph' she strode out of the room.

Wolf watched her tantalizing bottom snap side-to-side as she stormed angrily away from him. It was only a tiny swat, but hell, he wanted to rip those drawers off her and wail on that plump ass. He heard something. "Oh, sorry J, what were you saying?"

"Hey, Wolf. First thing, Dalton Bastovoi finally caught a glimpse of Giovanni Rana. I have men per your orders swarming the area searching for him. He was riding in an SUV with company, the windows were darkly tinted but that barracuda face couldn't be missed."

"Finally," Wolf grunted. "I knew he'd come in person for her. Rana will have heard enough about Ketherine by now. She's too intriguing at this point to send some lesser after her. And, knowing the deviant despot that he is, he won't kill her right off. He'll want to spend some time with her." The normal edge to Wolf's voice sharpened, it could cut through iron.

Johan chuckled. "Uh huh, we see how quickly she *intrigued* you, my brother."

Ignoring his comment, Wolf asked, "What did Dalton do?"

Another chuckle and Johan replied, "Dalton only got a quick glimpse yet he's sure it's Rana. He tried to tail him, unfortunately by the time Dalton got to his wheels the SUV was gone. I have men canvassing, but hell, bro, the land is vast with cottages and cabins scattered like mushrooms over every hill and dale, forest and mountain. Too many places to hide, especially since they are undoubtedly renting under a fake name."

"Okay," Wolf muttered. At least it was confirmed that the big man himself had come to Diggler's Rock.

A frisson of nerves fingered up his spine. He would tamp down the guards at the estate, he couldn't take any chances. Rana would find out pretty quickly Wolf had Ketherine stashed at his place and would make moves to try and get to her.

Rana was known to be bold and fearless, as well as deadly and sadistic. Rumor was he was savagely rough with his women, consensual or not. They didn't last long in his company. None ever made it to the police, or the hospital for that matter.

"What else you got?"

Johan's snort of disgust came through the phone. "There's a veritable den of creeps staying at that lodge, bro. Thugs in three-piece suits. Ansberry wasn't the only rotten apple in the bunch. One of the others," he paused as if he was checking his notes.

"Ah, Garrett Griggs. Griggs used to be mayor of Bryndale. It's a tiny town south of here. Like Ansberry, he has a shady history as well. Got caught with his hand in the cookie jar."

"Oh yeah?" Half of Wolf's attention was on his friend's imparting information, the other was being dragged upstairs where Ketherine would be getting ready for bed.

Although he'd had her clothes brought to her, he still insisted on her wearing his button down, long-sleeved pale blue shirt to bed. He allowed her to wear panties, but that was all. He was growing hard as he pictured her with her bare legs streaming from-

"Yeah," Johan continued. "He was embezzling from the town's coffers."

"What happened? Why is the man on the loose? None of them had come up with criminal records."

Johan answered, "No. Same as Ansberry. Griggs made restitution. The town didn't want it out there that their own mayor was robbing them blind, so he quietly retired."

"How long ago?"

Johan was silent as he reviewed his notes, then he said, "About five years ago."

Wolf pondered the information. "Both men were forced out before they could complete a full pension, how are they able to live such lavish lifestyles?"

"They are all involved with McMaster Lexington to some degree with Talon DeMar. The original co-founders both died before the business really got off the ground and it fumbled deep in the red for some time. But now, the business is highly lucrative considering none of the frat boys at the time they got involved really had much money.

"DeMar took out some loans and somehow in a short period of time, he came up with an influx of immense bucks and paid off the loans. He has contacts in foreign countries, it's unclear how he hooked up with them in the beginning.

"The records indicate he managed to procure several huge bridge building contracts early on. It was as if he was buying the materials and hiring the workers at the same time as he was starting up the bridge business aspect of the company, and building his first bridge. Something isn't copasetic, Wolf. There's no explanation as to where the funds came from."

Thinking about how long it can take to build a business, Wolf rubbed the back of his neck, they were missing something. "I need you to find out where he came up with the money, J. Still, they may be dirty beggars but it does not mean they would torture and murder some of their own. Where there are two rotten apples, it is probable there are more."

"*Jah*," Johan replied, "following the frat boys around and digging into their lives left a bad taste in my mouth. Those men stink higher to heaven than month old sardines."

"Keep digging, have Romet keep the men canvassing the area, and call Dalton and have him bring in a bigger crew to scour for that fucker Johnny Frog. I want him gone, J, and you know what I mean by gone. No trace of him."

"Gotcha, bro, on it."

"Okay, I have something to do, I will catch up with you tomorrow."

"Uh huh," Johan snickered, "does that something you have to do happen to be a green-eyed, long haired beauty that you are holding captive in-"

Wolf swiped his phone off and tucked it in his pocket and headed for the stairs.

Chapter Seventeen

Wolf closed the first door silently and engaged the lock then strode quickly through the living room and down the hall to the bedroom. Anticipation was making him hard as a rock.

Of course he had been perpetually hard since first setting eyes on Ketherine. He had known in an instant a roll in the hay would never satisfy him, he would need, crave her forever. He was bombarded with feelings and desires he'd never felt before. It should have scared him.

The room was dark as he entered shuffling out of his jacket. He pulled off his tie and tossed the jacket and tie on a chair. Tugging a few buttons open, he unbuttoned his cuffs and rolled the sleeves up to his elbows.

What he wanted to do was strip completely, then strip Ketherine completely and fall into bed with her.

His step slowed, she was standing by the window as she often was when he came to the bedroom. Wolf didn't know if she was planning her escape, pining for her home, or just trying to avoid him. Maybe all three.

He bent and unzipped his dress boots and kicked them off then proceeded to the beauty by the window. She looked so pensive, his heart clenched. He came up behind her. She was attired as he'd ordered, in his shirt and it was buttoned up to her neck. Of course. His modest, frightened little prude.

She had to have heard him coming, seen his reflection in the window, but she didn't turn to face him.

The drapes were pulled back, again not what he had instructed. The moon's silver glow lent cool illumination, the only other light came from the open bedroom door. Still, she jumped when he set his hands on her shoulders. Would she ever not fear his touch?

Standing behind her, Wolf curled his big hands over her slender shoulders and gently squeezed them, he bent and kissed the top of her head. Her response was to freeze, her body instantly became rigid with apprehension.

He moved his hands under her hair and curled them around the sides of her neck, and whispered, "Calm down, Ketherine, it will not be tonight. You," feeling her pulse flutter like mad against his fingers, he dragged in a discouraged breath, "have a reprieve."

God he hated it that she was terrified of him, of his touch, of his desire. "But," he whispered against her hair, "I need to touch you," his voice flattened, "and you will let me."

Her reaction was shivers that shook her shoulders under his hands, yet he could feel her slight yielding. Wolf lifted her hair from her shoulder and pressed a kiss on her neck and her upper body quivered under his lips. He couldn't tell if it was fear or arousal. God did he hope it was the latter.

He slid his hand around and cupped the front of her throat with his palm. His hand under her jaw, he tilted her head to the side and bent to kiss her temple, then her cheek, to the side of her lips.

Tasting the soft skin by her mouth, Wolf leaned his body slightly into her to barely brush her back, nudging his erection into her bottom, letting her know what he's feeling for her.

Another shiver roiled through her body. He touched the button at the hollow of her throat and undid it. She started, her hands rose to grasp his wrists.

Shaking his head, he murmured, "No."

She hesitated, then reticently lowered her hands, dropping them slowly to her sides. He methodically, slowly undid each button but stopped leaving the last two closed as she stiffened more and more with each opened button.

The shirt fell past the tops of her thighs, he unbuttoned it to just below her navel, keeping her privates still private, for the moment.

Wolf again gently clasped her neck with both hands, then skimmed his palms over her shoulders, down her arms, down the inner curve of her waist then spread to flatten across her stomach. Another quiver rolled across her shoulders.

She didn't try to move her body or push his hands away, encouraging Wolf to hope the quiver was desire and not intimidated resignation.

His lips softly licking, sucking her neck, he stroked his hands up and palmed her breasts over the shirt. Clutching them more tightly, he felt their full, soft weight, their round, chubby shape, a small moan of approval and lust growled in his chest.

Ketherine didn't move as he explored her breasts until he slid his palms inside the open shirt and covered them with his big hard hands. This time, a tiny moan elicited and she melted her back against his torso, and he smiled. She wasn't immune to him.

The priming he had done with her all week was finally coming to fruition. He had calculatingly seduced her body if not her mind into expecting, wanting his touch, his caresses.

Every moment they spent together he had provoked her woman's body to desire with mere nonsexual touches on her arm, her waist, her throat, belly, thighs.

He had slowly, carefully groomed her body to now crave more, more intimacy, to want to move on to sexual stroking. Her brain may not want him, but he could coax her body into betraying her.

Wolf leaned his body harder, fully into hers as he more roughly fondled her soft flesh. He wouldn't really hurt her, but he was not going to be a docile lover.

His growling moans tumbled out as he squeezed harder, more fiercely kneaded her breasts with his tough fingers. He pinched her nipples and gave them a slight twist and grinned at her exclamation of the mixed pleasure with pain, and rejoiced at the goose bumps that pinged up her arms.

"Oh! Wolfgang, I..." she trailed off as he stroked her bosom, her belly, her ribs, her collar bone, her lithe throat. With every caress she melted more into him with a faint purr.

Holding her in a tight embrace with his huge strong arms as he pleasured them both, Wolf swooned with fevered hunger. Ketherine was a wonder of beauty that a benevolent God had gifted him. He held a glorious treasure in his hands.

Her head nestled against his chest. Tussling back and forth over the broad pectoral muscles as her body reacted to his fondling, his roaming, skillful hands, his fingers plucking at her needy nipples that beaded tight in exquisite throbbing under his expertise.

His younger years as a soldier may have consisted of camp whores, but they had taught him how to bring a woman's stinging ache surging into excruciating peaks of orgasm, and hold her at the edge until she would beg him, scream for release.

When her breaths quickened and she strained against his expert fingers, Wolf slid one hand down to cover her mound, over her shirt.

With a gasp and sudden stiffening, Katherine made to move away from him. One hand tightened on her breast and the other over her mound, he murmured, "No."

Ignoring her struggles to stop his sensual ministering of her soft curvy body, he continued kneading her full flesh, his palm tautened over her sex as he pressed his fingers on it.

He simply wrapped his hand tightly over her mound to hold her still until she grew used to his touching her so intimately, and finally calmed like a skittish filly.

His lips brushed over her ear, he said softly, "See, my beautiful Katherine, I will not hurt you, I only desire to pleasure you, pleasure us both. The feel of your silken skin, these plump tits in my hands, for now, is pleasure enough for me.

"Once I make you come, detonate you to excruciating cries as you soar over the eclipse of your zenith you will be mine. The trauma of your past will be written over, dissolving it into nothingness, buried beneath our love making."

Katherine sighed and relaxed into him as he continued caressing, fondling her body until she felt her breasts swollen and aching in his hands, her sex throbbing under his palm that held her with slight pressure from his pulsing fingers. His heavy panting stirred her hair as he murmured nonsensical things in his own language in her ear.

Feeling her responding to his seductive stroking, Wolf slid his hand beneath the shirt, into her panties and drew his fingers up her slit and felt her silk ooze on his fingers, but she cried out and frantically struggled in his arms.

"No, please, Wolfgang, I- I can't-" Tremors of fear clogged her throat as she fought him for release. Her voice verging on hysterical told him he'd gone as far as he could tonight.

"Okay, okay, my traumatized kitten, I will stop, for now." He drew his hands up to clasp her upper arms. He turned her to face him and he about came right then and there.

Under heavy languorous lids her large eyes were glassy, dewy with burning arousal. Her lush lips parted and damp, her breasts heaving with heady passion. She was the sultriest, hottest thing he'd ever seen in his life. It took a willpower of steel for him to let her go.

"Fuck," he muttered closing her shirt.

Taking her hand, Wolf led her to the bed and pulled the sheet and blanket back. "Climb in, sweet." She obeyed in a daze.

"Good girl," he praised quietly. Drawing the covers over her, he bent and kissed her cheek. "I am taking a shower, you sleep, my pretty Ketherine."

Vowing to destroy the person who had hurt her so devastatingly, he kissed her again then reluctantly, yet quickly left her to head into the bathroom.

If he stayed another second he would break his promise he'd made a short time ago that tonight she would have a reprieve from him fucking her. He took care of his own needs in the shower.

When he dressed in a T and shorts and climbed into bed, she was asleep.

With a happy sigh, they had made progress, Wolf wrapped his arm around Ketherine and pulled her to his chest, and dreamt of her as he slept.

Chapter Eighteen

Ketherine and Wolf sat next to each other at the breakfast table. The dining table was long enough to seat twenty to thirty people. A buffet was set up along one wall for the occupants to help themselves.

Wolf's soldiers were in residence, they came and went following his orders. He had half the men and a few hardy females working on the serial homicides and the others on finding Johnny Frog, a few were involved in other missions.

Some women were present though, eager playthings for the soldiers. They all blatantly stared at Keti every time she was in view.

A few of the females observed her with hostility that she would steal the attention of the other males from them, while others watched her with lust filled eyes, and some viewed her with seething anger for taking Wolf out of the playing field.

"So," Wolf said as he watched Ketherine sip her coffee. Damn she was so elegant. "Tell me more about this archeology. Have you done any digs yet?" Dressed in a suit, he sat back, one ankle over a knee and held a piece of toast.

She set the coffee cup down on the saucer and nodded. "Yes, actually. I had a professor where I was at school in

Italy and she allowed me to intern with her. I heard she coincidentally happens to be near here right now. I had hoped to call her while I was in Diggler's Rock. There's word she's working on a burial site that they are moving and I thought I could assist."

Wolf's brows drew down in a frown. "Not now, Ketherine. It is too dangerous."

Her bottom lip pushed out in a pout. "But, no one is going to bother me at a dig site. Trust me," she smiled, "all that dirt and bones, tedious and boring, most people stay far away from it. I would be just fine."

Shaking his head, Wolf took a bite of the toast, chewed then said, "No. You are not safe anywhere. You stay here until I say it is clear."

At the unappeased sound she made, swallowing, he gave her a hard look. "Remember you are in my comfortable custody, when you could be incarcerated in jail."

Surprisingly, Keti didn't act terribly embarrassed at what they had done last night. Wolf thought for sure she would try to avoid him.

Her cheeks tinted pink when her eyes travelled over his body before shyly turning her gaze from him, yet a tiny smile lit her gorgeous lips. But right now those lips pushed out further in argument. "Oh, but Wolfgang, really I'm sure-"

"Hey," Johan interrupted.

Wolf didn't like the men near Ketherine so he usually sat with her at the end of the table and discouraged anyone from sitting near them, male or female. He trusted no one but his close friends with her.

He had given strict orders to the occupants other than his friends they were to stay way clear of her. And even now, his eyes narrowed at Johan who had managed to drag a chair to sit on the other side of Ketherine.

"I'm Johan, Wolf's friend." He introduced himself to her. "Wolf and I sort of grew up together. You must be the famous Rapunzel he has been telling me about." He shot Wolf a grin at his frown.

Keti tilted her head and studied Johan then smiled. "Oh, you mean Rapunzel because Wolfgang is holding me captive?"

"Johan," Wolf grumbled.

Johan tossed his head back with a laugh. "Yeah, exactly, Ketherine."

Her smile wide, Keti said, "Yes, I am trapped in an ivory tower but I'm not blonde like Rapunzel. Please call me Keti, my friends do," she cocked a brow at Wolf.

Impatience flashed in his dark eyes. Her name rolling over his foreign tongue he said tersely, "Ketherine, you are not being held prisoner for no reason. You are under my protection and in my custody, please recall you chose to be here. And, you have freedom, you are not confined to one room."

Wolf lowered an angry brow at her and slanted a glare of irritation at his friend.

"Humph." She muttered, "Here or a murdering rapacious jail, not sure what the difference is." Sipping her coffee, she commented, "And I am not allowed to leave the estate. Correct?"

Wolf's chest rose in a huff. He picked up another piece of toast then set it down irritably. "We agreed, Ketherine. You knew my terms, and it was here or in a cell. Where would you prefer to be?"

He'd known she hadn't a choice, Dutch had told him the horrors that had greeted them when he'd taken her to the jail.

It would have been a mess if she had chosen to stay at the jail. No way could Dutch leave her with the avaricious mutants incarcerated there, even the guards were miscreants and would have likely assaulted Keti the second Dutch had cleared the exit.

And, Wolf would have killed Dutch if he had left her there. Dutch would have had to bring her to Wolf without her acquiescence and agreeing to his terms. Terms he had yet to impose on her.

Although he could with good conscience bed her since she had agreed, he still wanted her to come to him freely, desiring him as much as he desired her. Or at least half as much.

Ignoring Wolf's pique, Keti said to Johan with curiosity in her gentle voice, "So, you say you two grew up together? I heard Wolfgang was in the military at a very young age."

An unreadable emotion flickered across Johan's face before he smiled again. "True that. It explains why *Wolfgang* is such a tough domineering bully, right?"

Keti's laughter tinkled out girlish and sweet, both men leaned in closer to her.

She commented Johan, "Your English isn't as heavily accented as Wolfgang's. His English is stilted, and he doesn't use contractions as easily as you do."

Johan's gaze flicked to Wolf who glared back with a stony expression. He petted her arm as he replied, "Uh, yeah, well, *Wolfgang*," he ignored Wolf's grunt, "was inducted as it were, in the military a few years before me. I had family, for only a short time unfortunately, but enough to smooth those coarse, rough edges from my decorum, unlike my growly ill-bred friend there."

Ketherine laughed at the dark look Wolf aimed at Johan.

Wolf's blood heated at seeing Johan continually touching her while they conversed.

Ketherine had turned her back to Wolf and she and Johan had quickly engaged in storytelling. Mostly about their exploits in the service.

While they spoke, Johan touched her arm, hand, now he was stroking her hair, and she was giggling. She ran like a berserking Bigfoot was after her whenever Wolf touched her like that.

"J, don't you have things to be doing?" he barked and scowled at the smirk Johan sent him. Johan was trying to provoke Wolf and it was working.

His friend pushed his chair back and rose to his feet. Grinning at Wolf, Johan grasped Ketherine's hand and kissed the back of it.

"Until we meet again, my lovely." He pressed his lips against her hand and stayed there until a growl from the other side of Ketherine threatened reprisal.

Grinning harder, Johan tapped two fingers to his head and said, "Yes, sir, I'm outta here. Later, lovely damsel," he crooned to Keti and turned on his heel and was gone.

Ketherine smiled at his back and murmured, "Isn't he just the nicest guy?"

Wolf's scowl deepened. "No, he is not. I could tell you tales, ah," he exhaled his jealous anger. He slipped his hand under her jaw to turn her from the doorway and to face him.

"I have work to do, I am meeting Sheriff Kross in a few minutes. I do not have to reiterate that you are not under any circumstances to leave the mansion."

Her brows knitted and her lips turned down. She opened her mouth to argue and Wolf bent and clamped his mouth over it. His hand strung around the back of her neck holding her from pushing him away.

He licked her bottom pout and then the top full lip causing them to part. He slid his tongue over her smooth teeth and entered into the valley of her sweetness, and he groaned with the ecstasy of her taste, her scent.

Wolf felt like a hound dog the way he lapped at her, bit at her lips, her tongue, the way his chest rumbled with arousal, he inhaled long and sharp pulling her scent inside him as deep as he could.

Slanting his head, he spread his hand on her back to pull her closer to him. Her breasts wedged against his chest and he deepened the kiss, chasing her tongue and biting it, sucking on it until she whimpered.

The whimper wasn't of fright though, Wolf's heart smiled. She was molten lava in his arms and was responding to his kisses. She wasn't experienced in kissing, love making, it was clear in the innocent way she followed his moves, and it was the hottest thing he'd ever experienced.

Growling his passion, Wolf held her tight to him. His fingers webbing her neck as he devoured her, chewed at her, sucked her lips, her tongue, he nibbled at her cheek and they both moaned. His erection throbbed in his pants,

Wolf moved the hand from her back to cup her breast. His fingers gripped her breast hard in his intoxicating, runaway lust, and she suddenly twisted her head from his and her hands came up between them.

Palms landing on his chest, she pushed at him as hard as she could, though they both knew she wouldn't be able to budge him even a hair if he didn't want to.

Eyes bleary with scorching passion, Wolf licked his lips, his gaze on her mouth that was cock-thumping wet and plumped and red from his kisses. *Hell*, he blinked, swallowed hard.

He was actually delirious, drunk on the taste, the fragrance, the aroma of Ketherine. Another few seconds and he would have her splayed out on the floor and gone thrusting between her thighs.

"Wolfgang, please," she whispered, gripped his wrist and tugged.

Dazed, Wolf looked down, he still grasped her breast. "Oh, sorry." He hadn't meant to molest her in public. Forcing himself to pry his lusting fingers from her soft globe, he dropped his hand and took a long deep breath.

He needed to adjust his pants but didn't want to draw her attention to the hard-on that was raging there.

Ketherine spoke with breathy puffs. Her eyes darting around, she said uncomfortably, "There are people here."

He found his voice, it was thick and husky. "No one could see you behind me, what I was doing."

The side of his mouth curled up, he said slyly, "So, you stopped me just because we were in public? You mean if we were in private you would let me freely fondle you, maybe do more? A lot more?"

Wolf realized he sounded like a teenager, but he didn't care. He knew someone had hurt Keti, damaged her psyche, made her afraid of men. He had known from the beginning he was going to have to move slow and win her over.

She didn't trust easily, and due to his deliberate coercion, she trusted him least of all. They were all barriers to overcome.

But, Wolf was nothing if not a warrior. He had patience and perseverance, he never backed down from a fight, or from obtaining something he truly wanted. Ketherine will be a battle, and a precious gift, he fully intended to win.

Flustered, still under the influence of his ardor, her mouth dropped, she blinked rapidly, her cheeks spotted with scarlet. "Yes, I mean n-no, I mean of course not-" Wasn't he the brute animal she was terrified of? A sketch of confusion painted her face, scrunching her brow.

He abruptly jumped to his feet. Grinning down at her he spoke right over her rushed objection, "Okay, good then. When I return we can pick up where we left off. We can have dinner in our suite and then continue this…" his gaze swept to her chest and back up, he grinned, "in private. It is time for our consummation, I am so glad you agree." He turned as she struggled to push the words out.

"Wolfgang, I mean, uh-" she gulped as he spun back around and grasped the sides of her head.

"Do not attempt to go outside, Ketherine," he admonished sternly. "I know you are bored, have cabin fever, but you must stay where you are safe. Mind me now, you do not want to experience my wrath, you will find my palm to your ass quite painful." He tipped her head up and landed a hard, passionate, hot kiss on her mouth then broke away and started for the exit.

He grinned over his shoulder and said, "Later my hot little kitten, we will finish this." He laughed at her stunned expression.

Chapter Nineteen

Wolf met Dutch at the police station. They were in his office seated at a small round conference table. Wolf had filled Dutch in about Ansberry the raping astronaut, and Griggs the embezzling mayor.

Dutch nodded wryly. "Your hackers are better than ours, Wolf. We are hindered by actually having to obtain warrants to access sealed information."

He motioned to a counter that held a pitcher of water, glasses and a coffee carafe and cups, condiments and pastries. "Help yourself."

Wolf sat back in his chair and set a hand on the small round table in front of him. "Thanks," he responded, but didn't get up.

Dutch's big fingers wrapped around his own cup of steaming brew, nodded for Wolf to continue with the rest of his information.

Wolf said, "I looked into a few of the others, there is stuff I want to dig deeper into about Miles Burton. He is an ex-police chief, I came across some shady trails, he may have used his contacts in the department to cover up that he was a deserter in the Army. I need to excavate further."

Deep in thought he went on, "And that fucker Stone Cash, no way is he anywhere near clean. No way. Malevolent corruption oozes from the man."

Dutch powered up a laptop on the table and pulled his chair closer to it. "Yeah, I always was suspicious of them, the group, but they don't reside here permanently so they are basically out of my jurisdiction. That blobby son of Cash's, Chester, gives me the creeps. No question though, is that Talon DeMar, the king of that frat kingdom is dirty down to his manicured fingertips."

He stuck a spoon in the mug of coffee in front of him and stirred the bit of cream he had poured in. His eyes canted wryly at his old friend from their soldier days. "So, how's it going with Ketherine? You know if you hadn't jumped on her so high-handedly I had planned to go after her myself."

Wolf leaned forward, his shoulders hunched, he powered on a second laptop Dutch had provided for him. "She is a suspect, you could not fuck her, Dutch."

Dutch grunted. "Not at the moment. But, we know she's innocent. If you hadn't staked your claim so quickly and acutely, as soon as the case is cleared I would have freaking pounced on that."

Wolf turned his head slightly to Dutch, his mouth hard. "Do not refer to her that way."

Dutch blinked at him, then smiled. "It happened, just as I figured. You're gone on her, aren't ya, buddy?"

Wolf lowered his blank expression to the computer. "We have work to do, man, less talk, more work."

Chuckling, Dutch tapped on a few keys on the laptop. "She's not just a plush, sexy, hot little thing to you. The big man has fallen, and hard. Well, they do say the bigger they are the harder they fall."

A low snarl from Wolf as he ordered, "Work, Dutch, work."

Laughter rolling off his tongue, Dutch grinned. "Okay. But I want deets later on you and her. And, if you decide to set her free, you let me know ASAP. So," he turned and narrowed his eyes at his computer then said, "What are we looking for?"

"Not gonna happen." Wolf started clicking away at the keys.

Answering Dutch's question, he said, "Something occurred when Talon DeMar came into his business. The company was in Chapter 11 and the balloon loans came due quite quickly, but he somehow pulled his fat from the fire and paid off all his debt, loans, back taxes with the IRS and managed to rapidly bring the company to a sky high earner.

"I want to see if we can discover who or where he got the funds from. Maybe it has a connection to the murders. We need to make our searches wide, encompass this entire corridor of the northwest to start with. Whatever happened could have been in DeMar's town or here, or anywhere."

Dutch scratched his head then combed his fingers through the light locks. "It's something to go on, better than twiddling our thumbs. Let's go." He hit the key pad.

Hours later, Wolf sat back and held his fist over a yawn. Shaking the tense weariness from hours of pouring over events that happened 20 years ago, he turned to Dutch.

Dutch had dark patches under his eyes and his jaw was clenched. He looked as tired as Wolf felt. Wolf said, "The only extraordinary thing we came up with was that massive fire that happened in the time frame we are looking at."

Rubbing his eyes, Dutch mumbled, "Uh huh." He yawned and drained his now cold coffee.

Setting the coffee mug down, he said, "Huge manufacturing plant burned to the ground in Fort Blair. There were deaths. Big insurance payoffs. The report said definitely arson, but no one was ever arrested for it. The plant was smack dab in the area where DeMar's and his frat buddies went to college. After the money started paying out, DeMar started paying off his debts. Too coincidental."

Nodding, Wolf peered blearily at the screen and agreed, "Yes. Now we just have to find out what the connection the fire was to DeMar and company. We need to follow the money. However," he pushed to his feet. "I have a date. I want to have a lot of time to spend with Ketherine, she needs heavy duty wooing."

"She tell you what happened to make her leave town when she was a young teen?"

He shook his head. "No. I am sure it is as we suspect. One of those fuckers assaulted her. She is too afraid of men, too reserved, cold, it has been hell to get her to even let me kiss her for fuck's sake."

Dutch's eyes popped in surprise then his brows lowered. "Are you saying you haven't banged her yet?"

Wolf narrowed his eyes with a growl. "She needs velvet gloves and patience. Besides, it is none of your business."

"Huh." Dutch sat back with a grunt. His smile at his friend cagey, he said with a mock in his tone, "I thought you were going to take her whether she was agreeable or not. You haven't even pushed her to adhere to your requirements of your agreement with her for your custody?"

Wolf snapped the computer closed and tucked his hands in his pockets. He said tensely, "I decided I want her willing."

"What?" Dutch's mouth fell open. "You gonna let her go without completing the deed?"

Fishing his keys from his pocket, Wolf replied, "No. If she does not come around, I will…" he shrugged. "I want her, Dutch, I am going to keep her. She will have to submit eventually even if a bit of force is involved. You know I would never hurt her, but I am not letting her go, Dutch. I told you that."

"Hmm." Dutch looked uneasy. "Not the way to start a relationship."

Wolf lifted his wrist and glanced at his watch and grimaced. Heading for the door, he grabbed his jacket off a chair. "I hope it does not come to that. It's a moot point anyway, I did not realize how late it was, she is undoubtedly long asleep by now." He would find out when he got home.

Would he meet a soft, sultry, willing Ketherine, or a hissing scratching kitten? Either one turned him on, but as Dutch pointed out, having her willing would do more for them in the long term.

He shook his head, what was he thinking? It was 2:00 a.m., she would be deep in snoozeland and he was not going to wake her.

He would have to keep it in his pants until tomorrow evening.

Chapter Twenty

*D*awn hadn't broken through the night clouds when Ketherine picked her phone up, surprised when it rang because she received so few calls.

Wolf had called the other day when he knew he was going to be too late for dinner. That was kind of...sweet. Almost domestic.

Rolling her eyes, she set the bowl she had yogurt and fruit in for breakfast in the sink and muttered, "Sure, the brute animal and me in domestic bliss, ha! Joke of the decade." A wry snort burst out at the ludicrous thought.

Assuming it was Bonnie on the phone, she didn't look at the caller ID just said, "Hey, Bonnie? How's it going?"

"Keti? Hey, it's Jardina Allison, how are you doing?"

Jardina had been Keti's professor in Italy. "Oh my goodness, Dr. Allison, it's so good to hear from you." A hint of question in Keti's voice wondering why her ex-professor was contacting her.

Allison chuckled. "Please, call me Jardina. Long time no hear." Her voice took a serious note. "Keti, why haven't you returned to complete your degree? Have you moved on to another university in the States?"

The thought brought a lump to Keti's throat. "No, I haven't. Remember I told you I had to join my stepfather in the family business?" She wondered if the call was about the professor's current dig.

There was silence for a brief moment, then Jardina said, "I thought that was only temporary. I...well I know how much you loved your studies in anthropology as well as archeology, I thought you would return to us. You were so proficient in osteology and told me you wanted to concentrate your further studies in that."

It took effort to hold back the tears of regret, Keti coughed to clear the grief from her throat. "Um, no. I don't want to play games here, Doct- uh, Jardina, I will be up front with you. I have to stay in the business, I have no choice. Maybe someday down the road I can return to...school. I had hopes to obtain my doctorate," she swallowed the hitch in her throat.

Before Jardina could comment, Keti said, "I have 50% ownership of the company and my mother's will stated I have to work at the business."

"But why? Why would she do that to you when it's clear to everyone who knows you that your interest in the disciplines of social science is in your blood?"

Keti pondered what, how much to tell her. She decided on the truth. "My...stepfather is a ruthless businessman. A good part of the business is we build bridges. Unfortunately, he tends to build his bridges overseas in disadvantaged places that can cause villages to plunge into dire indigence overnight and to cause some to literally die out.

"My mother used her veto power to force him to make the better decisions. I have been, well, corralled into doing the same. Without my veto many people could perish."

She would keep all the sordid Wolfgang, Johnnie Frog, and the serial murder business to herself. Really, how does one tell one's professor she has agreed to be a man's whore to keep herself alive and out of jail?

"I...see, I guess," Jardina said. "Well, if that's the case, well," a small embarrassed laugh bubbled out. "I am here on a project, near to Diggler's Rock where I heard you are staying. I called your home in Gladonia and they gave me your new number and told me you were here." She paused, took a breath.

"I called, because, well, I need to rush to my sister's side, she's been in an accident." Her gulp of worry was audible. "So, anyway, I thought maybe you, I mean I have only very green undergrads on the dig and I need someone to supervise them."

Keti said with surprise, "Someone? You mean me? You want me to supervise the dig?" A thrill bloomed up her spine and she grinned with delighted pride.

"Yes. You are more than capable. You interned with me so I know you know what you're doing. I don't, uh, don't expect you to do any actual digging, more like cataloguing, overseeing the students as they work."

The professor's voice came out strained, "It's just...I can't get anyone else here in this time frame. Maybe," she hesitated, then said, "maybe you could come on board for just a day, I can get someone qualified here by tomorrow if you can't stay. What do you say, Keti? Just a day, it would help me so much, those kids can get into so much trouble if someone isn't standing over them with a whip."

Keti laughed. "Yeah, I remember." The short time she had been at the university after she left the boarding school, while she studied, the rest of the class was out late nights partying. Gosh, she would so love to do it...but, Wolfgang would say no. "Listen, Jardina, I truly wish I could say yes but-"

"Oh, please, Keti, I'm begging on my knees here. Just one day. I'm already getting on a plane to California to be with my sister. If you could just go there for today I would be so very very grateful!"

Keti wanted to say yes so badly, but, he said he would punish her if she left the mansion. Hmm, Keti started getting mad. Who was Wolfgang Valdimar to tell her what she could and couldn't do, and where she could and couldn't go?

She wasn't guilty of any crime so she shouldn't have to suffer and be treated like a criminal or a child. "I'll do it. But I don't have a car, I don't think-" Her voice fell as she realized she couldn't get past the guards.

"Tell me a place to meet you and I'll have a car there to take you to the site." Hope filled Jardina's words.

Keti thought hard. How could she…she was near the window, she glanced out and saw the delivery truck pulling in with groceries. "You know what, Jardina? Let me get to where I can meet your car and I'll call you then. Okay?"

"Oh, wonderful, thank you so much, Keti! You not only will get paid a day's wage but you'll have credits towards your degree when you return."

That's not going to happen, Keti thought glumly. At least she'd have this brief opportunity to do what she loved.

Less than an hour later Keti was striding towards the dig site. It had gone so smoothly she couldn't believe it! She had dodged and ducked servants and soldiers and hid in an alcove near the kitchen.

When the grocery deliverer was about to leave, Keti snuck out a side window and dashed to his truck. As he turned it on, she had hopped into the passenger side.

To say the least he was quite surprised, and young, which was good.

It didn't take much for Keti to talk him into giving her a lift. His expression conveyed right off the bat he was besotted. The hard part had been getting rid of him once he took her to where she could call Jardina for the ride. He wanted to take her to lunch.

When she declined he asked for her number. She gave him fake digits and hurried from his truck. It wasn't nice but then neither would Wolfgang be if he found the driver on their doorstep with a handful of flowers asking her out on a date.

Tying her hair back in a braid, Keti eagerly walked quickly to join the group. Most were already getting the tools out that they would need to sift the dirt. Others were straggling in, yawning and slurping large containers of steaming coffee.

"Hey everyone," she greeted. Striding up to where the bulk of the group was gathered, she introduced herself. "I am Ketherine DeMar. I believe Doctor Allison advised you all I would be supervising for the day?"

She looked around at people that were about her own age. She had attended boarding school and graduated the high school two years early. Taking her classes online because she was leery of people, men, she absorbed everything she could like a dehydrated cactus.

Her foundation of knowledge was high and wide before she had physically entered Santatini University to do her internship.

She had a Bachelor's degree in both archeology and anthropology, and she was in the middle of her Master's in dual studies when Talon had forced her to come home.

Keti smiled at them. "How about you all introduce yourselves before we get started?" Her eyes glazed over by the time she heard the second Jason and third Megan. She would never learn all their names in the one day she was to be there, so she just kept smiling and they got to work.

Two hours later, "Hey Ms. DeMar," a handsome young man said, approaching her with a smile and a once over.

Keti tore her eyes away from the bones several students were trying to keep intact as they were transferred from the pit to a platform where they could be bagged and safely transported to the new burial site.

Actually it was quite surprising the bones were found undisturbed and in the shape the body had been when interred. The records she'd read noted the bodies had just been piled on top of one another, therefore it would be easier for the students to keep most of the body's bones together.

At least they wouldn't have to spend an inordinate amount of time matching bones. She understood the plan was to remove the deceased as fast as possible with as little detriment to the skeletons as possible because they were to be respectfully reburied as intact as they were when removed.

Keti opened her mouth, then pursed her lips with an embarrassed smile. "Hi, um…" drat, she knew she wouldn't recall their names.

His grin stretched freckles across his nose. He helped her, "Jessie." His grin widened as he continued appraising her.

"Too many of us to remember, no worries." Jessie nodded towards the flagged and rope-lined site that was crawling with students. Some digging, some sieving, some transporting, a lot of them chatting.

"Please call me, Keti," she said, returning his cheerful smile. "Yes, it's a large site. It's a good thing so many students could be involved, the transfer will get done more quickly."

He agreed, "Yes, and we're lucky it's not dead winter or dead summer."

The students doing the grunt work had long ago tossed their jackets. Others like Keti that weren't actively moving around still wore their jackets.

Jessie's lips bunched as he perused the site. "It's kind of sad, though, that these poor men have to be dug up and moved, and then reburied just so some condos can be built here."

"Hmm." Keti nodded, noting the bodies were too uniform to include women or children, which was to be as expected. "They were Chinese gold miners massacred in the 1800's by bandits. They were discovered 25 years ago when developers tried digging wells for water for plans even then to develop this area."

"Yeah," Jessie said. "That didn't go too well, huh?"

"No," Keti shook her head. "There was no water they could easily, cheaply reach and they lost funders. Lack of financial backing drove them to try again elsewhere. The county just tossed the dirt back over the bodies and forgot about them."

"Until now, and the ever persistent developers are back with more money and better methods of digging for wells. So," Jessie glanced at the bodies in the pit and said, "these poor fellows are being dug up and will be reburied in some Potter's field south of here. So sad," he shook his head.

"Uh huh." Keti's eyes narrowed on the bones still jumbled in the pit. The victims had just been tossed into the mass grave that had been quickly dug and then buried under several feet of dirt. Something didn't look right. Her brow furrowed. Keti said, "The records stated they were all male victims, right?"

"Yeah. Miners. There were no women this far northwest in the early mining days here, too dangerous. They, hey-"

Keti walked quickly to the cluster of bones the students were trying to separate from the jumble of bodies. "Wait," she called out, holding a hand up.

The students sifting the bodies stopped and looked at her with puzzlement. The body they were working on was almost completely brushed clean of dirt exposing most of the skeletal system.

One of the female students said, "We're being careful, Miss DeMar," she frowned at Keti. The girl resented being supervised by someone her own age. She wasn't actually working, she had been standing around drinking coffee and gossiping with some of the other girls.

Her red hair fizzled around her round head. Green eyes, masses of freckles and thin pink lips turned down filled in the rest of her pale face.

"No, that's not it, uh, Peggie." Keti pleased that she recalled the girl's name moved closer to the pit. She pointed. "I believe that skeleton is female."

Lips pushed out in consternation, shoulders shrugged in a so what manner. "What's the dif, Miss DeMar?" the girl's tone was sarcastic. Her disrespectful gaze rolled over Keti and a small sneer raised the side of her contemptuous lips as if she decided Keti didn't measure up.

Crouching, Keti leaned over to get a better look. She studied the partial skeleton for a few minutes. Then stood up. "The difference is, there aren't supposed to be any female bodies here, and judging by the color of her bones compared to the males, she hasn't been here nearly as long as they have."

Gasps rounded the area most closely surrounding them. The rest of the students stopped what they were doing.

Jessie said, "Are you sure? I mean, that can't be possible. The miners were killed and dumped. Sure, they were dug up 25 years ago, but hell, it was only about a week and they were reburied. Are you saying a woman just happened by, had maybe a heart attack or something and fell into the pit?"

Peggy said sarcastically, "Yeah, and none of the construction people noticed she had hair and skin and all, unlike the ancient bones already buried there." She said to Keti, "Get over yourself, the bones are of one of the miners."

Ignoring her, Keti shook her head, her eyes still glossing over the bones, she replied to Jessie, "No, I'm saying there could have been a murder. Not the one of the Chinese miners, but a more recent one. There were bodies piled on top of her indicating she was deliberately hidden amongst the copious bones."

She stood up brushing off her jeans. "We will need to measure the elements and averages to determine gender, race, age, possible cause of death. But, the pelvis is smaller, wider, more circular than the males'. Look," she said, pointing at the skull.

"Her jawbone is rounded and her brow not as pronounced. I think we need to contact the authorities and- ooh!" She cried out as Peggy suddenly tripped and her coffee flew all over Keti's shirt.

Peggy smirked and mumbled, "Uh, my bad. I'm so clumsy."

Jessie speared her a dirty look and hurried to help Keti. "Here, shit," he tore Keti's jacket off her while she pulled at her shirt to keep the liquid from burning her skin.

Chapter Twenty-One

*H*e was tired of staging car crashes then having to do the heavy lifting and haul his toys to the cabin. So, he used a truck parked outside the Dynamite Den Tavern as cover and waited for his prey to exit the bar.

He knew they had blown off dinner plans with their folks. He had spoken with Marc Burton earlier in town and he had told him they were having a few drinks and then Marc was taking his sister Libbie to meet her new beau.

Their father Miles was gonna have a conniption fit when they don't show. Only an hour passed when they appeared in the open doorway.

Libbie, wearing a tiny skirt and short rabbit fur jacket giggled and stumbled, her brother caught her arms and steadied her with teasing chuckles.

She slurred while still stumbling, "You were s'pposed ta be the deshignated, Marc so I could get mildly toasted and get my nerve up to let Rubal Brewerer have his way with me. Rubal Brewerere, shit, say that three times fast!"

Marc laughed and stumbled with her. "That's Brewer, Libs, and breaking news, you're already skunked. Soon as ol' Rube gets around to spreading them lily-whites you'll be passed out cold and snoring like an oncoming train."

"Marc," she scolded, playfully slapping his arm. "Y-you're my bro- other," the words spilled out sloppy drunk.

"Yer s'pposed to be takin' care of me. You were s'pposed to make sure I got tipsy so I looshened up, but not totally pa-las-tered," she dissolved into drunken giggles, staggering and tripping in her high heels. Her brother had to grab her arm again to steady her.

"Whoa, sis, maybe we need to get you a cup of coffee." Marc steered her to their car. "Or a gallon."

Hiding behind the truck, the man muttered silently, "Good, they parked off to the side, not under any lights, that'll be eas-"

"Hey."

The whisper startled him. He scowled at the man emerging from the shadows caused by the few parking lot lights. The man from the shadows joined him, stooping behind the truck where they could watch the couple from the bar.

The first male whispered in irritation, "'Bout freakin' time, Ren. I thought I'd have to do these on my own like I had to drag Ollie and his fat wife up a damned mountain."

Shadow man replied with a smirk, "Your fault. You were too impatient to wait for me." Crouching beside the first man, his whisper laden with carnal excitement he asked, "How're we taking 'em?"

Looking in a compact mirror she pulled from her purse, Libbie primped her hair.

Marc was opening the passenger door, his back to the parking lot, he never saw the Taser.

Chapter Twenty-Two

*W*olf answered his phone, "*Tere*, Romet."

"Ah, Wolf…"

Wolf heard the unease in Romet's voice and a miniscule hair of trepidation curled in his gut.

"What? What has happened?" He was sitting in a chair in the local library seeing if he could find information on Talon DeMar and his gang of thuggy frat buddies that hadn't been entered into the computer system.

He'd thought perhaps there were notebooks of hand-written records stashed away in this dusty archival basement of the library.

The town was small and rural, the cataloguing and scanning information, newspaper articles may not have been done as diligently as would in a larger more cosmopolitan library.

Wolf heard Romet clear his throat, and his trepidation deepened.

"Your girl, Ketherine is…ah, gone."

He was instantly on his feet. "What? What do you mean gone? Tell me specifically what the hell is going on," he demanded while starting for the elevator that would take him to the main floor.

Romet cleared his throat again. "I went to retrieve her to bring her to breakfast as you ordered, and she wasn't in her...ah your suite."

Striding quickly across the main floor heading for the exit to the street, Wolf barked, "What does that mean? Is she in the mansion?" To himself he muttered, *please be in the damned mansion, Katherine.*

Ripping it off like a Band-Aid, rapidly descending to their own language in his agitation, Romet sputtered, "She is not in the mansion or on the grounds. When we couldn't find her, I got a dump on her phone and viewed the surveillance tapes and, well," clearly he didn't want to tell Wolf what they found.

"Spit it out!" Wolf thundered as he ran to his truck.

"Ahem," Romet cleared his throat. "We discovered she'd received a phone call near dawn. The cameras outside picked her up climbing in the grocery delivery van. They weren't stopped leaving at the gate because the deliverer is well known. They thought nothing of Katherine sitting in the passenger seat as she was calm and smiling politely."

Slamming the door to his truck, Wolf growled, "I will fucking kill that man. Those men, the driver and the guard. Do you know where he took her?"

Turning on the ignition, Wolf kept the truck in Park. He couldn't drive out until he knew where he was going.

Sighing heavily, Romet replied, "Yes. We tracked him down. He took her to a gas station and left her off."

"What!" Wolf exploded, slamming his fist on the steering wheel. "He dropped her and left her there alone?"

"Yes. Calm down, Wolf, let me tell you all of it."

Scraping his taut fingers through his hair, Wolf groused inaudibly, *Calm down? Remain calm when Katherine was out there alone, in danger? For fuck's sake.*

When Wolf remained silent, Romet told him, "Wilhelm traced the call she received at the house. A Dr. Jardina Allison had contacted her."

"Who the fuck is she?" Sticking his fingers in the front of his hair, his palm flat on his forehead Wolf held it there for a second while he tried to cool his racing pulse.

"Well, she is apparently Ketherine's professor, and mentor from her college in Italy."

When Wolf didn't say anything, Romet went on, "Johan reached the doctor and she told him that she was in this area near Diggler's Rock doing a dig and was called away on an emergency.

"She needed someone to supervise the inexperienced students on the dig while she was gone, and she asked Ketherine to cover this one day for her while she got someone else to come in and take over."

Wolf blinked rapidly trying to understand what Romet was telling him, make sense of it while trying to keep his head from exploding. "There is more, Romet, I hear it in your voice."

Another heavy sigh, Romet said, "*Jah*. Apparently the doctor was duped. She was told her sister had been in an accident and that she was needed in California. When she," he took a breath knowing his friend was going to freak out.

"When the doctor reached the hospital she was told her sister had never been there. She called her sister and the sister confirmed she was fine and someone must be playing a nasty joke on them."

Wolf was quiet as he followed Romet's words. "So, it was a ruse to- what? Lure Ketherine to the site to- to grab her?" He shook his head.

"Does not make sense, who would have known the doctor had anything to do with Ketherine and that she would

180

call for her… but no, Ketherine is not qualified. I do not," he grunted, "I *don't* see unless the doc is involved in the scam that she innocently contacted Ketherine."

"Johan asked her that, Wolf. She said Ketherine had interned with her and she was quite proficient in anthropology, especially in osteology as well as archeology, and that the doctor could trust her to handle one day of supervision. Before you ask, osteology is the study of bones.

"Johan spoke at length with her utilizing all the threat he could induce, and Johan is convinced of the doctor's honesty. He is running a trace on her phone as we speak to see who initiated the call, although since it was used in a nefarious deed, the phone is more than likely a burner."

Wolf grunted. No doubt.

"The doctor said she had called Ketherine's home a week ago searching for her and was told she was at the lodge. When the doctor heard of her sister's emergency, she'd called the lodge and obtained Ketherine's new cell number.

"After she reached her, the doctor had sent a car to the gas station where Keti was dropped off, and had someone pick her up and drive her to the site."

"Where is the dig located?"

"It's way east of here, in Moose Gorge, an hour's drive if you or I were to go." He rattled off the address the doctor had given him. "Do you want me-"

"No. Dutch Kross' station is much closer. I will call you back." Wolf abruptly hung up on Romet and dialed Dutch's number.

When he answered, Wolf spoke quickly, "Ketherine has been tricked into going to an archeological dig. I believe it is a trap to grab her, or kill her. I'm at the library in town. You are much closer to the site than me, go get her." He provided the address Romet had told him.

"I'm on my way." Dutch didn't waste time asking any particulars, Wolf heard his footsteps as he hurried from wherever he was.

"Put the fear of God into her when you get her, Dutch. I cannot believe she would take this chance, she knows the danger she is in. When I get my hands on her I am going to tan her-"

Dutch cut off his tirade, "You gonna be at the estate? Shall I bring her there? I have to use the prison transport van. My truck isn't nearby and we were about to transport some prisoners to the jail in Opeka. I'll swing by, pick her up, bring her to your place then continue on to Opeka."

"All right. I will meet you at the mansion. Hell, Dutch," his concern gnarled through his angry voice like gravel over rocks.

"I know, Wolf. She'll be okay, we have to think that, I will call you when I have her."

Wolf had only been home from the library ten minutes when Dutch called.

"Yeah?" he answered on the first ring. He was pacing a tense trail through the grass in front of the mansion.

His skin burned hot with the scalding heat of his wrath. He unzipped his leather jacket and wiped a palm down the side of his black jeans. Today he was wearing a long-sleeved beige thermal and he had switched his dress boots to motorcycle shit-kickers.

"Got her, Wolf, she's fine. Uh, make that pissed." Dutch's chuckle was overridden by a rumble of male voices.

"Pissed?" Wolf said, incredulous. "She dares to be pissed? I will show her fucking pissed, Dutch. How long before you get here?"

"You will be pleased to know though at this point considering her current position, her ire of being bodily hauled away from that site has turned from angry to severely anxious." Dutch chuckled again, then grew serious.

"Some shit was going on at that dig, Wolf. Your girl determined that there was a more modern female body hidden amongst the bones of a bunch of ancient male miners. The female body did not belong there. She was about to call the local police department when some chick *accidentally* spilled her hot coffee down the front of Ketherine's blouse."

"Fuck, what? Is she hurt? Take her to the hospital, I will meet you there," Wolf ordered as he dug in his pocket for his truck keys.

"No, no, she's fine. One of the male students ripped her jacket off and helped her peel the blouse from her skin before she was burned."

"Shit, Dutch-"

"Fortunately she was able to quickly toss a bottle of water on the splash of coffee that soaked through her blouse to stop it from burning her, and she was able to borrow another shirt from someone else at the site. By the time she regrouped I was there. I called the Moose Gorge PD and apprised them of the situation."

His palm slapping his forehead, Wolf looked up to the heavens. What the hell else could befall that girl? "She needs a damned keeper, Dutch."

For the moment he needed to concentrate, he had to force the image of some jock ripping Ketherine's clothes off her out of his head.

He thought about what Romet had told him about the professor being tricked away from the dig. Then he pictured the scene.

Ketherine finding the body that didn't belong there. She's about to call the law when some bitch spills coffee on her, stalling the time before Ketherine could make the call, and the green students were not cognizant enough to call the police themselves.

"Yeah," Dutch agreed with mirth in his voice. "Girl needs a leash attached to a strong arm. Apparently the leash you put on her was too loose, bro. You need to tighten that shit right up."

His mocking laughter grated on Wolf's ears.

Dutch's mirth ended, he said, "Seriously, man, the very reason for her being with you was that you could protect her the best."

His sigh glancing off the phone, Wolf said, "I know. I did not think she would actually try to leave. She knew the perimeter was guarded. Who would have thought she has brains with that beauty and would quickly figure a way out of the estate without even being questioned?"

He grunted his annoyance. "Never mind. She will feel the sting of my leash, Dutch, and it will be fucking tight."

Wolf looked down at the keys in his hand. "Listen, I do not, ah, *don't* like the sound of what went down with that whole dig thing." He told Dutch about the doctor being tricked away. "Something ain't right there, you should look into-"

"I agree. Smelled to me too. I spoke with a few of the students. A young man," he paused to recall the interview. "Ah, Jessie Garrison. The guy that helped your girl out of her clothes."

His smile apparent in his tone knowing Wolf was already blowing his lid and Dutch was adding fuel to the fire, he went on, "Garrison told me about the body and that Ketherine was about to call the police when she was hit with

184

the hot coffee. When I asked him what he thought about the coffee incident, he admitted it looked almost deliberate to him.

"I searched for the girl, Margaret something, it's in my notes. They called her Peggy. I couldn't find her. I have a man looking into it, I'll let you know what we come up with. The body is still there. I called a lockdown with the cops as soon as I hung up with you.

"Anyway, we'll be at your place in about twenty minutes, give you some time to cool down, eh, bro?" He laughed at the harsh breathing hissing through the phone.

Wolf had in no way calmed down when the prison transport van pulled up the long drive and stopped where Wolf was standing waiting with his hands curled taut over his hips.

His boots planted apart, fuming anger fanned the air as if he was preparing for a titanic brawl with some bruiser instead of waiting on a soft petite female.

Dutch hopped out of the passenger side of the van and trod over to Wolf. "I'll get her out." He moved to the back of the van and reached for the door.

Wolf's head jerked back. "You have her in the back? What the fuck, Dutch?"

Sparing Wolf a spiked brow, Dutch reminded him, "You told me to scare her. I think she's scared." He unlocked the back of the van and swung the wide door open.

Inside, there were prisoners chained on both sides of the truck with their arms restrained behind their backs, and Ketherine was sitting smack dab in the middle on the right side.

So small compared to the cons around her, she was almost hidden. And Dutch was right, she was terrified. Her

185

horror-struck eyes wide with hysterical fright were bright with tears.

The prisoner on her right was leaning over trying to lick her neck, when she leaned away from him, the man on the other side bent his neck stretching, trying to bite her breast.

She was wearing a thin pullover sweater that was too small for her. Judging by the sweater that whoever loaned her, was not nearly as endowed as Keti.

The way she was restrained thrust her breasts out, and with her fright and the cold air, her nipples were tight beads poking straight out of the sweater. Every man inside the van was staring at her chest.

With her every twist and turn to avoid the males on either side of her, her breasts bobbled and jiggled. Wolf surmised there wasn't a soft dick in the van. Even a gay man would be gawking.

His face dark with rampant fury, Wolf ordered in low deep gusts, "Get her the fuck out of there."

Dutch shrugged one shoulder and jumped into the van. He reached around Ketherine and unlocked the chain that bound her to the bar behind all their backs.

He knew the prisoners were secured in a way they couldn't reach her with any part of their body, but she didn't. Her breathing was so panicked she was almost wheezing.

Dutch whispered, "Sorry, honey, but you needed a lesson. You're safe now." He glanced over at Wolf's furious stance. His lip tipped up at the corner. "Doesn't look that way at the moment, but I promise everything will be okay."

Looping his fingers around her upper arms he helped her to stand and said in a quiet voice, "Everything will be all right as long as you listen to Wolf and obey him. Let him do his job of protecting you."

Dutch needed to get a different key to unlock her cuffs. He had to bend over slightly to walk through the van but Ketherine was short enough she could stand up straight. He guided her to the end.

The van was up too high for her to get down, especially with her wrists bound behind her back. The prisoners complained about her removal amidst cat-calls and bawdy offers to help her.

Wolf moved to the van and tossed his jacket hitting Dutch in the face. Grinning, Dutch placed the jacket around Keti. He bent and slipped his arms under her and lifted her to the edge of the truck. Then he squatted and lowered her into Wolf's arms.

Keti's body trembled in Wolf's hold as he nodded to Dutch, and without waiting for the sheriff to unlock the handcuffs, he immediately started walking up the drive to the mansion.

A shit-eating grin on his face, Dutch closed the door on the rowdy cons and locked it then climbed into the passenger side and they took off to transport the prisoners to the prison in Opeka.

Wolf stalked silently across a short parcel of grass to the open front door where Absolom stood in a severe black suit waiting with zero expression on his lined face.

Wolf stomped past him and through the foyer to the stairs. Without pausing to take a breath, he carried Keti up the stairs and to their suite. Neither said a word, but both chests heaved with heavy breaths, Wolf's from anger and Keti's from fear.

The door was open, he kicked it closed behind them so hard pictures on the walls rattled. He strode through the sitting area, down the short hall and into the bedroom. The brown curtains were pulled almost completely closed so the room was only slightly illuminated.

The dark room matched the dark mood and fiercely angry face of the man that carried Keti. He traipsed to a divan and set her on her feet. She wobbled with her hands restrained.

Wolf caught her arm to steady her then quickly released her. Removing the jacket, he tossed it on a chair then stood a foot or so from Keti so he could scan her body searching for any evidence of injury.

His studying her without saying a word further unnerved Keti. Shuffling her feet, sniffing, she stared at the floor.

Wolf grabbed some tissues out of a box on the dresser and dabbed at her eyes, wiped the tears off her cheeks.

Her face red with mortification of the whole thing from Dutch Kross forcefully dragging her from the site, to having to sit chained in the van with unruly prisoners, and now facing the wrath of Wolf, a shudder hitched across her shoulders and down her body.

Sniffing and gulping, she turned her face away from him and asked so quietly he almost couldn't hear her, "Um, Mr. um, Valdimar, please, can you get these cuffs off me?" She partially turned to display her bound wrists.

She had been excruciatingly vulnerable for over an hour now and didn't relish standing there in front of the livid wolfman and not even able to put her hands up in front of her in some semblance of defense.

"Are you injured? The coffee burns, do you need medical care?" His voice was cold, without inflection.

Her lips pushed out in an unconscious pout when he didn't immediately release the cuffs, she shook her head. The long cinnamon curls bounced across the front of her.

"No, I got my clothes away from my skin before I was burned." Since he didn't start smacking her as she'd feared, the tears dwindled and her breath calmed.

Mouth thinning at the reminder that some guy tore her clothes off her, Wolf asked calmly, "Whose shirt it that? It is too small for you. Every cocksucker in the van was gawking at your tits."

Overlooking his crudeness since he appeared to want to throttle her, one shoulder bumped. With an embarrassed feeble grin, she told him, "I borrowed it from one of the students. My blouse was ruined and I don't know what happened to my jacket. Now, could you please-"

"Yes," his voice silky menace. "I heard a young man helped you out of your clothes." Wolf's lids were low, hooding the expression in his eyes. His shoulders a stiff line of bulging muscles, he clenched his fists at his side as if trying to keep himself from strangling her.

"Oh, well, he didn't really, I mean," Keti saw the barely restrained fury gripping Wolf. He looked like he wanted to commit murder. "Listen, Mr. Valdimar," she tried cajoling, knowing she was in deep trouble with him.

His mouth turned harder every time she called him Mr. Valdimar.

She said quickly, "I was perfectly safe, there is no need for you to be angry. I am a responsible adult, I wasn't fleeing custody. I would have returned when I was done."

Wolf took an imperceptible step towards her. "Perfectly safe?"

His tone still dark and silky smooth, he said, "Did Sheriff Kross tell you that your professor had been intentionally lured away from the site? Did you think there was nothing wrong with the discovery you made of a dead woman secretly buried? Did you think that not even

189

considering Johnny Rana's determination to eliminate you, that stumbling upon a likely homicide could have put you in danger?"

He moved closer, sneered, "Did you not find it the least bit suspicious that as you were about to call the law someone accidentally tossed hot coffee on you thereby stalling the arrival of the police?"

Shaking her head, her mouth opened and closed as she tried to explain. Suddenly realizing he was closer than arm's reach, she took a step back from him.

Her shoulders rose awkwardly when she moved due to the restraints. "No, I mean, there were tons of people around, I was perfectly safe. I said I would have returned after I finished the job."

Face darkening further with rage, fists clenching, he roared, "I told you not to leave the goddamned mansion, Ketherine! Your custody is not at stake here, you little fool, your damned life is!"

She shrunk from his wrath. "Bu- but I was safe, I told you." Lowering her head she peered up at him, said meekly, "Please, you don't need to curse and yell at me like I'm a child-"

Cutting her off, he ground his hands into tighter fists, his shoulders bowed, he shouted, "You act as reckless as a child, with no regard for your safety. With no goddamned regard for my directives. So," he reached out and strung his hands around her upper arms, "I will treat you as a child. You will think twice next time before you risk your life or ignore my orders."

"No, but-"

Gripping her arms, he gave her a sharp authoritative shake. "I warned you, Ketherine, I damned warned you."

Chapter Twenty-Three

*H*e hauled her to the divan and he sat down and pulled her to stand between his spread thighs. He'd yanked her towards him so fast her breasts were about thrust into his face.

The tips of his ears reddened, it took effort to tear his gaze away and to look down. "I gave you time, time to get comfortable with me. I could have made you fulfill our agreement that first night, but I…whatever, time to pay the piper, girl."

Wolf reached down and grabbed at the top button of her jeans and popped it open. Ignoring her gasp, he yanked the zipper down and gripped the waistband of the jeans.

Crying out, "No!" Keti tried to step backwards, out of his grip but his fingers were in the top of her jeans.

Wolf paused, his furious eyes rolled up to see her blushed cheeks and mussed hair, her eyes pleading with him.

"You agreed, Ketherine, you gave me your word you would not fight me. Are you saying you want to renege now that it is imminent?"

"I- I-" flustered, her chest heaved with frantic breaths. "No, I mean, can't we, can't we wait a- a bit? Just, uh, some more time?"

"You are out of time, Ketherine. If you want me to take you back to the jail, now is the time to tell me. It is jail or me and my terms."

He waited. She flapped her lids frantically at him, licked her lips in distress. Wolf knew he had her when her shoulders slumped.

She shook her head. "No, please…"

"All right," he sighed, pretending to misunderstand, "jail it is."

"No, wait, I," her voice came out quickly with a resigned exhale. "No, I will do what you want. I will stay with you and…" she took a breath, "do as you say."

"Good. Then we will proceed. You have assented. Again. But first, your punishment."

Her mouth dropped. "My punishment? What do you mean my-"

He spun her around, wrenched her jeans and panties to her knees, lifted her, then laid her belly down across his lap. Keti instantly started to fight to get off.

Wolf set a large strong palm on her back and told her, "You have agreed to have sex with me, even if you had not, you would still be receiving this punishment for disobeying me and putting your life in jeopardy. This will make sure you think twice next time before throwing yourself in the path of deadly danger."

The hair tie she'd tied around her braid was long gone. Burnished waves draping over her face, her wrists cuffed behind her back, Keti could do little to stop him. Nonetheless, she arched her back and kicked out her legs.

"No! Stop! This is ridiculous, I don't have to-to obey you like a-a child, like a slave! I didn't agree to- to being spanked!"

His hand smacked hard on her bare butt and she squealed and jerked back and forth.

Wolf told her, "When you consented to be under my care, my protection, my custody, you agreed to any methods I choose to deal out to you, to open your eyes to the danger you place yourself in. You are too naïve to the way this wicked world works. I tried to tell you, now I will teach you." He slapped his palm down smacking her again and again.

Keti screamed, flailing her legs, "Stop! You have no right!"

Pressing his palm on her back above her bound wrists, Wolf lifted one of his legs to lay over one of her legs to hold her still. "I am grateful for these cuffs, my Ketherine, next time we will use my own, but that will be in play, this is a lesson," and he slapped her bottom over and over, and Keti screamed and cried and begged him to stop.

When heaving sobs wrenched from her throat sore from screeching, and she started to drape limply over his knees, he slowed his smacks and pushed a thigh apart from the one he had secured with his leg. She froze.

Through her heavy sobs, she rasped, "Mr. Valdimar, what are you-"

His hand came down harder in four, hard fast thwaps on her butt. "You call me that again, Ketherine and I swear to God I will use my belt on your already very red ass."

He brushed his hand along her thigh, and smiled at the quiver that rolled through her leg.

"I- I'm sorry, but you…"

"Hush, we are done talking." He pushed her thighs further apart and cupped one of her sore butt cheeks and squeezed, smiling at the yelp of pain. "You are stunning all over, Ketherine."

Squeezing her flesh, his thumb slid into the crease of her bottom and he pressed his other hand on her back harder when she started struggling again.

Realizing it was futile to fight him, she was securely restrained, Keti stopped moving.

"Relax, Ketherine, the light spanking was only a lesson, I would never seriously hurt you, relax your legs. It is time you learned to trust me." He stroked her thighs, her bottom and waited for her to oblige.

It took a tense moment of time before he felt her loosen the rigidity in her limbs. "Good, now, stay that way, do not fight me." He moved his hand up her thigh and cupped her sex and she stiffened, tried to close her legs.

The foreign feel of his rough palm on her private parts panicking her, Keti tried to shift away from his offending hand with a frightened whimper.

"Relax, Ketherine. It is too late now to back out. You cannot get away or stop me, so give in to it. You agreed." His voice soft and coaxing, he stroked his fingers over the supple folds between her legs.

"You clearly will never get over whatever the trauma was that happened to you in your past to let a man in now. So I am going to force you to realize that sex is a natural part of life and to be enjoyed with your partner."

"I- I have no partner," she denied, sadness wisping her voice that rasped from her cries.

"Yes you do, Ketherine." He pushed her thighs as far apart as he could to more effectively stroke her slit and play with her swelling nub. Wolf smiled when after a few minutes he felt the silk of her arousal wet his fingers and she ceased struggling to get away from his strumming fingers.

He no longer had to hold her legs apart. With tiny mewing moans, Keti squirmed on his lap, her bottom pushing against his hand and his prying fingers that skillfully stroked up and down and around. Then he carefully probed her soft, wet channel and she jumped and twisted away from his hand.

"Shh," he cooed. "I will not harm you, tiny kitten. Trust me, please." He moved his finger slightly inside her then continued pushing until it was completely inserted, then he paused for her to calm down and bear his violation.

Her panting came shallow and fast. Her heart hammering, Keti sucked in a deep breath to force herself to relax and accept his penetrating her body. She had no choice at this point. She had accepted his rules, she had dishonored them and he punished her for it.

Once again she had said she would stay with him rather than go back to that hellhole jail, and now he was going to make good on his terms, now he was going to make her his. She was terrified…and excited.

Chapter Twenty-four

Wolf paused his fingers and moved the hand on her back to her head. Bending over her, he grabbed a handful of thick hair, lifted her head and turned it so he could cover her mouth with a searing, rough kiss that left her head spinning.

While he scourged her mouth, he slowly inserted a second finger inside her tender core. She was so tight he had to use more force than he wanted to. To distract her, he brought the kiss up to scorching. His fingers slid in more easily with her lubricating silk making the way slicker.

Pulling his mouth from hers, Wolf gently lowered her head, and started plunging his fingers carefully all the way in, then drawing them back almost all the way out before doing it again. Then he slowed inside and curved his fingers, stroking inside her soft walls, seeking her hot spots.

At first Keti was resistant to Wolf fervently imbedding his fingers inside her woman's channel, then she felt the magic he was creating, building. Warmth fired and zinged down below, rapidly sparking her sex in an empire of sizzling firecrackers-

But then suddenly, horrendous flashes of profane memories gunned bullets of raw hell into her mind, tugging

196

her away from the amazing feelings he was evoking. Fear quickly burrowed in to take hideous root.

Feeling her stiffening, her withdrawing from his sensuous plundering, Wolf whispered soft tender words in both languages while he stroked his spellbinding artistry, beguiling her delicate parts back into heady desire.

He would do everything in his skill and power to replace her vile memories with spine-tingling resplendent ones.

Soon he had drawn her back from the terrible chasm of agonizing memories and into a tailspin of prickling electricity. Thrilling tingling burned a path between her legs heading towards bursting prisms of mindless splendor.

His sinuous carnival of strumming, caressing, skillful plucking and pinching in concert with his plunging fingers shot Keti up to a soaring pinnacle.

He quietly said, "Go, Ketherine, feel it, let it go, trust me."

Her breaths strained, gasping, riotously standing on tiptoes at the precipice- with a strident wail she dove off into an explosion of spiraling iridescent stars.

Wolf continued playing her through her very first orgasm as her body arched and bent and spasmed wildly, he had to strengthen his hold so she didn't flail off his lap.

He would have loved for her to have shouted out his name as she writhed with his fingers still pronging and stroking, but he was satisfied, more than satisfied with her response. The only thing better would have been to see her face as she rocketed off. With him inside her.

Her gasps slowed down, the squirming lessened, panting hard, Keti fell limp over his legs and hung like a heaving noodle.

Grinning with delight at his success, Wolf waited for the little after-tremors to diminish then turned her over on his lap and shoved his hands under her, lifted her as he stood up and carried her to the bed.

Speaking soothingly in a hushed voice, Wolf told her, "Stay calm, little kitten, I am setting you on the bed."

Gently laying her down, he took in the rounded cheeks rosy pink with her orgasm, lips plumped and red from hanging upside down and his kisses, hair messy swirls of a mahogany river spreading over the blue sheet.

Under low lids, glazed green eyes misted in dazed bliss peered up at him.

Leaning over her he crooned, "So gorgeous, baby, you stagger my heart." Under his breath he muttered, "Hell, who knew I had a heart?" Wolf gripped her jeans and panties gathered around her knees and tugged them down her legs and tossed them to the floor.

Blinking through the fuzzy warmth enveloping her tingling body, Keti murmured a protest and struggled to sit up.

Wolf put his hand on her chest and gently pushed her down on her back. "No, pretty kitten, don't think, just feel. Trust me." Still stunned from her very first climax, she didn't fight him.

Dutch had told Wolf, Keti's friend Bonnie shared that it was pounded into the girls where Keti boarded at school that it was a sin, an abomination for a female to touch herself, and to do so she would burn in hell.

Keti had been too afraid of getting caught to attempt masturbation like some of the other girls had braved.

Even now as an adult, the nun's directives remained deeply ingrained so these feelings and sensations were new and startling. She was a virgin in every sense of the word.

He softly praised her, "There we go, sweetheart," and grasped the hem of the borrowed sweater and pulled it up and over her head to crumple around her still bound wrists.

Reaching under her, he unclasped her bra and lifted it, tucking it behind her back with the sweater. His eyes instantly lowered to her bared breasts, and his tongue slicked his suddenly dry lips.

His voice lowered to a scratchy rasp, "Damn, Ketherine, even more magnificent than I had imagined."

Setting a knee on the bed, Wolf sat back on his heel and covered her breasts with his hard hands.

At her sudden squirm and whimper, he hushed her, "Shh, baby, just feel me, close those beautiful eyes and feel my hands on you, feel the pleasure." He watched the apprehension flutter her lashes over ambivalent eyes trained on him, then she slowly closed them.

"Good, Ketherine, don't fear me, at least while we are together this way."

He wrapped his long fingers over her full breasts, his hands and eyes relishing the feast of the Ketherine banquet spread below him. Wolf squeezed and kneaded each globe finally able to savor the soft, lush feel of her, and letting her get used to his touch. He bent and sucked the milky skin of one breast until he'd raised a dark red mark.

Smiling at his brand, he went for more until her creamy breasts were covered with his mark and she was now squirming in renewed desire instead of anxiousness.

Grappling her breasts in his rough hands, Wolf bent and sucked a nipple into his mouth and bit it.

Tugging the puckered bead between his teeth and lips, he smiled at the soft groan Keti emitted as her body arched and twisted, hungry for more. He tortured that nipple until it was pinched dark and swollen and he turned his attention to the other one.

"Wo-Wolfgang, please," she cried while arching against his mouth, "t- take the cuffs off, please…" she trailed away into a mewed groan, her hips swiveling on the mattress in her novel lust.

He ignored her request. It would be easier for Ketherine he decided, to keep her bound then she would feel more forced to do this, and also not give into her natural instincts to fight him. Remaining restrained would eliminate any guilt or shame she would harbor for giving into him.

Grasping both breasts, Wolf licked and kissed his way down her ribs over her sunken belly and lower. Her protests started again and she drew her legs up as if she could stop him.

"Hush, now, Ketherine," he whispered firmly, gripping her slender thighs he pushed them back flat on the bed.

Then he promptly moved around the bed, set his big hands under her thighs and pulled her so her bottom was almost off the bottom of the bed. He knelt on the floor and positioned himself between her legs.

When he pushed her legs apart, and she felt his warm breath on her exposed sex, Ketherine again struggled to get up. With her wrists bound behind her, and Wolf's hands holding her down, she was not getting off the bed until he let her.

A resigned nervous sigh buckled out of her as she forced herself to stop fighting him and surrendering to his dominance.

His breath wafting over her bared succulence, Wolf sniffed her first, then nuzzled his face between her legs. Ignoring her attempt to wriggle away, he licked the length of her then immediately suckled her thrumming nub.

"Oh!" she squeaked, then moaned. "Oh, Wolfgang, that feels…that's so…"

His mouth grinning against her plump nether lips, Wolf sucked on the folds, her clit. Separating the plump folds with his thumbs he sucked, gnawed and bit every inch of her beautiful female morsels.

Gasping huffs and oozing moans, her body shifting under his firm hands that held her down, Ketherine's head thrashed back and forth on the mattress and Wolf slowly slid a thick finger inside her.

This time, there was not only no objection, she lifted her hips to meet the pressure of his digit pushing deeper inside.

After a few moments, when one finger moved more easily in her tight sheath, he added a second finger, he needed to prepare her to be able to take his girth without undue pain.

Wolf worked her until she was writhing so hard she was almost to the peak again and about to go over, and he suddenly withdrew. Getting to his feet, he quickly unbuckled his belt, undid the button on his black jeans and wrenched the zipper down so fast he thought he'd broken it.

"Shit," he cursed. He had forgotten about his boots. Shedding his boots, socks, shoving his pants and briefs down and off, Ketherine was squirming and moaning his name, calling him to come back to her.

"*Wolfgang*," a throaty whisper that enflamed his manhood beckoned him, "please…"

Wolf bent over, and lifted Keti up higher on the bed, then he climbed between her legs. Reaching over his shoulder, fisting his shirt he tore it off over his head and tossed it.

He lowered to Keti, caging her with his bulky forearms. He smoothed away a strand of hair from her damp cheek.

"Baby," he said softly as their gazes connected. "Are you okay" He held his breath worried she was going to tell him to take a hike.

When a line formed a frown between her brows, he stiffened in preparation for more arguing.

"Wolfgang," her lips formed an adorable pout, "you...left me before...I mean..." Cheeks already flushed with his lovemaking bloomed darker red.

Grinning at her, Wolf bent his head to suck at her lips before thrusting his tongue in her sweet mouth and taking her, hard, rough, with a no-bars-held passionate kiss until they both broke apart with harsh pants.

"Baby," he said, kissing her mouth again, nipping each lip, "you mean I stopped before you could come."

Sex talk made her uncomfortable. What a vast difference between her sweetness and the raunchy women he'd known. Damn but her bashful inexperience was hot, and fuck if the word endearing came to his weathered mind.

Talk about making him feel all dominant alpha. He wanted to teach her, revel in her, safeguard and care for her. She deserved to be cherished, and he craved to be the one to treasure her.

Grinning harder at her flustered expression, he maneuvered so his erection was pressed against her sex. His voice lowered into a deep, soft rumble. "That is because I wanted us to do it together."

She blinked up at him, but her lips curved in a shy smile, which disappeared as Wolf slowly nudged himself in, breaching her tender channel with his thick rigid length.

It was the hardest thing he'd ever done, but Wolf moved half an inch by half an inch, pausing in between for Keti to adjust to his breadth.

Her distressed breaths racing harsh in his ear, murmurs of pain and her abject tininess, she was so damned small, brought him to a halt.

Exhaling the tension of holding back, he watched emotions flicker across her beautiful face. Pain, fear, she wriggled, adjusting herself to better able to take him. And then she smiled up at him, and his heart broke completely into glorious pieces.

"Ketherine?" He didn't move, waiting tensely for her to either green light or beg him to stop. Hell, he had never given a woman any sort of concern before, but this little girl just tore him up, and he'd do anything she wanted to get that green light.

"I'm okay," she whispered shyly and wiggled her slender hips against his.

Every part of him except the steel rod inside her melted with relief. His own smile lit his harsh face expressing that relief as well as gratefulness and sheer agonizing desire for the sweet angel he cradled with his body, and he shifted deeper inside her.

Moving slowly, he studied her expression ensuring she was really okay with this and not just appeasing him to hurry up and get it over with.

But, an internal grin warmed him, her eyes now half hidden under lids heavy with passion glimmered with sultry heat as he finally buried his man's root to the very end of her, and he sighed, smiling down at her.

"Ready?" he asked gruff with such intense emotion and arousal, prodding his erection around inside her sleek sheath.

Nodding, her eyes flickered with hunger and need, her breathy, "Yes, Wolfgang," ignited him like sticking a fork in a light socket and he started to move.

Wolf slowly pulled out then slowly pushed back in Ketherine gathering her silk along the way making each plunge easier, and hotter, faster and harder, deeper. "Ah," he murmured and paused to reach to the nightstand beside the bed.

"What...?" she said breathlessly. "Are- are you getting the condom?" Her brows pinched when she realized that it should have been put on before now.

Keti was ignorant of intimate relations between men and women, but she did have sex education classes. But then again, she wasn't familiar with the expertise Wolf wielded on her body and she couldn't hold onto the thought of the condom. Besides, he was taking care of it now, right?

Not answering her, Wolf half turned her body so he could release the cuffs. Pulling them off her, he tossed them and the key on the table and, still deeply inside her, he rubbed her arms, massaging the tightness from behind bound.

When she raised her hands to press them on his chest, Wolf bent and kissed her. Threading her hands around his neck, she responded as lustily as he did, and he kicked up to a rapid driving rhythm.

He hadn't responded to her assumption that he was getting a condom. He knew he was clean, he had been on a long mission overseas when Dutch had called him to come and take care of the Johnny Frog situation as well as look into the murders.

And he knew Ketherine hadn't been with a man at least in recent years. As far as a pregnancy was concerned, he intensified his thrusts at the thought, he would be exceedingly pleased if that were to occur. Might not be fair to Ketherine, but, he ground his teeth fiercely, he never said he wasn't a selfish bastard.

Obviously inexperienced, Ketherine nonetheless pumped her hips to meet his plunges, and talk about striking a match- his brain and body instantly engulfed in fire.

Wolf gripped her shoulders, holding her down with his weight and he viciously stabbed into Keti's tender young body with vehement, utterly ruthless thrusts.

Growling and snarling like a voracious animal with each thrust, his own heathenish sounds reached his ears. It was a struggle, but Wolf pulled himself into awareness of how he was brutally assaulting Keti's small delicate body.

Tearing back from the raging abyss he was hurtling towards, fighting against his gorilla's nature to pummel his female into fully yielding submission, Wolf forced himself to slow his frenzied thrusts.

His chest rounded and heaved with heavy galloping breaths as he garnered control. Hell, this was his sweet fragile Ketherine he was ravaging like a feral animal.

Sweat beading across his forehead dampening his hair, he lifted his thickly muscled body off her soft form and braced on his elbows. He couldn't prevent himself from still rocking into her, there would have to be a bulldozer to plow him off her now, but he feared he was hurting her.

"Sweetheart," he said quietly.

Beneath him Keti's small hips were still rising to meet his, her chest was flushed, eyes closed, lips parted with panting exertions.

When Wolf slowed to barely oscillating in and out of her soaking channel, her lids fluttered, lashes rose revealing euphoric glazed green eyes that looked up at him in half-delirium.

She blinked, licked her lips, said between racing breaths, "H-have I done something wrong, Wolfgang?"

Relieved to see she wasn't in pain or scared, quite the opposite, she appeared as enraptured as he. Smiling gently, Wolf said, "I feared I was being too rough with you, my delicate little kitten." He grinned at the furrowed frown tugging her brows down in confusion and impatience.

"No, I…it, you…" she didn't know how to explain she was thoroughly enjoying his rough sex.

Wolf was absolutely taken aback, surprised that she had done a total turnabout from terror of him and sex to…his grin widened with wicked delight. His little girl was wanton and bursting with seething desire just waiting for him to spark her dynamite.

He lowered his head and ate at her lips, her tongue, kissed down to her neck and sucked hard then looked at her.

"So, since you appear to be handling me just fine, we shall proceed as we were. Okay?" One dark brow arched in amused question. Beside her shoulders his biceps bulged with the job of keeping most of his weight off her.

Licking her lips again, her eyes on his mouth, Keti nodded, murmured, "Um, yes, I'm fine, Wolfgang."

Wolf had always hated the name Wolfgang. He much preferred the shortened Wolf, it reminded people of the wild beast that lived inside him and that he wouldn't hesitate to take out anyone that merited it.

Plus, when people called him Wolfgang he often heard 'Vampire' uttered under their breath, and he didn't cotton to that moniker. He was aware how ruggedly vicious he looked and that's what people that called him vampire were thinking.

However, kissing her lightly, he damned loved hearing his Ketherine calling him Wolfgang. She was no longer looking at him with fear drenched in her wide eyes. It squeezed his heart and sent quivers to his nether region.

"Good," was the only warning he gave her before he powered into her and rejoiced at the sensual moan she gave and the milking reception of her body.

Wolf wanted to make the rapturous feeling of their bodies joining to last all day, all week, forever, but, he sighed. Ketherine was unused, tender, if he made her too sore he wouldn't be able to enjoy her again as soon as he would like.

So, reaching down between them, his fingers capered over and stroked her femininity until she writhed and thrashed almost violently on the bed, her breathing harsh and rife with sobs and throaty whimpers.

"Ketherine," he spoke firmly, yet tenderly. When her eyes stayed closed and the tiny frantic sounds she made increased, he said louder, "Ketherine, open your eyes, look at me. Now."

A few beats and her thick lids slowly rose, her chest heaving and pitching, breasts bouncing enticingly against his thick furred chest with his every lunge.

She smiled blearily up at him, and suddenly his thrusts turned erratic and fitful, he was losing control and was going to climax before her.

Wolf sucked in a deep breath, moved his forearm to brace along the bed and he pinched her nipple and clit at the same time and her lips parted in a silent scream.

Her neck arched, eyes rolling back in her head, Keti cried out, "Wolfgang!" and her body seized in convulsions so wracking her body bucked on the bed.

Wolf rolled his arms around her, hugging her body to his, and as she gasped and wept his name over and over, he couldn't hold out any longer. Her sheath clutched him, clenching around his swollen pulsating manhood squeezing the very hell out of it.

Wolf's spine knifed and his head fell back with a groaned rumble that ripped from his chest and up his throat into a roar- at the same time his seeds ejaculated from their sacs and blew up his engorged organ to spew like a raging squall into her small convulsing body.

His body shook and shuddered, he pushed up to straighten his arms, his entire body jerking and quaking until finally spent, he dropped with a groan, forcing his body to fall to the side and not crush Ketherine.

Chapter Twenty-Five

As Keti slowly woke, she became aware that her body ached, but not actually unpleasantly.

Her nose wrinkled, why was her pillow so hard? The pillow under her arm was hard too, she moved her hand to shift the pillow under her head and faltered.

It wasn't pillows she was lying on and clutching, it was a body. A hard, hairy, very male body. His body.

Memories of last night, all night danced through her head. They had done it. The fourth time she was barely awake, he'd played with her until she was wet and he slid inside her from behind.

She didn't even remember him coming. She had been used in such a heated frenzy, roughly, each time except the last. Wolfgang acted as if he couldn't get enough of her, couldn't take her fast enough. He took her so hard it was as if he wanted her to feel him in her body, her bones, her sore muscles for days.

Her body moved into a luxurious cat-like stretch and she lay back as she was, sprawled across his chest, her leg over one of his, his big hand cupping her behind.

"I can almost hear you purring, my sexy kitten," his sleepy drawl lazy and self-satisfied. He smiled up at her as she moved to brace on her elbows and look down at him. Her hair ruffled soft over his shoulders and chest.

"You are the most beautiful, exquisite thing I have ever seen in my life, Katherine." He raised his hand and smoothed the side of her hair off her face. She moved again and winced.

"Baby," he murmured and shifted to sit up. Fluffing pillows against the headboard, he leaned back and pulled her to sit beside him. Wolf frowned when she drew the sheet over her hips and pulled the shirt she'd put on sometime in the night closed.

"Katherine," he said, and waited until she raised her shy eyes to his. "My favorite pastime from now on is going to be gawking at that delectable little body of yours. I do not want you covering it up, hiding it from me." He tugged the sheet down past her thighs and pushed them apart.

"Oh, Wolfgang, please don't-"

"Don't what? Look at the most gorgeous thing, person in the world? You would begrudge me from viewing a Monet masterpiece, a vibrant flower, a castle in the sky?" He peered down at her, watching her nibble her lower lip. "You are a priceless piece of living art to be viewed, touched, enjoyed to the fullest, Katherine."

He ran his finger gently up the folds of her sex smiling at her slight tremble. Pushing aside the halves of her shirt, he cupped her breast, leaned over and licked then sucked her nipple enjoying another tremble that feathered through her body. He had marked a good bit of her silken skin with his mouth.

Her laugh slightly disparaging, she said, "I hardly think my body could be construed as a piece of art, Wolfgang." She felt awkward that he was staring at her private parts although he had done all sorts of things to them last night. All night. A blush rolled up her face.

He'd had his fingers, his mouth all over them and in them. Her breasts felt faintly bruised from the attention he gave them all night long. Even as they slept, when she would briefly wake, if they were spooned his hand clutched her breast, if she lay on top of him, his palm grasped her bottom.

Kissing each breast, he negated what he'd just said and closed her shirt and lifted the sheet to cover her lap to limit the temptation to take her again.

"Ketherine," he started. He sounded so serious her stomach suddenly quaked.

"What's wrong, will you send me home or to the jail now?" She bit her tongue to still the fearful quiver.

His brows daggered down immediately. "What? No, of course not," he said vehemently. "Why…after what we did last night would you think that?" He turned to face Keti then caressed her cheek with a strong finger gentled for her.

"You cannot tell me you did not like what we did, Ketherine. If I know anything, I know a woman who enjoyed my touch, my mouth," he smiled down at her covered breasts then her lap.

His gaze rolled back up to her anxious eyes. "You loved what we did. Baby," he said, then bent and gently kissed her. "A few times I recall you shrieking something like, 'Oh God, Wolfgang, yes, that's it! Faster! Faster!' " He chuckled at the blush that bloomed brighter.

He rounded his palm under her jaw and lifted her face for a deeper kiss then he sat back. "Did I hurt you? I told you to tell me right away if I did anything you did not like or that hurt. You never said-"

Keti shook her head, her hair dusted across her chest pushing the lapels of the shirt slightly open. His gaze dipped down, paused, then rose back to her face.

"No, no, I mean," if her cheeks could get any hotter she could light a fire in the fireplace. "You looked so serious just now, you said we needed to talk. I thought," her head lowered.

He raised her chin up. "I covered your temptation so we could talk. Your beauty strikes me blind, and your naked loveliness hammers me dumb. You thought what, darling?"

"Um, that you got what you wanted, had your fill of…of me, and that you were discarding me, um…"

His brow hopped in surprise. "Damn, Ketherine, the way your mind works. No, never. I will never get my fill of you. I have told you that, repeatedly." He hugged her to his chest, and kissed the top of her head.

"I knew I wanted you for life the second I saw you, I have told you and everyone else that. I have only been waiting for you to come on board."

He pushed her chin up and kissed her. "And, you have, right Ketherine? Tell me where we stand. I need to hear you say it."

Their gazes locked until hers lowered. He lifted her jaw again reconnecting their eyes. "Tell me, Ketherine. Tell me." The arrogant, confident bearing slightly wavered.

Confusion hazed her eyes for a moment, then, Keti set her hand on his chest. "I…I am surprised that…" she tried to turn her head away but he held her still.

"Surprised that what, kitten?" His voice stiffened with a hint of chill, preparing for her to tell him she loathed him, hated what they had done together, that she couldn't wait to get away from him.

"I…didn't think I would ever enjoy being with…a…man, ever. I've been so scared. The pain, the humiliation, the- the shame. But…"

His lips curved up with hopefulness. "But what, baby, talk to me."

Keti had expected to be consumed with revulsion for herself for the way she had responded to him. Shame for not fighting him, hatred for him for forcing her, she closed her eyes. She did feel shame nibbling at her innards, but the night had been too…miraculous, too wonderful.

Smiling shyly, her eyes lightened with joy, she said softly, "It was amazing, Wolfgang. I…loved it. I'm, um, sore right now." She said quickly at his frown of concern, "No, you didn't hurt me, I'm just sore from the many times we…uh…you know. But…"

Wolf kissed the tip of her nose. "But what?"

"I can't right now, but, as soon as the soreness, alleviates, I…" her gaze lowered to his mouth and she smiled. "I'd like to do it…again."

Her lashes dropped then rose showing him the desire that still swamped the vivid green of her eyes. "If, I mean, if that's what you want…"

"Oh fuck, baby," he crowed, gathered her in his arms and latched his mouth on hers and kissed her long and hard.

Leaning back, he smiled with happy relief. "Honey, that is not something you ever have to ask me. I will always want you more than I want air to breathe, food to eat."

Her brow beetled in consternation. "Then what did you want to talk about that's so serious?" Self-doubting shame starting to seep in. Keti moved to put space between them but he wrapped his arm around her holding her close.

He hesitated, not wanting to ruin the serene joy of their shared moment, but it the truth of her devastation had to be revealed before it could be burnt to ashes and scattered to the winds.

"I know you don't want to talk about your past, but I think it will help us move steadily forward. I can already see you withdrawing from me, your past is about to furl up into a big fisting wave and slam down on you, do its damnedest to drown you. It is trying to separate us." His lips bunched at the tell-tale reddening of her cheeks indicating he was right.

"Ketherine, I need you to tell me what happened. What happened when you were thirteen? What happened to make you run from your home?"

She tried to pull away but he held her. "No. It is time you told someone. You tell me. We have broken through the wall you put up, now it is time for you to tell about your past so we can remove its power."

He sat beside her, the sheet over his hips leaving his chest bared. His face relaxed, he leashed the beast, for her. For now. She needed his full support and focus.

Keti clutched the front of her shirt closed and stared down at the blanket and sheet that covered her lower half. Her shoulders rose with the deep breath she drew, then they lowered as she slowly exhaled like she was expelling the horror of her past.

It settled like an abominable mist around them. The stench of her obscene past was palpable to them both. Her body shivered as if she could shake the permeating horror from her being like a dog shaking wet fur.

Then she looked up at his face, the harshness gentled for once yet his strength radiated showing her that no matter what she revealed, he had her back.

The warm acceptance and affection gleamed in his dark eyes, and she inhaled peace and safety. Both of which Wolfgang had given her. He had unlocked her from the prison of her own body, her past, freeing her mind, lightening her soul.

Her lips trembled, but she forged on, like he said, it was time. He was her safety net, she finally had one that would catch her if she fell. He proved, even now that he sincerely cared about her, still wanted her.

The diligence in the way he had pursued her, how he coerced her, how hard he compelled her to stay with him, the way he held himself back from jumping her bones right away when he had every right to considering their agreement. Some would think stalker, an over controlling man…but…

The slow, gentle way he introduced her to lovemaking, and then showed her the delight of rougher, intense, even ferocious sex that had spun her on her toes and had her screaming for more. And the way he pleasured her well before he took his own release, and held her closely after.

Even the anger that unleashed when he found out she'd left the safety of his home, the fear he had genuinely felt that she could have been in danger. Yes, he had proven he really truly cared about her and wanted her long term. He is strong, he'll carry her if she falters.

Taking that deep, deep breath, she blew it out and nodded. "Ah, you're right."

Sucking in another calming breath she told him, "It had always been, but when I turned thirteen the festering boil burst into living hell and I had to get away. Most of my life, ever since I could remember, my father's friends, and their sons," her lips twisted in disgust, "grabbed at me every chance they could get."

His arm tightened around her, a deep growl rumbled with his grip. He didn't speak, he didn't want to say anything that would cause her to stop talking.

"Ah, yes, anyway, I managed to hide and dodge them. Mostly I would run to my mother's room. She was ill, even when I was a child, but she was my refuge in the hellstorm that was my life. At least I was safe when I was with her.

"She was bedridden, yet she was my security, no one would dare accost me in her presence. We had adjoining rooms so I was safe while vulnerably asleep."

When she stopped talking, he prodded, "But she couldn't always protect you."

Her face paled, shoulders slumped. "No, she couldn't. One day I was in my father's office, he had summoned me. I did some trifling work entering business information, mostly statistics into his computer for him. However," she took a breath. "This time, while I was working, um, Mr. Cash was there."

"Stone Cash," he stated.

"Yeah." Her mind travelled back in time as she described that day out loud. She was thirteen again:

"Talon, it's time." Stone Cash's coarse voice startled her, he had come up so quietly behind Keti.

She had finished entering current stats and was closing the paper file she had copied the material from. Without turning around and looking at him, she took a few small steps to the side hoping she could slip around him and leave the room.

Stone Cash had the coldest flattest eyes she'd ever seen, so cold she felt iced to the bone whenever his laser gaze laid on her.

The last year whenever he was around, she felt those stone cold eyes on her body, tracing her, following her movements. Whenever she looked at him those artic blues staring at her set panicked butterflies swirling in her belly.

He moved to stand between her and the door and repeated, "Talon. I've waited. It's time."

Talon didn't look up from his paperwork, he waved absently at his friend. "Yeah, yeah, whatever. There's a lock on the door to the den, have at it."

The way Cash stared at her, Keti's stomach cramped.

Lids low over those cruel eyes. Baby blue eyes that should make him appear friendly and boyish, but no, not those blue eyes. They were blank, yet evil loomed in their cadaverous depths, not unlike pictures she'd seen of the psychopath Hitler's eyes, twin vipers ready to strike.

Swallowing nervously, Keti sidestepped Cash and made for the door. "Uh, I'm done, Father, I have uh, homework, I'll leave you two-"

Cash grabbed her arm jerking her to a hard halt. "No, missy, you're coming with me." He started for the door literally dragging her with him.

"Why? What do you want?" Keti clawed at his hand but he marched her to the door. She cried, "Father! Help me! Father!"

Cash pulled her over the threshold, Talon never looked up.

His grip so tight it was punishing, Cash hauled her down the hall and shoved her so roughly into the den she stumbled and fell to the floor.

Stunned with fear and bewilderment, she climbed to her knees, asked him in a shaking voice, "M- Mr. Cash, what are you doing?"

He snorted and put his foot on her hip and shoved her to stay down. Unbuckling his belt, he said, "You're a teenager now, Ketherine, you know what a man wants." He stood over her unbuttoning his trousers.

Elbow bent, leaning back on her palm she held a hand up to ward him off. "No, stop, my- my father, he won't let you, stop-"

But Stone Cash dropped down and put his hand over her throat pushing her onto her back. His grasp deliberately painful, he pinned her to the floor making it difficult to even swallow.

He opened his pants and tugged his engorged penis out then he tore off her sandals and pulled her shorts down snapping them off, ignoring her shrieks for him to stop, for Talon to come rescue her. Not bothering to remove her blouse he just gripped both sides and rent it apart.

Depraved eyes gleaming with hunger of a shark about to tear into a baby seal, he smiled with amusement at her futile struggles, her whimpers of pain.

He lowered his big body over her and before she could draw another breath to scream, he violently slammed inside her. The pain, the burn, *agony*, her mouth opened in a silent scream-

"Noooo," she wailed, punching out, kicking, screaming!

Strong arms wrapped around her holding her to his chest. "Shh, Ketherine, it is Wolfgang, you are not there anymore, you are here with me, safe. Safe, baby, shh," he whispered gently petting her hair, caressing her back.

He wiped at her tears with his thumbs, kissed her temple, her cheek until she slowly calmed, yet, like a tuning fork she shook in his embrace as her chest heaved and pitched from the corporeal recalled fright.

"Ketherine," he said, kissing her forehead. "I will never let anyone hurt you again."

"It- it wasn't that one time," she sobbed. "The next time he took me to his home and locked me in his room. He kept me for- for a week, then," dragging a tormented breath up her throat, her hand went to her throat as if Cash still held her pinned to the floor of the den.

"Baby," Wolf spewed a sling of curses. "I will take care of him, he will pay for what he did to you."

As if he hadn't spoken she said, "Afterwards, when he brought me home, in the car he told me I was his, that any time he wanted me I was to- to oblige him. He warned me if I fought him he would knock me out with his fists. He told me when I turned sixteen Talon would turn me over to him to become his permanent mistress.

"As soon as I got through the front door I raced to my mother's bedside and begged for her to let me leave. I couldn't tell her what happened, Mr. Cash threatened that she was so helpless he would kill her if I told. A pillow held easily over her sick face and she'd die quickly."

While cuddling her, stroking her back, Wolf whispered how she was safe now and how he would get retribution for her.

Wiping at her tears, she leaned back and narrowed her eyes at him. "You did the same thing, Wolfgang. You decided I was yours, and you took me. You made it impossible for me to not agree to- to have sex with you, you are no different than him. Only you used the force of coercion instead of physically forcing me."

Wolf combed his fingers through her hair moving strands off her damp cheeks. "Ketherine, I know how afraid you are of men, of me. But, although you fought against me, and you were afraid of me, I saw your attraction for me. You are too young and inexperienced to hide it.

"And also too inexperienced to understand what you were feeling. Yes, I deliberately coerced you to stay with me. I believed I could break down your walls, show you how to enjoy life, sex, me. If I felt you truly did not like me, would never want me, I would have made other arrangements to keep you safe."

Keti nestled into his arms, sniffed and wiped at her eyes. "I don't believe you, Wolfgang." And she didn't. She knew what kind of man he was, the declarations he made to have her, his violent past, but…Tipping her head back she looked up at him, lifted her hand and caressed his rough cheek.

He still looked like an animal, a wolfman, grizzly, scary as heck, yet, she felt safe for once in her life. She felt cherished, she felt desired for her body but also for so much more.

She thought about how Wolf had spent considerable time and patience making her feel comfortable with him. He played games with her, chess, cards, made sure he ate dinner with her every night, took her for walks in the courtyard. It was like they were dating, like he truly wanted her to want him as much as he did her.

Last night he had been gentle, at first, careful with her as if she was a fine china doll, precious yet fragile. As soon as they ended one lovemaking episode he was quickly ready to go again.

Yet he wasn't just scratching a lustful itch like all the other filthy debauched letches like Stone Cash. He really wanted her, not just her body, he wanted all of her, otherwise he would have just forced her that very first night.

Keti shook her head to dispel the images of Cash raping her, but, wait, she pictured that day in the den before he attacked her, the files in her father's office floated in front of her eyes.

"Wolfgang," she murmured, mentally grabbing at the recollection. Her body stiffened as she remembered what she'd seen. She'd shut that time down so firmly in her mind that she hadn't dared pull it out and look at it until now.

Besides Cash's assault, what she had been doing just prior to it came barging back into her startled brain.

"What sweetheart, I am here for you, always."

"I- I recall when I was searching for the file to enter the stats in my father's computer, there was..." she closed her eyes tight and thought back. "Yes, I didn't comprehend it at the time, I was too young, but now... Now I understand," she turned to him, set her palm on his chest.

"They had this thing they called, uh, the Sater- no, uh, the Strathem-Link, yes that was it. It was an underground railroad. I mean, actually it was a real train. They were-trafficking, Wolfgang. I accidentally opened the file when I was entering information. It caught my eye because there were pictures of females.

"At the time I thought they were buying and selling dolls or maybe pen pals or something, but now I realize they used the train to secretly transport girls and women they abducted and were sending them to numerous locations where they were to be...sold."

"Sold?"

Nodding, she pinched between her eyes as she pictured the reports. "Yes. There was a record, descriptions of the women they were selling. Rating them, the prettier, younger ones were being sent to wealthy buyers, the others, God, Wolfgang," she covered her eyes with her hands as she visualized the graphs, the names of sites.

"It all made no sense at the time, but now I understand. I recall..." Keeping them closed, she rubbed her eyes as if bringing the writing up, imprinting it on her eyes so she could read them.

"Yes...I remember names, Easy Spread, Stick It, Passion Pets." Her hands dropped, she gaped horrified at him. "Wolfgang, they were sending the women to brothels, whorehouses. Here, domestically, and also out of the country. Apparently American girls pulled in a high price."

She frowned at the look on Wolf's face, he didn't look surprised.

He confirmed it by telling her, "We heard rumors about it from people we questioned around town. I have men interviewing people in your hometown, as well as where your stepfather and his merry band of delinquent cronies went to college. My men are digging into it. We will find it, Ketherine, shut it down, and arrest as many perpetrators as we can. We will search for the abducted women."

She turned to face him, brow wrinkled in vexation. "Wolfgang, my father, ah, stepfather, he was part of the train thing, he could have been the head of the whole industry. You need to tell the sheriff, he needs to arrest him! You need to save those girls," she sat back and cringed.

"It's too late to save those women I saw in the pictures, that was near ten years ago. But," she looked up at him again with hope, "maybe we can still find them and save them, or at least the new ones if they're still doing it."

He cupped her chin, said against her lips, "Yes, my love, we will do everything we can," and he kissed her until she pulled back,

"My stepfather, Wolfgang, the sheriff needs to-"

"Mmm," Wolf murmured, clasping her jaw to hold her still. "We need evidence, Ketherine, your memories of years ago are not enough. But, as I have told you, I already have people working on it. They are hacking into Talon's computers as we speak. We will get them all, now," his mouth closed over hers and he rolled on top of her forcing her down on her back.

"Let us see what else we can do until your soreness eases, hmm? Then I will draw you a big warm bubbly bath with some Epsom salts."

His hand stroked along her side. "You may have to share though, I want to play with my kitten in the bubbles."

Chapter Twenty-Six

Wolf entered the study with a mug of coffee when he heard his computer ping. It was a software program he had installed and it was announcing it found something.

He moved to the table and set the mug down. Hitting a key, the computer's monitor lit up, and he leaned over to study the information.

The second he read the report, he tugged his phone out and swiped it on, pushed the contacts selection and thumbed the number he wanted.

Dutch answered, "Wolf, I was just about to call you."

"*Jah*, Dutch, my program popped up with some interesting cross references." He could hear the instant attention in the sheriff's voice.

"Yeah? Do tell."

Wolf sat down so he could more easily read the monitor. "I had downloaded a program that would cross reference the parties and any criminal records they might have that we believe are somehow connected to the murder victims, and I got a hit. A big hit."

"Go on," an edge of excitement lit Dutch's deep voice.

"I entered everyone and also people that were peripheral to the folks staying at the resort, all their friends and relatives. I also included all residential males of Diggler's Rock between the ages of 18 and 65. I had a separate focus on ages 25 to 40.

"The younger generation at the lodge spent a lot of time in the town visiting and partying with friends they had made from previous visits over the years, and they were all quick to give names of anyone and everyone they could think of that were involved with everyone except their own friends."

"In other words, they threw the other occupants of the lodge under the bus."

Wolf's lip curled, his snort snarky in agreement. "Correct. I entered everyone Johan and Romet discovered. One of the lodge losers has a friend called Renner Zigfried. Thirty-one-year-old Zigfried is a registered sex offender with rape and aggravated assaults among other fun stuff in his criminal history. Shit came up all over the NCIC database."

"Uh," a hint of tentativeness entered Dutch's tone. "You don't have the authority to access the National Crime Information Center, Wolf. You have to be a criminal justice agency or someone under that umbrella, probation, District Attorney, otherwise it's illegal access."

Wolf chuckled. "Yeah. First of all, I cannot be caught, trust me. Second, you forget my credentials, Dutch."

There was a beat, then Dutch said, "I did forget. You are a foreign association, on a far extreme fringe connection with the CIA with very high security clearance. So, what about this Zigfried creep?"

Another chuckle then Wolf grew serious. "Guess who the connection is with Zigfried and the felonious tribe at the resort?"

"Wolf, spill it."

"Okay, you are no fun. Tomasso DeMar has a juvenile record."

"Ketherine's brother Tommy? His juvenile record would have been sealed, you can't access it-" He chuckled. "Okay, never mind. So, Tommy DeMar? My people should have found that record. It's time for some intense training in my office."

"Yep. Tommy spent time in juvy detention when he was twelve and again at fourteen. The computer cross-referenced all names connected with the correctional facility, inmates as well as corrections officers that were present at the same time as Tommy. Thank God for computers, it would take months for us to do that by hand.

"Anyway, when Tommy did his second stint in juvy at the age of fourteen, his cellmate was one Renner Zigfried. Zigfried was two years older than Tommy, he was in for strong-arm robbery."

"And Tommy?" The keen interest reveled in Dutch's voice, "What was he in for?"

"The first time, arson. He had set his school on fire. Apparently he hadn't studied for a test and figured the fire would delay things. Young and a first time offender, but there were injuries because he targeted his math teacher's office knowing the guy was in there.

"The teacher had tossed Tommy into detention several times for bad behavior. Evidently the twelve-year-old DeMar liked to hit smaller boys and lift skirts of little girls and pull their underwear down. Since the arson was his first offence he was only sentenced to six months juvy with a psych eval and follow-up. We can try to get those records, Johan should not have a problem-"

"Don't tell me, Wolf, I don't want to know. Those confidential records wouldn't be admissible in court."

"I know, but it will give us more insight into the freak. He started assaulting females pretty young, and clearly was a bully."

"What happened with the second incarceration?"

"Animals," Wolf answered flatly. "He butchered and burned half the neighborhood's pets. He was only in juvy for a few months for the offences they were able to prosecute when Talon DeMar got him court ordered to a psych facility.

"He was in lockdown for another half a year. Since then, there are vague reports that he committed other offences, but either he got smarter and did not get caught, the evidence vanished, or DeMar was paying off victims, the law and other shit. Tommy is a poster boy for serial killer. Arson and slaughtered animals, two biggies."

Dutch agreed, "The very basic traits of a serial killer. An accomplice would explain Tommy DeMar's squeaky clean alibi. We looked hard at him for the abductions especially since like Katherine, he had not arrived at the lodge until well after the others. The other occupants claimed they had stayed inside the first few days getting settled, and they were each other's alibis."

"Weak, but the alibis would stand up in court."

Dutch agreed, "Yes. It was difficult to investigate due to the time frame of the murders. We couldn't pinpoint when the cars were crashed, or when the victims were taken and returned to the crash sites.

"Ollie Duncan's car was found perched below a cliff and therefore wasn't located for some time. It had rained on and off for two days, which pretty much wiped out any traceable evidence of footprints or tire tracks. There were skid marks, however, there was no way to time stamp them or even prove they were Olli Duncan's or the killer's."

"What about paint transfer from another car if someone had shoved them off the road?"

"The car rolled and smashed into a tree. Not a lot workable to scrape off it. But, we have some samples of a black paint being tested in the lab."

Wolf said, "Every little bit will help. Anyway, thankfully the computer program I installed hooked up Zigfried's name matching it from the prison stint with Tommy as well as one of the other frat sons tossed his name out when questioned about people they saw in town."

Snickering, Dutch said, "These people would eat their young."

"Right. So the program matched Zigfried from the prison, the friends, and he also popped in as one of the male age-group we focused on in Diggler's Rock. From the prison match is where we got the info on Tommy. These are our perps, Dutch. What makes Tommy's alibi for the time of Ollie Duncan's abduction tight?"

"Good work, Wolf. Anyway, we checked out a couple of bars Tommy had claimed to have spent hours in the day Ollie and Annabella disappeared. The barmaids he'd made passes at all swore he was there. He would have needed a lot of time to cause a crash, snatch the bodies, torture and kill them, then return them to the scene. However, if he had an accomplice…"

"Yeah, he could easily swing it. And the Zigfried asshole would be in the clear since he was not previously on our radar to interview. Even so, there are wide spaces between sightings at the bars.

"Tommy would have had enough time to hit a bar, then leave and crash the vics' car, abduct the vics and stash them, then go to a bar for a while, then leave and go have fun with the vics and then maybe have Zigfried return them to their vehicle while Tommy went to another bar for his alibi.

Wolf went on, "Because we don't know when Ollie crashed, Tommy could have stowed him and his wife for hours, a day even." He set half his hip on the corner of the table and shook his head with exasperation.

"I saw Tommy DeMar briefly. He seemed rather benign, inconspicuous and unassertive, the kind that melts into the background. I would have sooner thought that creeper Chester Cash more likely as the killer."

Dutch nodded in agreement. "Yeah, chubs is sexually immature, doltish looking and gauchely non-masculine. I can see him sodomizing other stronger, more handsome, more aggressive, macho young men. Punishing them for being so much manlier than him. He's been a bane of Stone Cash's masculine ego since the cherub was born."

The corner of Wolf's lip tugged in. "It's always the unassuming ones that you overlook, exactly why they are able to pass under the radar. Chester is too big a pudgy white thumb, he sticks out."

Dutch commented with chagrin, "Still, Tommy DeMar never made a mischievous ripple when in town unlike the rest of the frats' sons. He would have been one of the last ones I would have considered as the sadistic killer."

Wolf said, "That's why he hasn't been caught yet. Tommy fits the bill all the way around. We just need to find the evidence and bring him and Zigfried in. Anyway, you said you were about to call me, what do you have?"

"Ah," there was a triumphant smile in the sound. "You are gonna love this. Your news is fantastic, and so is mine. I've had people working overtime on our theory about the arson and Talon DeMar and the frat bastards. They dug up the shitload, bro, the shitload."

Finally, the information was starting to pour in. Wolf moved to sit in a chair. "All right, hit me, Dutch."

It sounded like Dutch took a slurp of something, likely coffee before he spoke. "We were right. DeMar and the buddies got their filthy lucre from the arson. DeMar's father, Antonio, owned an insurance company. He insured a business, Goring Industries, they made ball bearings and other small wheel parts.

"Talon allegedly, according to one of the victim's relatives, talked his father into pushing the owner to insure the employees as well. Which he did. Antonio and the owner of Goring, Jack Mathers, were close buds. Talon let some time pass then he talked his father into convincing Mathers to throw a party for his staff in appreciation for their good work. It was a Christmas party."

"I get it, Talon torched the party and reaped the insurance dollars."

"Yep," Dutch said. "Due to so many victims, it paid off massively. My researcher dug up records that the rest of the frat rats were on the business payroll and listed as some beneficiaries, I suppose to deflect suspicion from investigators off the insurance company.

"Detectives never came up with anyone to bring charges against. They had suspicions, there were notes indicating they were looking at Jack Mathers, Antonio and Talon DeMar along with Stone Cash as he was a CEO of the insurance company. Talon and Cash were both CEO's of McMaster Lexington as well. But the detectives could never come up with any evidence to indict them."

Fury raced through Wolf's brain. Fucking assholes murdered innocent people then went on to destroy lives in other countries with their greedy bridges, and the alleged sex trafficking. And, the hell they rained on Ketherine.

His hands rolled into tight fists, if only DeMar and Cash were present right now, they would never leave the building alive.

Wolf sucked back his wrath and said, "So, with all that highly suspicious paying out the benefits, what about now? Can they prosecute them now? Is there an issue with the statute of limitations?"

"There may be a limitation in the arson, but not the deaths, the murders of the victims. Sadly, they found nothing to tie them to the crime then, so it would be unlikely if we could now. Doesn't mean we won't try, I've already got the wheels in motion."

"Hell," Wolf muttered.

"Ditto. Hey, I didn't tell you the other interesting part. Antonio DeMar and Jack Mathers both perished in the fire."

Wolf's brows shot up. "Oh *jah*? Shit. He killed his old man." Shaking his head, he said, "That guy gives sociopaths a bad name. Then you have Talon and Tommy, father and son arsonists. Apparently that rotten apple didn't slither far from the tree."

"No kidding. Plus, that body Ketherine discovered at the burial site?"

"Yeah?"

"I have my suspicions, now that I know what Talon DeMar is truly capable of. Around the time of the second burial, Talon's first wife disappeared. The story was she ran off with a lover, but her relatives said she'd never leave her two boys, and no one ever heard from her again. She's the same height and the ME said the body is Caucasian and the age range he believes she was matches DeMar's wife. We got DNA going on it."

"Holy shit, Dutch, the man is a Satan in waiting. Sounds like he could even teach the old devil a thing or two about the word insidious." And his Ketherine had been raised by the bastard.

It's amazing she turned out so sweet and soft, and lucky she got the hell out from under DeMar and that other fucker Cash. Wolf's body burned with rage, he ached to get his hands on both sick freaks.

Silence rose as the men contemplated all the reprehensible information they'd learned and shared.

Dutch broke the silence, "All right, I'll get backup and go scarf up Tommy and Zigfried. I'll call you when-"

"Okay, Johan is calling me. I will be in touch, later Dutch."

Chapter Twenty-Seven

Wolf disconnected with Dutch and answered Johan's call. "*Tere*, J."

"Wolf." Johan's normal mischievous voice was spiked with glee.

Hearing the eagerness, Wolf ordered impatiently, "Don't gloat, J, just damned spill it." The conversation continued in their language.

Johan let out a whistle causing Wolf to hold the phone away from his ear with a grimace. "I am impressed, my brother," Johan's teasing grin came through on the wire, "you have graduated to using contractions. Only one so far, but still, you rock, you-"

"Johan," Wolf groaned.

"Okay, okay, keep your panties on. Speaking of Ketherine, how-"

"Goddammit J!" Wolf exploded with exasperation.

"All right," Johan snickered. "You'll fill us in later on how the love affair is going. Now there's an oxymoron, Wolf and love, hah!"

He spoke quickly over Wolf's curses, "We found what those weird markings are that were burned into the victims' chests. We scanned them into the program and it took a while, but a match came up."

When Johan paused to peak Wolf's curiosity and to annoy him, Wolf sighed, "J…"

"Okay, but you'll be proud of me. I reviewed notes and photos of our searches of the lodge and cabins. In Talon DeMar's room was a paddle on display. A frat paddle. The same symbols on the paddle were what were burned into the victims. They are a fraternity symbol."

"Damn." Wolf smiled. "I am proud of you. The older generation males at the lodge were all in the same frat. What was the name of it? I have it written down-"

"Yeah," Johan said, he'd already researched it. "Brothers in Hell. Apropos, eh? The Greek letters depicting the frat name; Beta Iota Eta, are the symbols burnt into the bodies, BIN. I'll text you the Greek spelling and shit."

Wolf looked at his screen when it dinged. He saw Αδέλφια στην κόλαση, Beta Iota Eta – the symbols of the letters are BIN- β ι η. "J, this was not the specific branded design, I recall it slightly different."

"That's why they pay you the big bucks my smart friend. Yes, there were lines, like an X slashed through the β ι η. The brandings were so crudely done each one looked slightly different and without perfect lines."

Picturing it, Wolf murmured absently, "The killer was X'ing out the fraternity, crossing them out. Eliminating, destroying it. He hates the men, the fathers, Jared Duncan, Devis McShane, probably Talon, Cash and the rest of them."

"That's what I was thinking."

"So," Wolf pondered, "the Frat Rats did something terrible to Tommy, something so heinous, instead of killing the older men, he is making them suffer worse by torturing and murdering their spawn, Ollie Duncan and Michael

McShane. I have a feeling their women were collateral damage."

Silence commenced as the two friends considered assorted angles to the motives.

"Money, love, betrayal, those are the basics, Wolf."

"Hmm." Wolf scratched his head then dragged his hand down his face as he thought. "No, it has to be something worse, so bad he tortured them horribly, viciously sexually. The torture, the particular acts are telling." Closing his eyes, he pictured what could have been the scene.

Going over it out loud he said, "The killer had stripped the couples, branded the males while they were alive according to the ME, he then fucked them then killed them. The males were horribly tortured and branded and killed, the girls were sexually assaulted then murdered without the extras."

"He raped the women with his body, but he used something long and hard that caused tremendous internal damage to the males," Johan said.

Cringing at the recalled photos they had seen of the deceased, Wolf rubbed his eyes running the scenes through his head again and again.

Then, "Hell, J, it is like a copycat revenge. He did to them what was done to him." Although Johan couldn't see him, Wolf nodded at Johan's sharp gasp.

"Uh, then, he was repeating his own tortured assault..." Johan floundered taking in Wolf's theory.

"*Jah*, the killer himself had been brutally assaulted and branded. I am thinking he was sodomized that is why he is so viciously cruel to the males, but does not want people to think he is gay, so he is proving that he is straight by also fucking the females.

"He is repeating history on the victims, his history. Once we find our perp no doubt he will have that frat brand somewhere on his body." Wolf picked up his mug of coffee, sipped, made a face at the tepid brew and set the mug back down.

Johan remarked, "Except he kills them when he's done."

"*Jah*, J, the ultimate pain, killing their offspring. Plus, he eliminates any witnesses."

The silence grew again. Without expecting an answer, Johan ruminated, "The question is, is he done? Did he complete his retribution-"

"Or were there other degenerates in the group that had tormented him, not just Duncan and McShane and therefore there will be more victims?" Wolf needed to call Dutch Kross.

"We must haul in the bunch of them again, Johan, one or more of them knows something. We need someone to re-interview the couples that have returned home to bury their kids. I want our people doing the interrogations, I want the gloves off. Dutch has to follow too many rules, he will not be able to beat the damned answers out of them."

"Okay," Johan said. "I'll call Romet and the others and get the ball rolling."

"All right, later," Wolf said, hanging up then he called the sheriff.

Chapter Twenty-Eight

After Wolf filled him in, Dutch said to Wolf over the phone, "It ain't done, Wolf. He's not done. We got more people missing."

"Ah, shit."

"You said it. Like the other victims, the missing folks are also family members of the frat gang, so everything you surmised appears to be accurate. It's not a couple this time, however. They're siblings. Mark and Libbie Burton."

"When?"

"I was just about to contact you. We got the call about ten minutes ago. They were supposed to meet their folks in town for dinner last night. They never showed and they aren't answering their phones. I called over at the lodge to see if their car was there and it isn't. I've got deputies scouring the area for their vehicle. Wolf-"

"Yes, I know. At this point they are undoubtedly dead, but, maybe not." Wolf tried to think.

"There has to be surveillance cameras somewhere in Diggler's Rock. We might be able to track their route and also see if another vehicle is frequently in the pictures with them. You need to pull the videos. There has to be film of their car somewhere at some point in town. Tommy or

Renner Zigfried likely stalked their victims before abducting them."

He didn't tell the sheriff he was going to have Johan do the same thing, only not quite so legally, but without the legal binds he would undoubtedly be quicker and more effective and more comprehensive.

He'd only just hung up with the sheriff when he heard sirens. Alarms.

"Oh shit," he swore, "the estate has been breached!"

Whipping his phone out, he called Gaven, head of his security as he raced up the stairs.

Boots pounding down the carpeted hall when Gaven answered, Wolf barked, "Tell me."

"Yes, sir," Gaven responded, his breathing was as rushed as Wolf's, the adrenalin flowing.

"A large truck drove through the gates. The only reason why they could break through the iron was because the gates were partially open to allow some people to leave. They must have been hiding down the street waiting for the opportunity to happen. The truck burst through and raced over the lawn, it's heading for the front door of the-" He broke off to shout orders, his voice bounced as he was running as well.

In the background, Wolf heard shouts, then gunfire. He was at the back of the estate while the commotion was at the front. By the time he reached his suite, the door was already flung open and Keti was hurrying out, fear and confusion streaking her face.

Without speaking to her, his phone still plastered to his ear, he grabbed her arm and pushed her back inside the suite and slammed then locked the door. He told her, "Get in the bathroom, lock the door, do not open it for anyone but me, Johan, Romet or Gaven."

Keti didn't move.

"Sir!" Gaven shouted from the phone.

"Here," Wolf responded to him while waving at Keti. "Do as I say, Ketherine, immediately."

Still she stood, the fear and confusion stealing her ability to move. More gunfire and her shoulders rose to her ears with a wince at the terrifying sounds.

"Goddammit." Wolf grabbed her arm and forced her to walk swiftly through the hall and into the bedroom. At the bathroom, he thrust her inside and commanded her again, "Do not open that damned door, now lock it," and he slammed the door in her white face.

"Update, Gaven," he ordered as he ran back through the suite. He was torn between staying and protecting Ketherine and rushing to the uproar to secure the estate.

"Sir, the truck broke through the front doors of the mansion and burst into the foyer. Our men are on it, they've stopped the truck with firepower but soldiers poured out of it and we are working on containing them."

Wolf could hear the pop-pop and harsh bangs of guns firing through the phone as well as from the hallway.

"All right, I will start assault from the second floor on down, keep me apprised." He hated to leave Ketherine but he would be of better benefit to stopping the men before they reached their floor than trying to fight them off once they approached the suite.

Other doors flew open as he ran down the hall, he was quickly joined by his own people.

Wolf and his men scattered to each end of the hall and towards the main staircase. Shouts and screams rang out amidst the barrage of firing guns from downstairs.

Keeping their backs against the wall with weapons up and ready, they cautiously moved down the staircase- rapid

239

gunfire pinged bullets along the wall blasting plaster fragments in all directions.

Wolf and his men ducked and paused. Wolf signaled his team that he was going to go first and they were to cover him.

Peering quickly, he curved his arm around the wall and fired, heard a grunt, and he dashed forward with his head down. His own men's bombardment of gunshots rappelled over his head as he moved down the stairs.

The man he'd shot lay groaning on the steps, blood poured from a chest wound. Wolf took his weapons then left him and continued on down.

His soldiers were right at his back. The shouting and fireworks were growing fewer and farther between.

When he reached the first floor he saw the floors and walls spattered and pooled with blood and numerous bodies lying on the floor, some with eyes wide-open in death, others writhing and moaning in pain.

Wolf's people were interspersed amongst them, clearing the wounded of their weapons and quickly restraining them.

Gaven hurried up to him. Wiping sweat off his forehead with his sleeve, he holstered his weapon and said, "We got them all. They're either dead or dying. I'll initiate the cleanup." Snow blew in from the gaping doorway.

Surveying the damage to the house and the bodies littering the floors, Wolf nodded. "Who are they? I am guessing Johnnie Frog's people."

"Yeah, we questioned one of the soldiers. He answered quickly once my blade sliced into his shoulder. Johnnie Frog was the one who ordered the attack. He wants your woman."

Holstering his own weapon, hands on his hips Wolf grimaced. "*Jah*, I was expecting an assault, just not to this brazen extent." He walked over to the truck that had blasted through the front doors.

It was a massive black tank of a machine. Steam poured out from under the crushed front end. All the doors were still open from the soldiers' rapid exiting.

Gaven followed him. "The truck is mostly bulletproof, the windows too. But they didn't hold up to our exceptional firepower. It was a good thing you insisted on us purchasing the uber weapons. It took a bunch of that firepower, but we broke through the windows, that's why they bailed and tried to rush the house."

Wolf watched his men working, cuffing all the soldiers whether they were dead or alive and dragging the bodies along one wall for easier policing.

He should go check on Ketherine, she's probably terrified, but he wanted to wait to ensure all was in control and cleared.

"You mighta gotten us, asshole," one of the restrained soldiers spat blood at Wolf, then grinned showing a missing tooth, "but Rana got what he came for." One of Wolf's men near him kicked him, told him to shut up.

Crossing his arms over his chest, Wolf was about to ignore him, when, he spun around narrowing his eyes at the man. "What do you mean came for? Rana is here?" He'd scanned each attacker, none were Rana.

He stalked over to the soldier.

Blood poured from his shoulder, his camo-shirt was drenched in blood. The soldier spat again, told him caustically, "Of course. Rana runs his own missions, shithead. You may have won this little battle, but he stole the war."

Wolf swung around to Gaven. "You have any sighting of Giovanni Rana here?" He quickly glanced around at the prisoners again, Rana wasn't among them.

Gaven tapped his earpiece and parroted the question. Shaking his head, he told Wolf, "No, sir. No sign of him. That asshole is just trying to stir-"

"Oh, fuck," Wolf cursed a streak, broke and raced for the staircase. Taking the steps two at a time, he fished out his phone and called Johan.

When Johan answered, Wolf barked out, "It was a distraction. Johnnie Frog is here to take Ketherine. Call the men to secure the perimeter and the rest of the house. I am on my way to my suite."

His heart beat frantic in tandem with his footfalls as Wolf raced to where he'd left Ketherine alone and vulnerable.

"Goddammit!" He swore under his breath when he saw the door to their rooms was wide open.

As he reached the suite he noticed the splintered wood. Someone, Rana, had kicked the door in. The worst thing that stabbed terror into his gut was he didn't hear a thing from inside, no screaming, no begging, no gloating laughter, nothing, just dead silence.

Wolf ran through the living room, saw the kitchenette was empty he hurried down the hall. Passing two bedrooms he could quickly tell they were vacant, he rushed on to the master bedroom, and his gut twisted with the acid of fear.

That door was broken open as well. Sweat sprung along his brow as he moved inside and saw a table knocked over, a candy bowl lay on the floor the candy sprawled on the carpet.

Dragging a shaking hand through his hair, the bathroom door was also kicked in, he peered inside, it was empty.

"Where the hell," he muttered, trod quickly to the large window that overlooked the back perimeter of the estate.

His heart gripped as if in a clenched fist. This portion of the estate was the most secured by the electrified fence that bordered the woods beyond, so his men had not yet reached the area to search.

Down below, Johnnie Frog grasped Ketherine's arm and was dragging her quickly across the lawn.

Snow cascaded from dark grey clouds. Dried colored leaves dusted up around their feet as he fought to haul her to the waiting helicopter that just landed. The propellers whooshed the leaves tossing them in swirling circles like papery Skittles.

Rana and Keti were halfway to the chopper when Keti twisted, jerked, and stuck her leg out tripping Rana.

When Rana stumbled he released Keti and she ran-

Wolf shoved the window open and drew his gun. But, Rana had easily caught her, he was twice her size. He slapped her, she staggered and he bent to toss her over his shoulder.

"Dammit," Wolf barked a curse, he couldn't take the shot, he'd hit Ketherine.

Chapter Twenty-Nine

*H*anging upside down, the blood rushed to her head as it bounced hard on Johnnie Frog's back.

Ketherine put her hands on his back and pushed up. Her brain blanched, they were almost to the chopper and the pilot was opening the door.

If Rana got her inside she was a goner. He could toss her body into a river and no one would know she was dead.

She would only be declared missing, therefore, Rana and Talon could make all the wonderful deals they wanted to without her interference, or anyone else stepping in with their inheritance of her half-ownership of the company.

Her body jolting, she could hardly think, barely draw a full breath as it was slammed out of her again and again with each of his running strides.

They were almost to the helicopter. Even if she managed to get away from Rana at this moment, he would only quickly catch her and beat her into submission. But, she'd be damned if she would give up without a fight.

Keti hit him all over, everywhere she could reach- he kept running. Her hand hit something in his pocket. With his frantic race carrying her to the chopper, Rana never felt her pull out the extra pocketknife he kept in his back pocket. It was tiny, but could still cause damage.

She couldn't wait until he reached the helicopter to do something, she would only wound Rana with the small knife and the pilot could shoot her. So she swiftly opened the knife and stabbed it into Rana's lower back.

He screamed, skidded, his feet staggered with short choppy steps, he dropped Keti to reach for the knife.

With a cry, Keti slammed to the ground knocking the wind out of her. Her mouth open, hand on her chest, she struggled to draw air into her shocked lungs. Her body was too stunned to try to crawl away from Rana, to get up and run.

"Argggg," Rana roared, yanking the tiny knife from his back. His eyes bulged with rage as he turned to her. He tossed the knife aside and pulled a gun from an inside holster strapped over his chest.

Lifting the weapon, he bellowed with fury, "You bitch!" Stepping closer, spittle slung from his mouth as he cursed her. "I was gonna keep you for a while, play with you, I might not have killed you right out you bitch, but now," he aimed the gun at Keti.

She tried to roll into a ball, a smaller target, but she knew she was done, the man was standing over her, she was trapped. Her head tucked down she screamed as she heard the gunshot-

The shot reverberated through the woods, Keti waited for the pain, then the blackness that would take her under forever… but, she heard a thump and raised her head.

Rana was lying on the ground on his back, spread eagle. A hole in his forehead oozed blood, it trickled out and slid down the side of his head.

"Ketherine!"

Keti heard Wolf's shout and looked up. He was standing at the window of their suite, the gun still raised. His hard face solid iron didn't show what he was feeling, but it was the most beautiful thing she'd ever seen in her life.

She heard shouts and saw the pilot was trying to get back inside the chopper but Wolf's men were charging towards him with guns out, yelling for him to get out of the machine.

"Hey, Keti." Johan bent to her and offered his hand. She put her hand in his, it shook so badly he clasped his hand around hers to calm it and pulled her gently to her feet.

Men streamed out from everywhere, a couple ran to check on Rana, one kicked his gun away from his prone body, others went to yank the pilot from the helicopter.

More soldiers hurried into the woods through a now open gate to check for any more of Rana's people lurking or running away.

It took several minutes before Wolf was sprinting across the yard to Keti and Johan.

Johan stood with his arm wrapped around her shoulders. Her body quaking from head to toe in a havoc of emotion, adrenalin zapped, short-circuiting her brain. Keti felt like she was in a blender, the world whirling around her while her body spun in the opposite direction.

A string of curses tumbled from Wolf's mouth as he approached her. He glared at the grinning Johan, and Johan removed his arm from around Keti's shoulders and she flung herself into Wolf's open arms.

He crushed her in a fierce embrace, his face pressed into her hair. She cried her relief against his chest. Wolf stroked her hair, her back, whispering that she was okay now, safe, he had her.

If Keti didn't know better, she would think she felt a slight tremor in his hand that caressed her head and down her hair. She must be mistaken though, his aim and firing at Rana had been rock steady and true.

Around them, Wolf's people quickly with efficient skill saw to taking care of Giovanni Rana, the pilot and the helicopter. His arm curled tightly around Keti, Wolf walked her across the lawn to the house.

Inside, Wolf led her to a parlor. Settling Keti on a flowered settee he fixed them both a strong drink. "Here, baby," he said, handing her a glass of amber liquid.

The only thing revealing the emotion in him was the tautness of his voice and the grit of his tight jaw. Even as affectionate as the term 'baby' is, in Wolf's harsh voice and guttural accent the note of endearment was more implied than sounded.

Keti was pleased the tremors in her hands had lessened as she took the drink. "Thank you, Wolfgang," she said quietly.

Taking a tiny sip of the strong alcohol, her nose wrinkled at the taste. With a small cough, she blinked and gave Wolf a tremulous smile as he sat down beside her with a heavy sigh.

Throwing back a big gulp of bourbon, Wolf set his hand on Keti's thigh. "Sheriff Kross will be here to take our statements. Rana will no longer impact your life or anyone else's."

Holding her glass with both hands, Keti leaned back, a small moan slipped out and she shifted uncomfortably. Wolf studied her with concern. "Were you hurt, Katherine? Did he hurt you? Do I need to get you to a doctor?"

She shook her head. "No, I'm fine. Just a little bruised." A smile softened the anxiety that had constricted her features from her terrifying ordeal.

"At least now I can move about freely now without worry that Mr. Rana will get me." Staring down at the liquor she said, "I should go home." Lifting her glass to sip she missed the frown on Wolf's face.

He squeezed her thigh in consternation. "You forget, Ketherine. There is a killer out there that is targeting your group. You are not any safer than the rest of them. He may come after you next."

One shoulder bumped, she twitched her glass and watched the liquid slop side-to-side. "I just need to stay inside, Wolfgang. The killer is grabbing people outside, and he's taking couples. I'm not a couple, so if I stay inside I should be fine."

His jaw clenched, mouth a hard line, he narrowed his eyes at her. "Ketherine," a slightly angry note entered his voice, "I thought we…" he waited until she looked at him.

"I hoped at this point, I mean, now that we have been intimate, gotten to know each other, that we are a couple."

"Um." Keti's lips pursed, she leaned over and set her glass on the coffee table in front of them. Setting her palms on the cushion she moved to get up. "I think I should pack my things, I'm not sure, um…"

His hand tightened on her leg holding her down. His face a stony mask, Wolf growled his irritation. "You forget, darling," anger seethed through his clenched teeth, "that you are here in my custody. You will stay here until the murderer is caught."

Lashes flung wide, Keti gasped. "But, really, you don't think, I mean the sheriff doesn't really think that I am the murderer? That's preposterous!"

His jaw worked, thick fingers dug into her thigh, he said, "Does not matter, you are still a suspect, therefore still in my custody. You will not leave the estate." He kept to himself the possible latest abductions of Libbie and Marc Burton.

Cinnamon brows daggered down between eyes filled with pique. "Now Wolfgang, this is all quite ridiculous, I can't believe you think that I-"

Wolf bent and smashed his mouth over hers effectively squashing her protests. He cupped the back of her head with one hand, the other slid up her thigh, up her side to her back. Slanting his head, he ground at her mouth, pushing her lips apart to plunge his tongue inside to attack hers.

At first Keti froze, then she put her hands on his chest to push him away, but he gobbled her, bit her lips, sucked her tongue and she slowly softened in his arms and kissed him back.

His hand moved from her back to palm her breast. He wrapped his big fingers around her full flesh and kneaded it, gently at first, then at her moan his grasp roughened, and she purred at his lips.

She whimpered when he slowly released her completely and moved an inch away from her.

Puzzled, lids half-mast with the desire he had instantly aroused in her, Keti whispered, "Wolfgang? You...don't want me?"

His smile eased some of the hard lines in his face. "Baby, I would be dead and I would still want you. But, you just had a terrorizing assault. Abducted from here, dragged across the lawn to a waiting helicopter. You were well aware of what would have happened if Rana had gotten you inside and it took off. Then he was seconds away from shooting you."

A shiver pinched his spine showing how afraid he had been when he'd seen Rana accosting Keti and almost making off with her, then aiming his weapon at her heart as she lay trounced on the ground at his feet.

All thoughts of packing her things forgotten, pushing her long hair off her shoulder, Keti set her hand on Wolf's knee and smiled back at him.

"And you rescued me, Wolfgang. You're my hero. I…want to…" the smile turned sultry with a tilt to her head, "thank you."

All thoughts of leaving him had drifted away with his intense kisses. She leaned into him, pressed a hand on his thick chest and grinned up at him. "I want to show you what you've taught me. Let me thank you properly, Wolfgang."

He wound his fingers around her arms to hold her back. "Katherine, I would like nothing more than to have you show me how…grateful you are, show me what you have learned from my tutoring, but," he brushed her arms with his thumbs.

"You have had a traumatic day. I…don't want to take advantage of your…distress. You are feeling the rush of adrenalin. That is what is making you so…" the side of his mouth curved up with a sinful glint in his eyes to match, "amorous."

The smile flattened. "But," he stroked her cheek, "there is always a crash after the adrenalin burns off, and, I do not, *don't* want you to regret-"

Keti scooted close to him, set both palms on his chest and lifted her chin and slowly licked his upper lip then bit his lower one, her coo a sensual invitation.

"Wolfgang, how about we burn off our adrenalin together, then crash together?" Sifting her hands up his broad chest she slid them around his neck and pulled his head down to kiss him.

They kissed, hands roaming bodies, hers all soft abundant feminine curves that he worshipped; his pure iron musculature, a hundred percent virile man. Wolf leaned back. "I don't understand. You were just fighting me on staying here, and now…?"

She smiled shyly. "You are forcing me to say here, so," she shrugged with a sexy pout, "I figure I might as well make the best of it. Come on," she tugged at his hand.

"You don't have to say it twice, sweetheart," Wolf stood up quickly, bent and scooped her up in his arms and headed for the stairs.

Her arms threaded around his neck, their mouths glued together they heard Absolom call to them that the sheriff was on the phone.

They grinned and Wolf sped up his step and hurried up the stairs.

Chapter Thirty

*F*or hours Dutch Kross and his deputies reviewed camera videos from all around Diggler's Rock searching for a shot of the Burtons' car.

Deputy Barnes leaned back in his chair with a yawn. Scratching over an ear he yawned again. "How much more, Sheriff, how freakin' many more of these tapes are there? This is a needle in a hay-"

"There." Dutch bent forward pointing at one of the monitors. "There they are, watch." He clicked a few keys, rewound the video the Wolf's team had forwarded to them and pressed play and watched it again. His finger pointing at the screen, he said, "See the blue Kia, there on Buckman's Bridge."

They watched the blue car crossing the bridge that arced over Rainbow River. The other three deputies that were studying the tapes jumped up and hovered around Dutch to view the video.

"Zoom it in, Sheriff," Deputy Sharon Sudner said leaning over Dutch's shoulder. "Make sure that's the Burtons in the car. Enlarge the tag."

Dutch enlarged the tag first, the deputies all nodded in unison.

"Yep," Barnes spoke, "that's their tag. Zoom in, see if we can see the occupants."

Dutch tapped the keys and the car grew larger, then larger. A few of the deputies gasped.

Barnes said, "That ain't Marc or Libbie Burton."

"No." Dutch peered in at the screen. "That's Tommy DeMar."

"Doesn't appear to be anyone else in the car," Deputy Sudner said. "It looks like he already killed them and is disposing the car. That sucks big time."

"I don't see the black truck Tommy DeMar usually drives," Barnes remarked.

"Look," a deputy spoke excitedly and pointed at a red car behind the blue Kia. "That Chevy fits our BOLO for Zigfried. That's Renner Zigfried right behind him. What the hell did they do with the Burtons?"

A grim silence followed as they watched the cars travel over the bridge to the other side.

"Hey," Barnes said, "they aren't staying on the main highway, look, they're turning off onto that side road, it's a dirt road. You know, Junction Path, runs parallel with the river for a mile then forks off to the west into fields and then woods."

His eyes on the screen, Dutch ordered, "Barnes, get a team headed out to Junction Path," he swiped his phone off the table and dialed.

Wolf was partially lying over Keti, who was lying on her stomach. His hand was under her cupping a breast, his breath stirred her hair.

They were naked, replete, satiated. Neither had an inkling to move.

Absolom had put the sheriff's questioning about Johnnie Frog off, and Johan saw to the clearing of the house and yard. But now, Wolf's phone rang. The tune playing told Wolf it was Dutch Kross.

"Damn, baby, I should get it," he growled. Rolling slightly onto his side, he reluctantly snatched the phone off the nightstand. Keti murmured incoherently and snuggled under his big body.

He pressed the button, "*Jah*, Dutch, I am kind of busy right-"

"We found the cars, Wolf. At least we found where they are headed to. Tommy DeMar was driving Miles Burton's car with Renner Zigfried tailing right behind him. They turned off Buckman's Bridge onto Junction Path."

Wolf rose up on one elbow, the sated languidness snapping away.

Dutch said, "Because it's a path and not a road it isn't on a map. I have deputies heading out there to search the area. Thing is, we're talking miles and miles of scrub and forest and foothills. We need somewhere more specific to head to."

"Ahh," Wolf groaned, raking his hand through the front of his hair, he looked down at a naked Keti buried beneath him and smiled. Then he frowned.

"You want me to go after someone to pinpoint an area. But, hell, Dutch, we questioned all of the Frat rat pack but they all said they had no idea of any property in or around Diggler other than the lodge."

"I know. But listen Wolf, the frat brothers and their spawn spent most of their lives visiting the lodge here, it makes sense that someone owned something. A townhouse, a cottage, a cabin, something. If anyone knows something, it's Talon."

254

"Why haven't you arrested him?" Annoyed impatience radiated in Wolf's growl.

Dutch replied, "We plan to arrest him when we get more evidence regarding the assault of Tommy DeMar when he was a child, and the arson, insurance fraud and the murders as a result of the arson." He took a breath, the rough exhale came through the phone.

"Hell, we're going to bring him in regarding the discovery of his murdered first wife. The State Attorney wants more proof of his deeds. The point is, right now he's not in police custody. I sent a deputy to his home but he lawyered right up. *We* can't question him…"

With a snort, Wolf said, "I see. Since you cannot be involved in…forcing him to talk, you want me to…interrogate him."

"Yes," Dutch said tersely. "I don't care how you get the information. Beat the shit out of him, break bones, don't care and don't want to know how you do it, but, hell, Wolf, there are two young people out there, if they're still alive are about to be savaged and butchered. We need whatever you can get, ASAP. We find them, you can always tell me for the record you just happened to come across them on a search."

Wolf sat up, his gaze on Keti. She lay curled on the mattress with a happy sigh. Damn, he hated to leave her when they were making such amazing headway. She had instigated sex with him, bringing his dream to fruition.

Next would be convincing her to stay with him of her own free will, even after all this murdering shit was done. He picked up a lock of her hair. It curled around his fingers like it was hugging them, he sifted the curl through his fingers feeling the utter silky softness of it. Like her skin.

He sighed harshly, said to Dutch, "*Jah*, of course, I will go right away."

Dutch said, "We could use your team, Johan, Romet, a few of the others to help us go after Tommy DeMar and Zigfried. Our deputies aren't as experienced with gun fighting, combat, we have no SWAT here, we could use their expertise."

Wolf paused, let the curl drift through his fingers. "I would have to leave Ketherine with a skeleton crew, Dutch. I don't want to leave her at risk."

Keti rolled over, Wolf's gaze fell to her breasts, his mouth edged up as hunger for her began a burning gnaw starting in his groin.

Looking thoroughly relaxed, like a woman that had made love all afternoon and was satisfied and content, and sexy as hell, she said, "Go, Wolfgang."

"Ketherine, I don't want to leave you unpro-"

She heard most of the conversation. "Marc and Libbie's lives are at risk. I'll be fine. The killers are out there with them, I'll be safe here. I'll call Bonnie to come stay with me."

"Huh," he snorted. "I doubt that blonde bimbo will be much of a shield between you and danger."

Her lips pushed out, she rebuked him, "Wolfgang, Bonnie is not a bimbo. She's been my only friend over the years."

His jaw twitched. "She may seem like Snow White to you my little softie," he stroked her hair, then fondled her breast. "But you have clearly missed her flirting. Hell, babe, the girl brazenly grabbed my balls the first time we met. She is lucky she moved off quickly at my expression, I wanted to break her fingers."

She looked surprised. "Really?" Her brows lowered and she smiled. "Oh, she's just, flirtatious, she's about to be engaged to Kyle Griggs. She was just playing. I'm sure she grabbed you accidentally."

"Hmm, sure."

"Go," she ordered him, pushing his hands off her. "The killer could be murdering them as we speak. Please, I'll be perfectly safe here, you need to save them. Go."

He hated to leave her, but she was right. Lives hung in danger, and she should be safe at the estate. "Okay, beautiful. I will call you."

He kissed her hard then moved off the bed before he relented and rolled back on top of her. Or pulled her up on her hands and knees and moved behind-

"Go, Wolfgang," she giggled at the heat in his heavy-lidded gaze.

He kissed her again then called Johan and Romet to gather the others to join the posse as he headed to take a quick shower.

Wolf hurled Talon at the wall for the second time, the man struck it with a crunch of cracking bones. They were in Talon's suite at the lodge in his living room.

When Wolf rang the bell to the lodge and Nigel let him in, Talon showed up a minute later.

Wolf told him he needed some information, could they speak in private. As soon as they entered the suite, Wolf grabbed Talon's blazer lapels and heaved the older man at the wall.

"Fuck!" Talon howled, slapping his palms behind him against the wall to keep from sliding down. He shoved his black hair out of his eyes and glared furiously at Wolf. "What the fuck, man?"

Talon was a big muscled male, but Wolf had more height and thicker muscles, and he'd been a trained fighter and he'd been battling guerillas in jungles when he was but a toddler.

Wolf cracked his knuckles and moved a few steps to where Talon leaned against the wall. "That was an extremely mild example of what will only be the beginning if you do not answer my questions."

Talon tugged his shirt down and straightened his blazer, snarled at Wolf, "Fuck you, boy, I'll have you run out of the country in one second flat. I have friends in the state police depart-"

Bam-

Wolf socked Talon in the jaw so hard Talon's head snapped to the side almost breaking his neck.

"I don't give a shit who you know, DeMar. By the time I leave here you will not have teeth to hold back the drool, or a tongue to speak with. You cannot use a phone if every bone in your fingers are broken."

He took a step to Talon and Talon jerked his head away expecting a blow.

"Trust me, DeMar, I would thrill to fuck you up even without needing information. The things you allowed to happen to Ketherine." Wolf could barely see through the red haze of fury that covered his eyes at what she had told him of her childhood. But he couldn't kill Talon, not yet.

His arms curled, biceps bulged, hands rolled into fists, he stalked closer to DeMar.

Coarsely pushing the words through grit teeth, he said, "I dream of killing you for what you did to Ketherine, your stepdaughter. What you did to your servants' innocent children, I could break you in half, rip your nuts off, twist and shatter your fucking spine with my bare hands for the sadistic torture Ketherine told me you wrought on them to get her to cooperate with you."

"Back the fuck off," Talon barked, holding his hands up to ward Wolf away. "What do you want? You want money? I'll write you a check-"

Whack-

Wolf bashed his fist in Talon's dark brown eye and Talon roared in pain.

Slapping his hand over his eye, Talon slumped over with a wail, "What do you want! What the fuck do you want you fucking maniac!"

Wolf stood back, his boots akimbo, crossed his arms over his chest and said calmly, "There is property out here somewhere, in the vicinity of Buckman's Bridge. One of you owns something, a house, apartment, cottage, barn, shed, something. You tell me right now or I will-" he put his hard fist to Talon's bleeding face.

"Okay, okay," Talon cried, ducking his head he held his hands up. "There is- I'll tell you, back off you fucking bruiser."

Not moving a step back, Wolf set his fists on his hips. "Tell me, right now, no fucking around. First stall, first lie, I will snap your leg over my thigh and break the fucking thing like you did to that kid's arm." He pushed his face into Talon's with his eyes blaring the dark threat.

Cringing from the fierce man, "All right, I said okay," his voice taking on a panicked shake, Talon wiped the back of his hand over the blood seeping from the side of his split lip.

Looking at the blood, he took a deep breath, sighed it out in a pained shudder. "There is a cabin. In the old days, when the kids were young, I took Tommy and Roger out and tried to teach them how to hunt. Little pussies," he spat out a wad of blood and gingerly patted his swelling eye.

259

"Little fuckers hated every second of it. Chicken shit, lily liver-"

Bam-

Wolf slammed his fist into Talon's gut. Talon bent over double with a gagging retch.

Wolf stood a bit to the side in case Talon vomited. "Tell me where it is. Right now, or I will box your fucking ears until your skull crushes and they meet, you asshole."

Tears pouring from his eyes, Talon whimpered raising his arms to cover his head. "It's six miles east of Buckman's Bridge, a- a hunting cabin. H-hard to find."

Wolf whipped out his phone and dialed Dutch.

"Kross here."

"Okay, DeMar, give Dutch directions to the cabin."

When Talon completed providing the directions, Wolf said into the phone, "I am on my way to help with the take-down, Dutch."

"There," Talon sniffed, swiping the back of his hand across his snotty bloody nose. "You got what you wanted, now get the hell out of here you fucker. Get out of my-"

Wolf hit him so hard Talon slammed into the wall again. Before he could right himself, Wolf was on him.

On his way to his truck, he called Johan. "J, I am coming out there. Tis a cabin, Dutch Kross will tell you where it is. There is an overgrown path to the back that you can take, the killers will not see you coming."

"You got the info from DeMar?" Johan asked. Wolf could hear sounds of the truck rumbling as he drove.

"*Jah.*"

"Anything left of him?"

"Not much. It will be some time before he will be released from the hospital before he can stand trial on whatever charges Dutch can get on him." He hopped in his truck at Johan's chuckles.

"Don't laugh, J, I wanted the bastard dead, but," he sighed and started down the street. "Dutch would kill me if he could not arrest the prick. So, I left him alive, sort of."

He headed towards the highway leading to Buckman's Bridge.

Chapter Thirty-One

"*O*h, Bonnie, I'm so glad you could come! Did you bring Kyle with you?" Keti opened the door to let her friend pass through.

Absolom was busy out in the back of the mansion helping the mechanic fix a snow blower.

Removing her knit hat, Bonnie shook her blonde hair out and smiled. "No, he's off with his dad doing father-son bonding shit." She tugged her gloves off and stuffed them in her jacket pocket.

"Oh, okay, I thought you said he and maybe one of the girls was coming with you. I've prepared lunch. I made enough Mexican chicken pasta, garlic bread and salad for an army. Maybe you can take some back with you. I can-"

"I didn't bring Kyle, Keti, but I did bring someone." Bonnie gave Keti a sly grin and stepped aside.

"Oh?" Keti looked to the door with interest and a welcoming smile. "I hope you brought your appetite with-" Her eyes widened, she stumbled backwards as Stone Cash stepped through the doorway.

"Ketherine." His gaze swooped down her body and up with a smarmy sneer. "I am hungry," his eyes swept her figure again with a leer, "but not for food. I've hungered to get my hands on you again now that you're all grown up, and filled out."

Expanding pupils in his savage gaze publicized he liked what he saw. She wore pale jeans, a yellow blouse with pearl buttons and ankle boots.

Keti's brows lanced down with startled horror, she took another step back. Her attention swiveled from Cash to Bonnie who stood grinning at her.

Bonnie raised both arms and chirped, "Surprise!"

Her mouth falling open, Keti stared at her friend in bafflement, Bonnie knew Keti went to great lengths to avoid Stone Cash. Keti had hinted strongly why she avoided him.

"Why," she asked, her eyes flicked to Cash and back to Bonnie, "why would you bring him here?"

Cash pretended to frown but his smile leached menace. "That's not very friendly of you, Ketherine." He took a step towards her, his menacing smile sharpened as she shrunk from him.

Swinging her head to Bonnie, Keti cried, "Why, Bonnie?" She winced at the cruel bent to Bonnie's thin lips painted pink. She wore black leggings and a pink jacket. Her blonde hair wisped around her face from static electricity from the knit hat and dry air.

Looking down at her nails, Bonnie shrugged. "I have a real hankering for that hot he-man of yours. I hit on him when he first showed up but the tough guy only had eyes for you. Really, Keti," with an eye-roll she brushed her nails on her sweater.

"I'm doing you a favor. You said you wanted to get away from the big ape, here's your out. Mr. Cash will take you to the lodge, and I will stay here and welcome your heathen home."

"What? No, Bonnie!" Keti's hands curled into fists, her shoulders drew up rigid as she looked from one to the other.

Stone Cash with his sandy blond hair and innocent blue eyes that stabbed lust and predatory danger at her, Bonnie with her Joker's grin pretending as if she was really helping Keti.

"Come, Katherine." Cash held his hand out to her. "Don't be difficult, just come along with me, we don't need histrionics."

Keti backed up further, her hands came up, palms out. "No, no, I am not going anywhere with you. You- you need to leave, right now." She struggled to sound strong and commanding, but she knew her voice was strained thin with fear.

Shaking his head wryly, Cash made a grab at her, and she side-stepped his hand. Scowling, Cash said, "Don't make this hard, Keti girl, I am in no mood to play games. If you don't come with me peacefully right now I will hurt you, and you know how much I can hurt you."

"Oh go on, Keti, don't play hard to get. He wants you, and I want the wolfman. You see? We're all happy," Bonnie told her with a wide grin.

"No!" Keti glanced towards the hallway, but she knew there were no servants in the mansion today. The soldiers were out on missions, and Absolom was out back. No one would hear her scream, she was on her own.

"Get out, both of you!" She turned and made to flee for the hall but Bonnie blocked her, waving a finger at her. "Uh huh, bad Keti."

Keti darted to the right to get around her, and she screamed when Cash stuck his hand in her hair and snatched her to a hard stop.

Keti batted at his hands, kicked at his legs- Bonnie stepped in front of her and slapped her face. "Stop being such a baby, Keti. He wants you, he's hunky for an old guy, what's your problem?"

Tears springing from the betrayal, her neck wrenched back, Keti cried to the woman whom she thought was her friend, "My problem is he raped me when I was a child, Bonnie," she twisted to get Cash to release his grip on her hair but he just laughed and shook her roughly.

"Oh don't be such a drama queen," Bonnie chided rolling her eyes again. She spoke snidely, "You were lucky to have an older man to show you the way. You didn't have to have the ignominy of losing your virginity to a pimpled sweaty teen in the backseat of his rusty car. What a bore. I bet Mr. Cash was anything but boring, am I right?" She smiled up at Cash who ignored her as he dragged Keti to the door.

He reached the threshold and Bonnie called out, "Mr. Cash, are you taking her to the train you told me about?"

He turned and smirked at her, twisting his fist in Keti's hair forcing her neck to arch back painfully so he could more easily control her. "You bet, hon. After I've had my fill of her she'll be sold, taken out of the country. You don't ever need to worry about her again."

Eyes rounded in dire fright and terrible confusion, Keti couldn't move her captive head from Cash's steel grip. She cried, "Bonnie, you knew he would do this. You were my friend, how could you do this to me?"

Bonnie moved into Keti's sight. Her laugh humorless and nasty, she sniped, "You always took all their attention, Keti. The young guys and the older ones, didn't matter, they all wanted you. We were all just blah paper dolls whenever you were around."

She took a step closer and sneered in Keti's bent back face. "Finally, you are gone, out of our hair. None of us liked you, we'll all be happily rid of you. And I get to have the king of the jungle. I bet the wolfman is a raging beast in bed. I can't freaking wait. Good riddance, Ketherine," and she slapped her again.

Cash's mouth pulled in dryly. "Who knew you were such a bitchy shrew, Bonnie? Come on Keti girl, let's get you on that train before Miss Fisticuffs here damages my property and your price lowers."

Gripping Keti's hair in his tight fist, he forced her out the door. Keti screamed, scrabbled at his hands, tried to dig her feet into the ground, but he jerked her so hard she thought she'd lost half her scalp.

He dragged her to his car, hit her hard enough to stun her, then he lifted her and all but threw her into the back of the car. Keti fought to catch her wits to fight her way out, but Cash was prepared. He had rope.

Grabbing her arms, he flipped her over on her belly and jerked her arms behind her back and he quickly tied her wrists, then he bound her ankles and tied her wrists to her ankles. Pulling a handkerchief from his pocket he tied it over her mouth effectively muffling her screams.

He climbed in the front of the car and rolled his eyes at the gay wave Bonnie sent them as he drove off.

Keti's body tossed side to side and bounced on the seat, Cash drove at breakneck speed unheeding of her discomfort. Her heart beat a frantic drum, her worst nightmare had come true.

That Stone Cash would get his hands on her again. This time, there would be no refuge, no protection from her mother, no rescue from Wolfgang. Certainly Cash would not take her to the lodge knowing Wolfgang would come after her with guns blazing.

Wolfgang would never know where Cash took her. Bonnie had said something about the train. Her stomach pivoted with fear, not the underground railroad, not the sex trafficking… he couldn't.

The longer he drove, the higher her despair rose.

****

Dutch radioed everyone to come to a halt. Judging by Talon's directions they were within a mile of the cabin. He didn't want Tommy to hear them coming, if the Burtons were still alive, he might kill them and run.

Cars and trucks pulled up in the woods near the foothills parking helter-skelter.

Dutch hopped out and went to his trunk. Opening it, he pulled out a shotgun and a box of shells. He stuffed the box in his leather jacket pocket and traipsed over to where his deputies were parking.

Johan and Romet were first out, before Dutch's men. They were dressed in camouflage and armed to the teeth. They trod quickly over to where Dutch was setting up his command center.

When everyone gathered in a huddle, the sheriff said in a quiet voice that wouldn't carry through the thick woods, "Okay, turn off the sound on your radios and phones. Any contact will be done in silence by text." He glanced around at the group as they each did as he instructed.

"We will break into pairs and circle the cabin. According to Talon DeMar, the cabin is tucked deep into the woods surrounded by dense shrub. It will be tough to find even with the explicit directions. Whoever locates it first will send a text to Jenson," he nodded to a deputy with a barrel chest, red hair and beard. Jenson gave him a nod.

"Jenson will send an all contact text to the rest of you with instructions. Johan," he nodded to Johan and Romet.

"You and Romet are the most experienced with combat and infiltrating stealth. You two go around that back trail we crossed, that should take you to the rear of the cabin. Do reconnaissance, determine where DeMar, Zigfried, and the Burtons are all located inside, or outside the cabin."

Dutch checked to see if the gun at his hip and the shotgun were loaded then he glanced around.

He gave Johan a chin lift. "Wolf called, said he was on his way. You two take off first because you have the furthest to go, I'll start the other pairs off and-" A car engine rumbled, the group turned to see the dust rise from the trail.

Wolf slowed his truck then came to a stop. Opening his door, he climbed out and silently shut the door behind him.

He started towards Dutch and Johan when his phone buzzed in his pocket. Frowning, he slid it out and read the name on the ID.

"Absolom," he spoke sharply yet quietly into the cell. What on earth could the majordomo want?

Chapter Thirty-Two

"*B*ad news, sir," Absolom spoke firmly as always but his voice was knit with anxiousness.

His eyes on Dutch, Wolf said tersely, "Tell me."

"Stone Cash was here-"

"What the fuck? You know I would never allow that fucking piece of shit in my house, Ab, what the hell!" he barked so loud Dutch frowned at him.

Johan and Romet strode over to stand with Wolf.

"Sir," Absolom spoke quickly, "I wasn't present. I was out back with Williams the mechanic helping him repair the snow blower. When I came inside, a girl, Bonnie something, was sitting in the living room making herself at home. No one else was present in the estate."

"What the hell, Ab, what-"

"I quickly discovered Miss Ketherine was not in the residence. I questioned the girl, uh, she wasn't cooperative at first. I had to...use methods to make her answer me."

"Of course, Ab, whatever you needed to do. What happened?" Wolf rubbed his palm over his heart, it started aching with awful trepidation. He wore a leather jacket over a beige thermal and black jeans, motorcycle boots.

Dutch left his team and tramped over.

Absolom said, "Uh, she's a tough bitch, sir," he cleared his throat. The majordomo was the epitome of decorum, his spine iron rod straight, he never lost his cool, actually he seldom said a word other than, 'Yes, sir.'

He said to Wolf, "After some...persuasion, she told me she brought Stone Cash to the estate. When the guard called up to the house for permission for entrance, he told Miss Ketherine only that this Bonnie was at the gate. Of course Miss Ketherine said it was okay for her to pass through. The man, Cash, was hiding in the trunk."

After sucking in an apprehensive breath, Wolf ordered in a rough voice, "Tell me Ketherine did not leave with that prick, Ab."

"Sorry, sir. This Bonnie said she brought Mr. Cash so he would take Miss Ketherine away so this Bonnie person could, uh, have you."

"Me? That is shit, Ab, what the hell?" Wolf scraped his fingers down his face, growled, "Whatever. Where did Cash take Ketherine? Make that whore tell you, Ab, anyway you need to."

"Yes, sir. I did get that information out of her, but it's not enough. The girl said Mr. Cash was taking Miss Ketherine to a train. She said it's some sort of transport for...abducted women to be...sold."

Rubbing his head in agitation, Wolf ground out, "I know about the train. Where is it located?"

"That's the thing, sir, she doesn't know. Trust me," he said quickly, "if she knew she would have told me."

Wolf had brought Absolom with him from Estonia where they had both fought in the military.

Wolf had saved his life more than once and he had Absolom's complete loyalty. They both knew many ways to get information out of the most weathered operative.

270

Their methods were quick, up to the edge of deadly and even beyond, their victims gave in quickly to stop the pain. Wolf had had the baddest of bad men beg him to kill him to stop the agony.

Dragging his palm down his face again, Wolf's head hung. "*Jah*, Ab, call me if you learn anything else, thanks." He hung up.

Raising his head, he squinted at Johan, "Stone Cash has taken Ketherine to that underground railroad." He turned to Dutch. "I have to go."

Dutch nodded. "Of course. We have this handled. Johan," he looked to Johan and Romet, "you guys go with him."

"No," Wolf said, turned and hustled towards his truck. "Your people aren't trained. It is likely Tommy and the other asshole have weapons. Johan and Romet will start the assault of the cabin. You need them."

"Wolf," Dutch called out, "you need backup!"

Wolf cranked his head, said over his shoulder, "I only need to know where the fucking train is."

One hand on his hip the other forearm laying across his forehead, Dutch said loudly as Wolf threw the driver's side door open, "One of those other frat creeps, Wolf, they have to know."

A sharp nod, Wolf jumped in his truck. He turned the key and the passenger door opened. Glancing over, he growled, "No way, J, Dutch needs you here."

"Yeah, just drive, bro. Romet will cover it." Johan settled into the passenger seat and clicked his seat belt on.

Wolf couldn't waste time arguing with him, that damned train could be taking Ketherine anywhere in the country, including an airport for foreign delivery.

Smashing the pedal to the floor, the truck fishtailed in the dirt then it quickly disappeared into the dense foliage on the way back to the main road.

It was a pity Wolf had given Talon such a beat down he wouldn't be able to get any information out of him. When the prick comes out of his coma besides broken bones and damaged organs, DeMar will be drinking his food out of a straw through his wired mouth for a long time to come.

The other frat rats had to know about the damned railroad, he'd have to go after one of them.

He floored the truck all the way to the lodge.

The truck roared down the road, when they reached the turnoff to the street the lodge was on, Wolf wrenched the wheel, the truck skidded across the asphalt turning onto the road.

Johan grabbed the handle above the window to keep from getting thrown about. Speeding up the lane leading to the lodge, the truck raced over the asphalt onto the driveway then came to a screeching halt- Wolf was out of the vehicle before he slammed it into park.

Sprinting to the lodge, Wolf didn't bother knocking, he flung the unlocked door open and stormed inside.

Diane Ansberry, Jeanie Griggs and Rein van Baer all looked up at the door ricocheting off the wall.

Wolf studied each of them to decide who would cough of the information he needed the quickest. He barked, "Where is Miles Burton?"

The three just gawked in stunned surprise at him.

Wolf stomped across the throw-rugs to an over-stuffed chair Rein was lounging on. He bent over, grabbed a fistful of Rein's white button-down and jerked the husky man to his feet.

"Oh!" the women gasped.

Rein's eyes popped wide, he exclaimed, "What the hell do you-"

Wolf tightened his hand, squeezing the collar around Rein's heavy neck. The auburn-haired male's face turned beet bright as he sputtered. Wolf couldn't trust that Rein would lie to him, he needed a sure thing fast.

Rein was a hefty male but Wolf lifted him up to his tippy-toes and shook his fist making Rein's head flop back and forth. "You have two seconds to go and get Miles Burton and bring him the fuck here right now or I will twist that ugly head right off your fat neck."

And Wolf was dying to do just that. The perv and Talon DeMar were trying to force Ketherine into marrying the bastard who was Talon's age.

That the old pervert would think to put his hands on his precious sweet Ketherine- he squeezed harder and gave Rein a violent shake. "Go get him," he commanded, slammed him into the wall then released him so abruptly, the man staggered sideways.

Gasping for air, Rein put his hands to his aching throat and glared with shocked fright at Wolf.

Wolf stomped his foot at him and roared, "Go!"

Rein looked like the cartoon character whose feet pedaled but didn't get traction. When Wolf took a step towards him, Rein gave out a tiny squeak and rushed out the door. Johan trailed after him.

Diana and Jeanie with their mouths hanging open like dimwits gawked at Wolf, neither moved nor said a word.

His big chest heaving, fists rolled on his hips, Wolf's jaw worked as he waited with zero patience for the men to return.

It was mere minutes and Miles Burton came huffing into the lodge with Johan behind him. Johan stopped then reached outside the door and yanked Rein inside.

The coward was going to run and call the police but Johan shoved him into the living room.

Panting and wheezing because Johan had made him run, Miles glanced around the room at the women. Seeing their white faces and rounded eyes, he looked with fear at Wolf who appeared to be about to huff and puff and blow the whole damned lodge down.

Sweat shone on Miles' almost bald head, his belly joggled with his gasping breaths. Wiping a pudgy palm over his damp pate, he said to Wolf, "What on earth, man, what the-"

"The railroad, Burton, the underground railroad," Wolf started.

Blinking rapidly as the guilt flooded his fleshy face, Miles said, "I don't know what you're talking about, I- *oof*!"

Wolf punched him in the stomach and the women screamed.

Ignoring them, Wolf said, "You know what happened to Talon DeMar. I will fuck you up like I did him if I have to ask you questions twice and you don't give me fast, specific answers." Squinting one eye, he leaned into Miles, "You feel me, frat boy?"

His wide hand on his rubbery stomach, "Uh- uh- uh-" Miles chugged in pain. Terror fried his brain and tangled his tongue.

"Okay," Wolf crossed his arms, "let me put it this way. As we speak, Dutch Kross and his deputies are about to charge the cabin where the killer is holding your children, Marc and Libbie."

He slid his phone out and set his thumb on the front of it. "You talk fast or I will call Kross and tell him our information was bad and to give up the rescue and tell his men to go home. Now, speak, and speak fast," he swiped his thumb across the face of the phone and typed in his password.

The ruddiness moved from Miles' face up to his sparsely haired head and tears sprung out the corners of his eyes. "No, please, please, my children! I- I'll tell you what you want to know, just please, don't call them off, please save my kids, please!"

Holding his thumb on the phone, Wolf said, "The sex trafficking, the train they are transporting the females, how do I find it?"

Lids flapping up and down in guilt mixed with fright for his children, Miles glanced quickly at the two women sitting on the couch who stared back at him in disbelief.

Rein's face had flushed with his own guilt. Apparently all the men knew about the railroad, but the wives did not.

Wolf raised the phone to his ear about call Dutch.

Letting out a heaving breath, Miles said, "Okay, okay, please just," but Wolf started to speak into the phone.

Miles sputtered, "Okay, the train has already left the banking station. This one is going- uh, let me think," he squeezed his eyes with his fingers as he tried to recall where the particular train was going to.

"Yeah, Kross," Wolf said into the phone. "I think we might have been given bad info."

"Okay, stop!" Miles wiped the sweat and tears from his podgy eyes. "It- it's going first to Kennewick, Washington. There they will put some of the women on a boat to go up the Columbia River, others will be taken to an airfield where they will smuggle them out of the country."

"How will they get the women to the river or the airfield?"

Miles' eyes flit to Diana and Jeanie who stared back at him in shocked horror. "Ah, by truck."

"Name and description of the train, the location of the tracks, and same with the trucks," Wolf commanded him.

When Miles just blinked back, Wolf rammed his fist into his gut again. Miles bent over with a retching grunt.

"Speak or you will get another, Burton, and the next time you see your kids will be at their funerals."

Gulping in a wheezing breath, his hand pressed over his stomach, Miles tried to straighten. "All right." He pulled his phone out.

Wolf said, "Tell me your password, do not fuck with me, Burton."

"Yeah, yeah, it's MarcLibbie2." He swiped the cell on and entered the password then clicked to a file and handed the phone to Wolf. "All the information is there, write it down and-"

Wolf snatched the phone and ran to the door.

At his heels, Johan followed him out and sprang in the truck as Wolf was shoving the gear into drive.

Chapter Thirty-Three

"*F*uck, Tom, come on," Marc wailed over his sister Libbie's muffled sobs. "Don't do this, what did we ever do to you?"

Tommy DeMar and Renner Zigfried were rolling Marc onto his stomach. Marc's hands were tied with plastic ties behind his back. Tommy held a gun to Marc's temple.

"Don't try anything, Marc," Tommy ordered him as Renner cut the zip ties and Marc's wrists were freed.

Lying on his front on the bed, Marc rubbed the red skin scraped raw. He didn't fight when Tommy snagged his right hand jerking it above his head and tied it to the bedframe then did the same with his other hand. They had already stripped his shirt from him.

Once he was secured, Renner tucked the gun in the waistband of his jeans and gripped Marc's hips twisting them to turn up at the side, then he proceeded to unfasten the jeans and rolled Marc back over onto his belly and he tugged the pants down his legs taking his underwear with them.

Ripping Marc's shoes off and tossing them to the floor, Renner peeled the pants and socks off at the same time.

Propped in a corner of the room, Libbie's Persian cat smushed-in face was swollen crimson from crying and screaming. Her blonde hair awry, damp with her tears it stuck up in places.

Naked, she was hogtied and laying half against the wall, her butt on the floor, legs bent, ankles and wrists tied and then tied together. She blubbered and pleaded and screamed into the sodden gag wrapped around her mouth.

After Renner bound Marc's spread legs to the bedframe, he stood back with a huff. "That good?" he inquired of Tommy.

Tommy's dank fair hair flopped over his eyes as he surveyed Renner's work. "Yep, that's good. Wait, you need to tuck a pillow under his hips so his ass sticks up in the air."

Renner turned back to Marc. "Okay. Since you got to do the others on your own, I have some catching up to do, eh?" He grinned at Marc then snatched a pillow that had fallen to the floor when Marc had struggled with the two men. He stuffed it under Marc's hips and stood back to enjoy his work.

"Nicely done," he complimented himself, then looked over at Libbie vibrating in terror against the wall.

When she saw his attention turn to her, her eyes ruptured in blind hysterical horror. Her body wriggled in a frenzy of movement as she squirmed trying to get away from his predatory gaze, but she was trussed like a Thanksgiving turkey, she could barely move a finger.

Renner grinned at her raving terror. "Oh yeah, Tom, my friend. I wish I coulda had a piece of the other two bitches, but, this one is the best looking anyway of the bunch. Well, not counting that bitch Keti DeMar. I want her next, what do you say?"

Tommy shrugged. "Whatever."

"Geeze, Tommy," Marc cried from the bed, "Keti's your sister for God's sake."

"Unh, stepsister. I'll take a piece too when we can get her away from that mercenary asshole Valdimar. But, for now," he trod over to a backpack he had set on a table. "I need to get my branding shit set up. You go ahead and do the bitch while I'm getting shit ready."

He stared down at Marc then clicked his fingers. "Hell, I forgot, we need him on his back first so I can carve him up. Help me, Ren."

Renner shoved his gun into Marc's temple while Tommy untied him. But Marc knew he would be dead anyway so he fought back- and Renner slammed the butt of his gun into his head stunning him. The two killers quickly repositioned him on the bed and tied him back up.

Once that was done, Renner made his way from the bed over to the wall where Libbie huddled into herself crying, trying to stay in a bundled ball of protection and skirt away from him. He unbuckled his belt and slid it out of the loops and wrapped an end around his hand.

Grinning at her he said, "I like to tenderize my bitches first," and he lashed the belt out striking Libbie's thigh. She screeched into the gag and a red welt rose immediately from the lash.

Wriggling against the wall, tears gushing, chest heaving, Libbie screamed as Renner raised the belt to strike her again.

Meanwhile, Tommy whistled a tune as he took out his branding supplies and set them on the table next to the cowboy lamp. Firing up a tiny blow-torch, he turned his head to wink at Marc.

Marc shook his head to clear the bleariness from the hit. He cried, "Geeze, Tommy, shit, why? What did we ever do to you to deserve this?" and sobbed into the mattress under his face.

279

"Hmm, since you ask," Tommy stuck the end of the blade into the flame, "I'll tell you. You see, while you all were being pampered and petted, loved and given everything you ever asked for, one summer, one very long summer, my old man passed me around to your dads."

"What? No way!" Marc stopped crying, shocked at his words.

"Oh yeah, he did. Andrew Ansberry was the first, he digs both chicks and dudes. There isn't anyone he wouldn't hump."

"Whoda thunk it of that stringy wimp, huh?" Renner said as he lashed at Libbie again. Her muffled screams banged off the wooden walls.

Tommy grunted. "Uh huh. So, Garrett Griggs was next, then Devis McShane, then it was Ollie's dad Jared Duncan, your dad Miles Burton, and even Rein van Baer. That guy is one freaky perv. He'll do anything with a hole, need to keep your dogs away from the freak. Anyhoo," Tommy smiled at his branding blade burning scorching hot in the torched flame.

"Almost ready. So, all summer, each man had his fun with me. Sometimes they did it as a group, there's a few voyeurs in the gang, ya know? It was a contest. Whoever didn't make me bleed had to buy drinks at the club later."

Marc shrieked, "Sick, that's sick, you bastard, my dad would never do something like that!"

While the men talked, Renner's belt made whipping sounds as it slashed through the air before lashing Libbie's body and her screams came muffled sodden through the wet rag.

"Yeah well, they did." Tommy sounded angry, and hurt. "This," he gestured to the branding equipment, "this is what they did to me. Thought it was cute to label me, brand me as theirs. They burnt their goddamned fraternity letters into my young flesh." He suddenly lifted his shirt and the BIN was scarred all over his torso.

Marc's eyes bulged as he fought back bile ratcheting up his throat. His tongue heavy, he croaked thickly, "*Oh God.*"

"Yeah." Tommy tugged his shirt down. Filled with bitterness he groused, "You and the rest, Michael McShane, Ollie Duncan, Kyle Griggs, Eddie Ansberry, not a finger touched your lily-white skin. So now, you will pay for your fathers' sins, and your fathers will pay when they have to live the rest of their lives knowing your torture and deaths are laid right at their front doors."

"Please, Tom, it's not our fault, it's not Libbie's fault, please let us go, we won't tell a soul, bro, I swear." Marc gulped down a noisy globby sob. "Why did Talon do that to you? His own son?"

His lips pressed tight, Tommy's face hardened. "Because he isn't my father. At least he doesn't think so. Look at me, bro, who do I look like?" He waited with a blank expression as Marc stared at him through sodden eyes.

Marc stuttered, "I uh, I don't know, I mean how could I..." he blinked once, twice, red blotched his white face as recognition struck.

"Fuck me, Stone Cash. You're fair like him, but tougher, more masculine looking than Chester. Talon and your ma were both dark-haired and dark-eyed." He gulped. "You mean-"

"Yeah," Tommy snorted. "My dad told me once that he believed my mom and Cash had an affair and I was a result of it. No one has ever admitted to anything. My mom left us," he said bitterly.

Marc gawped wide-eyed at Marc. Tommy continued, "She didn't want Cash's bastard son I guess and feared my dad finding out about the affair. She didn't know he'd always suspected it. I'm the only blond and blue-eyed person in our entire family. Grandparents, aunts, uncles, all of them dark on dark."

"B-but still," Marc sniffed and swallowed loudly. "Why would Talon do such a thing to an innocent kid?"

Tommy shrugged. "Dunno. I think he hated looking at me and seeing the results of his wife's adultery, the utmost of betrayals. He was punishing my mother by punishing me."

"But Stone Cash? Why are they still friends?"

"You don't see how close they are, Marc? I think my father cared more for Cash than he did for my mother. And, Cash is such a stone cold sociopath he wouldn't have comprehended how his fucking his best friend's wife would be wrong. Their lives, money, histories are bound together with blood chains, if you only knew the whole truth. Whatever. We have things to do, story time is over."

Libbie screamed hoarsely as the belt lashed her again and again. Renner grinned at the red bleeding gashes laid out in crisscrossed stripes all over her bare skin.

"This is hot, Tom, I'm pissed I missed out on the first ones you did. I wanna fuck her now." Renner laughed as she cried and still struggled, whimpering in agony, squirming to get away from the sadistic madman. He unbuttoned the button on his jeans.

"Okey doke," Tommy responded in gleeful singsong. He said to Renner, "I think the blade is hot enough, you wanna watch while I do Tom and then you can do Libbie? You can fuck her after you cut her up."

Renner's brows bunched between his mean eyes. "What? No, I wanna fuck her before she's all carved up and bloody. You didn't carve up the other bitches."

"Check it out, Ren, she's already cut and bloody." Tommy bent over Marc and whispered, "Same as you'll be, same as Ren will be."

"I thought you didn't brand the women, Tom," Marc said on a hitching gasp.

Tommy looked at him and shrugged. "I decided why should the girls miss out on all the fun. Like Ren."

Marc's head twisted to the side so he could see Tommy. He blinked in question over pouring tears, not sure what Tommy was saying, he could barely hear him.

Renner had removed Libbie's gag so he could get off on her screams, and she was obliging. Blood curdling shrieks vibrated at the top of her lungs.

"Yeah," Tommy whispered near Marc's ear. "I brought Ren along as a scapegoat. I plan on setting it up to look like Ren did all this kidnapping and killing, and somehow you got loose and you two fought. You got Ren's gun away from him, but sadly, just before you shot him he stabbed you."

He leaned in closer with a scabby grin. "Everyone but me dies, and I walk away as innocent as a newborn babe. Great plan, eh? Everyone thought I was dumb as a rock, they'll think differently now because they'll believe I was involved in this because of my relationship with Renner, but it will drive them nuts that they can't prove it. I walk away scot free. Pure genius, am I right?"

Tears leaked from Marc's eyes soaking the sheet under his face. "B-but what about Kyle Griggs and Eddie Ansberry? H- how come they don't have to suffer this?"

Tommy turned back to his branding equipment. "Don't you worry you jealous thing, I have plans for them. It's just getting too hot around here, I have to do things differently once we get back to Gladonia."

Libbie's screams hacked and rasped mingled with Renner's sadistic gleeful chortling as he continued striking her.

"Tom, please," Marc strained at his restraints, tried to kick his legs free. The bed shifted a few inches across the wooden floors from his frantic struggles. He yelled, "He's going to kill you too, Renner!"

Tommy and Renner grinned at each other. "Nice try," Renner said.

Marc shrieked, "No! Really! He told me he was framing you- me- us!"

Renner chuckled at him not believing his friend would turn on him.

Tommy called out, "Okay, Ren, I'm ready to carve Marc up, leave Libbie for a minute and come watch me, this is totally fun!"

****

Sawdust, that's what her mouth tasted like, Ketherine swallowed, licking her lips that were as dry as ancient papyrus.

Her jaw throbbed with jolting pain, she was lying on something that felt like rubber, firm plastic. A continuous sound resonated, a rumbling and clacking, her body jostled with movement. A groan escaped as she struggled to open her eyes and sit up.

"Ah, I thought you would never come around, Keti girl. Playing with you is no fun if you aren't conscious to…enjoy it." The familiar baritone spiked quills of instant fight-or-flight into her brain.

One eye pried open and squinted up at Stone Cash. He was a wobbling blur. Then she realized he was wobbling because what they were in was moving, jostling, rocking back and forth. She turned her head slightly and saw windows ran along the wall as far as she could see.

They were on a train. Both eyes flashed up to him, she whispered as her stomach cramped with comprehension, "The underground railroad?"

A polluted grin spread across Cash's boyish face. Even fifty something, he still had that sweet, young look about him. How contradictory, such evil on the inside and so angelic on the outside. Like a bright shiny apple with a rotten core.

"Damn," he said with admiration, "still a smart beautiful package, Katherine. Too bad I can't keep you, you would make a fine queen to my king."

Keti looked at him as if he were insane, her brows lifted in derision. "King? You're right."

She licked her dry lips, swallowing scraped her parched throat. "Satan is king of the underworld." She moved to sit up and realized her wrists were cuffed behind her back.

Cash grinned watching her push back on her elbows rolling and twisting to sit up, his gaze on her breasts shimmying with her movements. He wore the same dopey lustful look on his handsome face that his son, cherub Chester had.

He chuckled. "True, you wouldn't be the first to call me the devil."

"Where are we going?" She glanced around. They were alone in the car, trees whizzed by the windows.

Cash sat down beside her, smirked when she shifted away from him. "We're getting off at Kennewick."

Keti didn't want to look at him, she kept her gaze on the bouncing windows. "And then what? What happens in Kennewick?"

"You go on to the next leg of your journey, and I head back home."

Reluctantly, she turned to see his malevolent grin. The man was pure unadulterated evil. "My journey?"

He nodded, eyes suddenly heavy hooded with the lust he didn't bother hiding. "We need to get rid of you, Talon doesn't want you dead, yet. He can get another seven years out of you like he did after he murdered his first wife. As long as you are alive but missing, he has full control of McMaster Lexington. We decided it was best to keep you alive for now."

Her shoulders stiffened with her sinking heart. "Where am I going?" She pictured a dark grey cell somewhere with no windows that she'd have to endure for seven years before they killed her.

"Sheer Palace." He smiled at her confused expression. "It's a brothel in Shanghai. At Kennewick you and a few of the other women here," he motioned with his head to the front of the train, "will be trucked to a private airstrip and loaded onto a plane as cargo."

His smile darkened with heated excitement at what her fate will be. "When you reach Shanghai you will be trucked again to the brothel where you will spend the next seven years on your back. Hell, Ketherine, I hope for your sake they keep you high on heroin so you don't suffer quite so much."

Tears slipped out in horror of what her doomed destiny will be. "How can you be so…so heartlessly cruel? I have never done anything to deserve this- this fate."

One shoulder bumped up. "It is what it is. Maybe if you had cooperated with Talon when he wanted you to sign his papers, or," he moved closer to her, smirking as she plastered herself to the side of the seat with a cringe of fear and revulsion. "If you had agreed to be my concubine like I intended."

The smile turned to a scowl. "But no, you fled to that boarding school, then stayed out of my reach whenever you were home. And now, that fucker Rein has laid claim on you. So," he shrugged elegantly again, "I can't offer you my protection."

Her head swimming in mind-boggling terror, Keti gasped, then acted so afraid she couldn't catch her breath. Bending forward, she pretended to fight to draw air into her paralyzed throat.

It wasn't like she had to seriously fake her despair, she was clinging to her sanity like the last leaf on a tree on a windy winter day. But, she needed a distraction so she could work on the cuffs binding her wrists.

"Oh, fuck, you're having a panic attack. Hold still," Cash ordered. He put his hand on the back of her neck and pushed her down so her head was below her knees. "Breathe slowly, long deep breaths, you can't fucking croak before we get our dough out of you."

While her head was down and she was gasping for air, Keti twisted and pulled on the cuffs. Her hands would be scraped and bleeding, but that didn't matter, getting away from him was the only thing she could think about now.

Pretending to be in a frantic hysterical panic, she rocked and shook her body as if in extreme distress while tugging and wrenching her hands while he rambled on about taking deep breaths.

Finally, as he was tapering off, she could feel one hand slipping halfway out-

"Okay then." Cash sat back and pulled her up with him. His gaze latched on her heaving chest, he reached out and grasped her breast, and squeezed with delight at her pained yelp. Keti jerked to the side to break his grasp.

He grinned at the sight of her, her hair falling in a mess over her face, bosom shaking, tears streaking her cheeks and wetting the blouse.

"Come on, Ketherine, don't be difficult. I gave you too much of the sedative, you slept the whole way, we will be pulling into the Kennewick station any minute and I want my piece of you before you're shuffled onto that truck."

Keti frantically shook her head while twisting her hands behind her. The rumbling wheels of the train were becoming quieter as the train appeared to be slowing, the trees weren't flashing by so fast.

Cash went on cheerfully, "You'll probably be raped ten times over by the men running the trucks and the planes long before you reach Shanghai. Let me give you something special to remember, just like when you were thirteen, remember that week?"

He caressed her cheek, his fingertip brushing over a tear, he licked the tear off his finger. "The best fucking week, pun intended, of my life."

"No!" Keti turned on her hip and kicked at him catching him in his knee.

"Ow, bitch, that hurt," he barked then hauled off and slapped her, she slammed back into the hard seat bruising her spine.

"Enough niceness, girl," Cash muttered. Grabbing the sides of her blouse he yanked it apart, the buttons flew clattering over the seats and floor.

He wound his fingers around her upper arms and pushed her down on her back. Shoving a knee between her legs, he climbed on top of her and opened his mouth on her breast molding out of the peach bra.

"No!" Keti screamed, not expecting anyone to come to her aid. His mouth sucking on her breast, Cash reached down to open her jeans, and one of her hands sprung free from the cuff with a great deal of pain and loss of skin.

She twisted hard and shoved her knee up hitting him in the groin, then she hurled her arm hitting him in the face with the opened handcuff.

Cash gripped his balls with a yowl and curled away from her. Keti pushed him and squiggled out from under his heavy body and fell to the floor.

She immediately jumped to her feet and raced for the door as the train came to a sputtering whistling, rocking stop. The wheels rotated squeaking one more time.

A second later, the door slid open and Keti ran for it.

Scrambling down from the train, Keti worked to control her panic and keep ahold of her racing terror. She needed to get away from Cash before he came after her, and before any of the men climbing out of the trucks saw her.

Her feet tripping over gravel, she sped along the side of the train, she couldn't run straight out because there were three trucks lined up there. Then she heard Cash's bellow and knew he was up and out and onto the chase.

Burying the scream that scuttled up her throat like desperate sharp nails, she bolted down the row of train cars, then her feet backpedaled to stop her momentum as she reached a car that the door was sliding open.

Keti could see inside were dozens of females crammed into the railcar, some looked as young as five or six. They were all restrained, clothes filthy, profound hopelessness blanking their dead eyes.

"Oh, Lord," she cried, she couldn't leave them here, how can she help- *oomph-*

Stone crashed into her, slamming her body with a bang into the side of the train car. "Damned bitch, I would break your fucking neck if you weren't so damned valuable!"

He caught her hands, snapping them behind her back and jerking them up so roughly hard it felt like her shoulders were dislocating.

Keti screamed in agony catching the attention of the women squashed into the car. Their eyes stayed blank, they had been beaten, tortured and raped, nothing fazed them anymore. It was heartrending to see the same grave hopelessness staggering out of the children's eyes.

Gripping her wrists in one hand, Cash fisted her hair, dragging her head back so far she felt he would break her neck like he threatened, and he jerked her arms up further. A smile of satisfaction lifted at her cry out of pain.

"Get used to it, girl," he growled in her ear. "You think you can get away from me, never gonna happen, not until I turn you the fuck over. Now, I am still getting my share of you."

Releasing her hair, he shoved his hand to the middle of her back, pressing her hard into the metal train car. So brutally hard, her lungs strained to draw in air, her breasts were painfully smashed, the metal scraped the side of her face.

"I gotta do this quick before those assholes see us. Any minute they're coming for the women. The way you look, they'll be fighting over who gets you first." He reached around her and ripped the button open on her jeans with one hand, and started pushing them down, shoving so forcefully the zipper spread open.

Keti didn't dare scream, it would only bring more men. She was to suffer Cash's rape before she was handed off to more men that would ruthlessly, endlessly assault her for whatever was left of her life.

Her will to fight withered, it was no use. Cash had her pants halfway down her bottom and was snatching at his own pants.

No, she shook her head, she had to fight, for herself and those other poor victims. She would have to endure his rape, but it would make him weak at some point.

He would be preoccupied either while he was climaxing or right after he finished and was fixing his pants, and she would make her break before the other ruffians came to take her.

As if reading her mind, Cash grabbed her hair again, pulled her head back and slammed it into the side of the train, and she felt herself fading out.

Chapter Thirty-Four

Marc screamed, his back and hips writhing on the bed, tears spurted with the searing slice. His body arched off the bed and to the side trying to get away from the blade.

Tommy just laughed and said, "Shit, Marc, what a sissy. I've only just begun, that's just the first line of the B. You know, for the Brothers in Hell, our dads' fraternity. Well, you'll be seeing that hell soon, but not before I get my fun."

The smell of burning flesh flared like a lit human match in the cabin.

Libbie stayed silent huddled against the wall, for the moment Renner's attention was not on her. He was grinning in malicious delight at Marc's suffering.

Renner commented, "Hey, man, I think it's cooled down. You need to heat the blade again for the next letter, gotta love them Greeks!" and he smiled broadly at Marc's face contorted in torment.

"Yeah, you're right," Tommy agreed, and turned away reaching for the torch on the nightstand, next to the cowboy lamp. Over his shoulder he said, "I think I'll-"

The window suddenly burst in, shattering glass exploded across the room. At the same time the door crashed open smashing into the wall, shouts of "Police! Freeze! No one move!" boomed about as police stormed into the cabin.

Dutch Kross barreled through the wrecked door- just as with his jacket over his head and arms, Romet vaulted through the broken window curling into a summersault as he hit the floor then sprung to his feet.

In a flash, Renner Zigfried whipped his gun out from his waistband while Tommy froze with the blade in his hand.

"Unh uh," Romet grunted, twirling around he kicked the weapon from Zigfried's hand, it flew across the room.

Zigfried yelped when Romet's foot struck his hand. Zigfried threw his fist out at Romet's jaw, but Romet ducked his head to the side and grabbed Zigfried's arm, and slammed it over his knee just like Talon had done to the servant's child, and grinned at the satisfying crack and scream from Zigfried.

As officers charged into the cabin, Tommy took several long running steps and jumped headfirst out the broken window.

Dutch had hurried to where Marc lay moaning, he shouted to a deputy, "Call a bus!" His eye caught Libbie trussed up against the wall. "Make that two ambos."

A deputy bent his head speaking into the radio on his shoulder requesting the ambulances.

Another deputy moved to Libbie crying huddled naked in the corner. He ripped off his jacket and gingerly laid it across her mindful of her gaping lacerations then crouched to cut off her restraints.

Dutch shouted to Romet, "DeMar might get past the officers that were covering the back-"

"On it," Romet replied, and copied Tommy taking several running steps then dove back out the broken window.

Another somersault and jumping to his feet, Romet quickly glanced around and saw a deputy lying on the grass, blood gushing from a wound in his chest.

Romet yelled, "Dutch! Get out here, cop down!" and he raced to the only opening in the lush, prickly woods that surrounded the cabin.

Branches slapping his face, an experienced tracker, Romet jogged silently, years of stealth training built muscle memory, pure reflexive action.

Ahead of him lay a path of smashed down grass, it appeared to be an animal trail. The woods were too thick for Tommy to have gone in any other direction. The snow had halted overnight so there were no footprints for him to follow.

Romet ran calmly for several minutes before he noticed a few broken branches on some shrubs indicating something or someone had just passed through the foliage.

He needed to keep moving, but he had to be prepared for an ambush since he didn't hear any thumping shoes or branches cracking as Tommy would have caused running through the woods.

Romet had to slow down to listen. Hearing nothing, not even a bird or a swaying limb creaking from the breeze, he came to a stop and perked his ears.

He heard a faint rustle and looked up, Tommy dropped from the limb he perched on with his knife in his hand.

Romet leaped sideways, Tommy roared with the knife raised like some murderous Tarzan and partially landed on Romet knocking him to the ground.

Cursing himself for not thinking to look up while he searched, it was an amateur move on Romet's part. Wolf and Johan will chap his ass with rookie jokes forever about it.

Kudos for Tommy for achieving the surprise attack, and to climb the tree so quickly and silently. The son of a bitch must have been practicing in case of this event.

Thanks to Romet's hypersensitive hunting skills he was able to detect Tommy just before he dropped, but it was close. Tommy's body hit Romet slightly but it threw Tommy off balance as he landed. Romet rolled with the fall and jumped to his feet.

Tommy landed on his feet in an awkward crouch. He stumbled a few faltering steps before catching his balance. He bent in a fighter's stance, back hunched, arms bowed out, knife in one hand, his legs spread to stabilize himself. With the solid foundation, he would be able to spring in any direction.

Romet grinned at him and wiggled a couple of fingers challenging him to come at him. "Come on, boy, come at me," he taunted.

"You foreign-assed motherfucker!" Tommy thundered. "I'm gonna cut you into such tiny grisly pieces, your own mother won't recognize you in your coffin!" and he charged at Romet, hacking his arm in an arc with the knife blade down aimed to stab into Romet's head.

Ducking and twisting his body, long moppy hair lassoed around his head as Romet easily side-stepped Tommy's attack. He laughed a jeer as Tommy stumbled past him almost tripping and face-planting.

Steadying himself, face contorted with fury, eyes bulging with raging hatred, Tommy ran at Romet again. And again Romet easily dodged him, with his hands clasped behind his back, a mocking taunt saying that Tommy couldn't beat Romet even with Romet's hands tied behind his back.

Losing all control in his blinding rage, breaths heavy and fast, Tommy charged again slashing his knife up and down, lashing back and forth mindlessly berserk.

With cheeky laughter and his hands still behind his back, Romet danced and leapt, dodged and spun, avoiding even the wind of the knife as Tommy now recklessly hacked at him in his frenzied rage.

Tommy's fair hair darkened with sweat flopped over his blue eyes. Those infuriated eyes squinty beads of murder, he charged again and again slashing, stabbing, hacking, verging into self-combustion of furor, growing even more enraged at Romet's mocking laughter as he easily dodged his parries and thrusts and stabbings.

"Okay," Romet sighed, "enough of this sandbox playtime." He stood as if a statue, instigating Tommy to run blindly at him, knife engaged to kill.

Tommy was a hair away when Romet spun on his toes, twirled and bashed his steel-toed boot into Tommy's neck.

Tommy's eyes popped, his tongue expulsed from his open mouth with a gacking sound, and he dropped like a sack of mud.

Pushing his mop of hair back with both hands, Romet stood over the unconscious Tommy. "Sorry about that bloke, it's gonna be doubtful that you will ever able to speak again with that crushed larynx. Maybe they can poke a hole in your throat and put in one of those gizmos that speaks like in a buzz for you."

He rolled Tommy on his belly, pulled a plastic tie out of his back pocket and bound his wrists.

Standing straight, Romet pivoted hearing brush rustling and crackling from down the trail. He stood calmly waiting as Dutch broke through the dense vegetation, cursing as a twig poked him in the head.

Dutch looked at Tommy splayed out on the ground and shook his head. "Gonna need another damned ambo, bro."

He ambled over to the body and bent down, put two fingers on his neck. "Good."

The sheriff smiled crookedly up at Romet. "I know it was a temptation to kill him, but we want all our strings tied up in pretty bows. I need him so he can tell us the broad picture. Here, grab his shoulders."

Romet started. "What? Why?" He blinked newly falling snow from his eyes.

Grasping Tommy's legs, Dutch said, "We have to carry him. No point in the paramedics having to fight their way through this bramble and then have to drag his ass out. Come on."

"Aw, hell," Romet grumbled as he bent and caught up under Tommy's armpits. "Why do I havta carry the heavy end?"

The men trod in tandem back through the shrubs and thick trees carrying Tommy.

Dutch told him, "Because instead of playing with him like a cat with a mouse, you should have taken him out right by the house. Quit whining like a little girl. You wanted the hunt, so you let it happen so you could chase him. Your punishment is to carry the heavy part."

He bit back a grin at Romet's muttered cursing all the way back to the cabin.

****

Huffing strenuously against the back of her head, Cash yanked on Keti's jeans with one hand, the other hand pressed against her lower back to keep her from fighting him or fleeing.

The punch had stunned Keti, making her so dizzy she floundered to stay standing, but then she turned into dead weight in his hands as she passed out.

"Fine, little bitch," Cash grumbled and lowered her onto the ground. "It'll be easier to fuck you on the grass rather than up against the train anyway. Just gotta get these fucking jeans off-" Cash yelped as he was suddenly body slammed.

Wolf didn't wait for Cash to stop rolling, he jumped right on him and started throwing wicked punches.

Cash yelled, instead of hitting back he tried to protect his head with his arms. Blood and sweat sprayed everywhere as Wolf's fists pounded the older man into the ground.

Wolf's snarling grunts as he struck Cash, and Cash's screams for help were drowned out by shouts and authoritative commands flooding the area behind them.

Johan held a shotgun aimed at a belligerent group of males that he was ordering to line up in front of the trucks. As he commanded them, vehicles rolled into the station and parked haphazardly on the grass.

A slew of Wolf's men climbed out and hurried over to Johan. Johan barked orders at them as well, and they rushed to take the positions he instructed.

Soldiers forced the truck drivers to face the trucks and they quickly restrained them until the police could arrive and take over.

There were two dozen males and three females detained against the trucks. They would all be charged with kidnapping and sex trafficking.

Two soldiers pulled Wolf off Stone Cash's pulverized body. Several more went to help the women confined in the train cars.

Staggering when the soldiers released him, Wolf wiped sweat out of his eyes with his arm and looked for Keti. He saw her curled on the ground, one hand encased in a handcuff, and he stumbled over to her.

Crashing to his knees, he touched her face, and her lashes fluttered. "Babygirl," he uttered anxiously, "talk to me, sweetheart."

Her lids flickered then slowly opened. A bruise turning purple decorated her cheek, but she smiled limply. "Wolfgang, you found me..." her voice trailed off weakly, "you came for me."

He scooped her up and held her against his chest. Kissing the top of her head he murmured, "Always, my Ketherine, always."

Chapter Thirty-Five

Wolf watched Johan making a peanut butter and jelly sandwich. A can of Coke with the tab open sat on the wooden island. They were standing in a commercial kitchen.

When Wolf rented the estate he had brought in a big crew to help with both finding the serial killer as well as neutralizing Johnnie Frog. He hired a cook and servants to take care of the squad.

The males as well as two female soldiers spent most of their time in the field, when they were in the mansion they kept to a separate wing enabling Wolf to enjoy his privacy. They all utilized the kitchen, gym, library as well as the dining room.

"You know," Wolf said, "there is deli meat, fried chicken, potato salad, leftover pasta, meatloaf, and a bunch of other good stuff in the fridge. Why are you eating peanut butter?"

Johan set the butter knife on the countertop, put the sandwich together and took a huge bite, a quarter of the sandwich was gone.

Chewing the wad then swallowing, before he took another bite, his eyes on the sandwich he held, Johan replied, "I like peanut butter and jelly."

Wolf leaned both forearms on the counter and watched Johan eat. "Someday you will grow up, J, and develop an adult palate."

Johan shuddered. "God forbid." Gulping some Coke, he sighed, "Ahh," then set the can down and grinned at Wolf. "So, instead of critiquing my appetite, you were telling me about the fab frat fops."

Wolf's head tipped back with his laugh. "*Jah.* You have a way with your English vocabulary, much more refined than mine."

Nodding while chomping, Johan said, "You bet. And you could take a lesson from me, my friend. But I have to give you credit, you've been working on those contractions. So, Talon DeMar?" Behind him outside the window, snow fell, sunlight sparkled off the showering powdery flakes.

Wolf snagged a beer from the refrigerator. Using a bottle opener, he popped the lid off and swigged.

Wiping his mouth he said, "The warrant for his mansion, Blackslade in Gladonia came through with the goods. In Talon's vault, Dutch found weapons. One of the guns, a Colt 45, ballistics matched the bullet they pulled from his wife's skull, thankfully it was still there. Only Talon's prints were on the gun, and a partial match was on the bullet. So, they got him for her murder."

"Good," Johan said with a nod, stuffing the rest of the sandwich in his mouth. Speaking around the wad of bread, he mentioned sarcastically, "For such a smart man he's pretty stupid."

Wolf went on. "True that. Dutch's people picked up the rest of them, the Brothers in Hell frat pack; McShane, Ansberry, the whole group of them for the sex trafficking. Talon DeMar and Stone Cash will be arrested when they recover from their…injuries."

Watching Johan stuff the rest of the sandwich in his mouth, Wolf said, "It is doubtful the law will ever be able to pin the arson of the warehouse where they got all their startup money from on DeMar or any of the other men. Or the murders of the victims that perished in the fire. Too long ago and no evidence."

Nodding while licking his fingers, Johan replied, "Also, probably unlikely they can be prosecuted for Tommy DeMar's rapes and torture when he was just a young child."

"*Jah*." Wolf said, "You can feel bad for the fucker, J, but a savage childhood is no excuse for what he did to those innocent people."

"I heard Talon let Tommy be abused because he's really Stone Cash's spawn. And that Cash never had an inkling that Tommy might be his son. That true?"

Wolf shrugged, took a few sips of beer. "That is the word. They have to agree to DNA testing if anyone wants to know for sure. That is all unlikely though as all of them will be in prison. Personally, I could give a fuck."

Finishing off the soda, Johan crunched the can in his fist then looked for the recycling receptacle. "Speaking of the murdered wife, what was all that at the burial site with Keti about anyway?" He wiped the breadcrumbs off the wooden island onto his palm and brushed them into the sink.

Wolf looked up at the snow drifting past the kitchen window. "Well, when Talon got wind of the burial site being dug up and the bones to be removed, he feared exactly what happened. That someone would notice his deceased wife's bones.

"He had originally thought he had gotten lucky coming across the open pit when the developers were seeking to build, and he heard that they were going to cover the pit back up. He managed to toss his wife's body in the pit. And, I suppose he climbed in to mix her body in with the others. The next day the pit was covered. She decomposed along with the rest of them."

Johan's nose wrinkled in distaste. "Guy is the sickest freak, that he could be so coldly inhuman that he climbed into a burial pit, stomped over dead bodies, set his wife's body in and covered it with the skeletons. Even weirder, the woman would have still had flesh and hair and shit, he stuffed her amongst those old bones. Sick." He shuddered at the picture of what Talon had done.

Wolf nodded in concurrence, no denial from him. "Yeah, so Talon lured the professor away thinking if the green students were the only ones there they would probably not notice the difference between her bones and the others.

"They were not analyzing the bones, just trying to keep each persons' skeleton bones together for transport. They would all eventually be reburied but properly, in their own coffins, graves."

Johan trod over to the pantry where he disposed of the can and came back. "It was just serendipitous that circumstances had Keti here at the perfect time, and it was her professor working here in this country on a break from her academics in Italy, running the dig to call Keti to cover for her. It appears God had his fingers in the pot, stirring it so Keti would be the one to provide evidence of her stepfather's first wife's murder."

"*Jah*. Romet located the student that spilled the coffee on Keti. She admitted she had been hooking up with Talon, he'd liked them young. She said he told her to make sure she was at the dig site to keep an eye out for anyone recognizing that the bones were wrong."

"Did she know he had buried a body there?"

Wolf shrugged. "He didn't tell her why, and she didn't care why. She was not an archeological student but she had volunteered to help with labor. She was on speed-dial with Talon. Talon told her to stop Keti from calling the cops, ergo the spilled coffee. The stupid thing was he wanted her to grab the body and hide it."

Johan burst out a laugh. "Sure, how ridic, the girl was probably like 110 pounds. Like she could have grabbed up the bones, the loose bones, and run off with them without anyone noticing."

Agreeing with a nod, Wolf said, "DeMar really had not thought anyone would catch on about the bones, he only had the student there as a precaution. He was so caught off guard when the girl called him that he clumsily improvised.

"He would have been better off to have the chick set fire to the place. He could have maybe had his men slip in during the aftermath and steal the body. But thank God he didn't tell her to do that."

"Not as smart as he thinks he is. Anyway, you been in the grand room today?" Johan asked, lifting the lid off the teddy bear cookie jar.

Wolf's lower lip pushed out. "No, why? I just got home, I was going to grab a chicken leg to eat while hunting Ketherine down."

Shoving a whole cookie in his mouth and snapping up three more, Johan said, "Follow me, bro. This oughta be fun."

Canting Johan a quizzical look, Wolf followed him from the kitchen down a hall and to the grand room. The two men stood just inside the large room.

In the center of the room, Keti was sitting on the cream colored thick rug. She was laughing with delight and surrounded by a parade of boxes.

Romet, Wilhelm, several of Wolf's close team either stood or sat on chairs circled around her. A few held colorful items in their hands, others hammers, various tools.

Wolf leaned over and whispered to Johan, "What are they doing?"

Johan grinned. "Decorating the room."

"What for?"

"Christmas."

"Why?"

"Come on, Wolf, you didn't live a normal childhood but surely you know people decorate their homes and fir trees for the holiday."

Taking in the cheerful spectacle, Wolf's brow knotted. "*Jah*, reindeer and Santa and all that foolish shit morons indulge in. It is childish make-believe."

"Yeah, well, you better not let Keti hear you say that. She's had the men putting up most of the stuff, see?" He waved his hand over the room.

Green branches of fir draped along the mantle of the fireplace, twinkling white lights strung through the fir and down the side of the fireplace.

A Nutcracker soldier stood sentry at all the doorways, Santa Claus candles sat jolly on tables and on and on.

"Where did all that shit come from?" Wolf asked.

"She went shopping. Romet and Wilhelm took her right after lunch when you were meeting with Dutch Kross."

Keti glanced up and saw Wolf watching her. A big smile brightened her face already rosy from the laughter. Christmas carols played in the background, a few men hummed along as Keti had been singing with the tunes.

Wolf could smell hot chocolate, and plates of cookies dipped in sprinkles were on plates presented on various tables.

Wolf growled, "Shopping? She knows she is not allowed out of the house. Romet for fuck's sake knows my orders, what the hell-"

"The danger is over, Wolf. She is no longer in danger, she should be free to roam as she pleases." Johan's grin spread as Keti climbed to her feet. A string of Christmas lights dangled around her neck. She wore reindeer antlers on her head.

Stepping carefully over the strewn ornaments and boxes, she made her way to Wolf. All the males in the room were grinning like Johan at the look on Wolf's face.

"Hey, Wolfgang," she greeted him, stood on tiptoes and kissed him lightly.

He frowned at her, said gruffly, "J tells me you left the estate, you went shopping. You know my orders-"

"Stop fussing," Keti scolded him with a cheerful smile. The men stifled their chuckles.

"Fussing? You call my protective commands fussy? Listen Kether-"

"The bad guys are all locked up, Wolfgang. I'm safe now and you know it." Slinging her hands around his neck, Keti kissed him again, this time longer.

And he could never resist her, he took over the kiss, his hands gripped her hips and pulled her tightly against him.

But they weren't alone, the room was filled with his soldiers, who were making teasing smooching noises, he set her from him.

"What is all this, Katherine?"

Beaming up at him, she turned to view the room all holiday colorful and twinkling. The men holding hot chocolate topped with whipped cream, grinned happily at them.

"This," she said gaily, "is Christmas. You are just in time to take me out to get our tree."

His gaze glued to her mouth, he repeated vaguely, "Tree?" The only plans on his mind since leaving the meeting with Dutch at the station was getting Ketherine naked and into bed.

Who was he kidding? Those plans relayed over and over in his brain as Dutch talked about the felony charges they were filing.

Nodding vigorously, Keti grabbed his hand. "Come on, let's get our coats. Johan can come too and help you carry the tree."

Johan's turn to look consternated. "Me? Carry what tree?"

Keti tugged on Wolf's hand. "The Christmas tree. I found a place where we can go choose our own. Don't worry, they'll cut it down for us."

"Cut it down?" Letting her pull him, Wolf shared a look with Johan. Johan grinned with a shrug.

"I'll get my coat and meet you guys in the car." Johan chuckled all the way out of the room.

It had snowed for several days, the land was covered a foot high in some places with the white stuff.

Johan parked the SUV in front of the lot. A hand painted sign announced 'Christmas Trees, you pick it, we chop it.'

Keti tumbled out of the car before Wolf could get his door open and chase after her. Johan pocketed the keys, laughing at his pussy-whipped friend.

The two men patiently followed Keti as she raced from one tree to the next.

Finally, she stopped and jumped up and down. "This one! This is it!" She pointed with excitement at a tall thick fir tree.

She demanded, "Call the man to come cut it down for us!"

Wolf and Johan cranked their necks to look up at the tall wide tree, and shared another glance. It will take more than just Wolf and Johan to put that huge-assed tree up.

While they waited for the man to come and chop the tree, Keti danced around checking in case another tree was better.

"Damn," Wolf muttered, "how the hell do I get dragged into this shit. When did-"

Splat-

A snowball whacked him in the back of the neck. He swung around with a curse, "What the hell-"

Johan stood twenty feet away sniggering while he bent to scoop up more snow for another snowball.

"Oh, *jah*? That is how it is, J?" Wolf crouched and scooped up a big handful of snow and quickly shaped it into a ball. By the time it nailed Johan in the head, Wolf was gathering snow for another ball and ducking the one Johan hurled at him.

While the workman took an ax to the tree and wrapped it in netting, Keti stood shaking her head at Wolf and Johan who were now wrestling and rolling around in the snow.

Twenty minutes later, Johan and Wolf carried the bound tree and tied it to the top of the SUV and Johan drove them back to the estate.

The entire way Wolf kept shaking his head. He could not believe he spent the afternoon trudging through the snow to get a tree, had a snowball fight and wrestling match with Johan. He and Keti sat in the back.

Wolf couldn't take his eyes off her. She glowed, she was happy, her cheeks were round and rosy, sheer joy radiated from her shining eyes. And Wolf fell deeper and more madly in love with her than ever. His life was about to change in a way he had never expected, and he was thrilled.

After dinner, they and the crew spent the evening drinking spiked eggnog and apple cider, decorating the tree, and later Keti made them all sit and watch 'Rudolph the red-nosed Reindeer and It's a Wonderful Life' while they nibbled more cookies.

His arm around Keti as they sat together on one of the sofas as the last movie ended, a warmth swarmed Wolf as he looked around astounded. His men watching sentimental drivel and a cartoon, and they all seemed quite content.

He hugged Keti, kissed the top of her head, and he realized he was content as well. His life of brutal savagery was going to soften, and he wasn't afraid.

He was eager to start a life with Katherine. Only his woman could make a bunch of hard-bitten mercenaries sit peacefully sipping eggnog and watching sappy TV.

Christmas Day arrived white and serene. While Keti sat amongst a plethora of colorful wrapping paper, Wolf's close friends were sitting around chowing on cinnamon coffee cake.

Keti had insisted on buying each man a present, as well as Absolom who appeared horrified, and a few of the servants she felt close to.

Surprisingly, the gifts were reciprocated, and the room was one big haven of laughter, perfume bottles, sweaters, cuff links, chocolates, and wrapping paper spread everywhere.

While everyone was occupied showing their gifts to one another, Wolf stood up from the recliner where he had a bird's eye view of the festivities.

He sauntered over to where Keti sat on the floor, and he lowered to one knee in front of her, his hard face still harsh, but his dark eyes glowed with love. The room fell silent.

Her eyes wide and large, Keti put her hand over her mouth.

Wolf smiled. "Babygirl, I know it is too soon. I know you are not ready. But, I want to show you I am serious. Everything I have ever said to you, I meant. I want to marry you, spend the rest of my life with you, raise a family of our own. You, ah," he paused, swallowed, "do not have to answer me now. I just," he held out a small box and opened it. "I just wanted you to think about it. Take the ring, and think about it. Okay?"

She had been talking about leaving and he wanted his claim on her finger. He feared she would leave his house now that the danger was over and never come back to him.

Keti sat and blinked at the ring. Wolf lifted her hand and slipped the ring on her finger. Her lips slightly parted, she gazed in awe at the diamond sparkling on her finger then she looked up at Wolf.

He stared stone-faced back at her, then a lopsided smile tilted one side of his mouth. "Just think about it, Ketherine, no pressure."

Holding her hand up, Keti admired the ring, she said, "You know I have to leave, Wolfgang." It was only a flash, but his face tightened before it turned back to stone.

"I need to…to see to the business. My brother Roger is taking over McMaster Lexington. I can trust him, but I need to finish some tasks. I need to…" her gaze lowered, then raised to his hard expression. "As you say, think about…things."

They celebrated the holiday with a turkey and all the trimmings, wine flowed and people chatted and laughed.

Christmas music played softly. Several of the men had women with them, it was a joyous dinner. For everyone except Wolf. He was broody and cranky because the next day Keti was leaving.

They spent hours making love during the night. But now, the time had come. Wolf stood by solemnly while Keti packed her few belongings. Then carrying her suitcases he walked her to the limo waiting outside to take her back to Blackslade.

With Talon and Tommy in jail, Roger would be taking over the business and Blackslade Mansion. As long as Roger did right by the people where they built the bridges, Keti was more than happy to turn everything over to him.

"Ketherine, I will, ah, call you." Wolf stood by the open door of the limo.

Keti raised her hand and caressed his cheek. "Okay." They hadn't discussed how long she would take to think about things, or how they would progress while she did.

She had work she needed to finish up, and Wolf had to prepare to break down the compound, send his men off to other missions.

The trials for Talon, Cash and Tommy and the rest of them, unless they took pleas, wouldn't happen for at least a year. Meanwhile they were all being held without bond.

Wolf wanted to push her for a time limit to decide. He hated every second that they would be apart. Every second while he worked he would be wondering if he'd ever see her again. She was young, she was a good, sweet, kind person, and he…was not.

He feared letting her out of his sight, but he had to let her go. For now. Trying not to think about other men that would be flocking around her vying for her attention, he cupped her chin, bent and kissed her slow, languorous, sexy and loving. Then he let her go.

He stood watching the limo follow the curve of the driveway to the far gate, until it was out of sight. Johan came up and stood beside him.

There was nothing for Johan to say. They couldn't tell the future, and they both knew Wolf was way out of Keti's league, the type of man he was. Still...

Epilogue

It was New Year's Eve, loud music blared from the grand room. His people were celebrating, waiting for the fireworks and the big silver ball to fall. Wolf couldn't stand the frivolities.

He had called Keti only once. He didn't want her to think he was badgering her or stalking her, she had to be left alone to make her own decisions. However, he hadn't heard from her. Not a peep.

He decided he'd wait another week, then, he couldn't help himself, he was going after her. He had to. He couldn't live without-

The doorbell rang. Then it rang again. "Dammit," Wolf bit off a curse. Everyone was busy.

He mumbled and grumbled all the way down the stairs and through the corridors to the front double doors.

"Great," he muttered. "Now I have to welcome one of my soldier's damned guests, some floozy he picked up to spend the New Year celebrating, in bed. Lucky him."

Of course he didn't have to spend the night alone. Woman relentlessly threw themselves at him. But, every touch and invitation from the women only made his stomach pitch and his heart ache more. He only desired one woman's touch, body, heart. And it appeared she didn't want him.

Feeling sorry for himself, Wolf angrily jerked the door open. It was his home, he didn't need to be polite. His head down, with a glower he barked, "They are down the hall to the right. There is food and drinks. I think some are dancing. You can go find-"

"Oh? Can I go ahead? I thought I would have a chaperone. A tall, handsome man to lead me, guide me, see that I was safe and…you know, adored."

His head shot up, mouth dropped.

Keti stood in front of him with a teasing grin, wearing a white cashmere coat and holding a bottle of champagne. She was so beautiful his heart hurt.

"You- you are here, Katherine," he whispered, gawking like a mindless fool at her. Then he realized the cold wind was blowing her hair and snowflakes into the house. He quickly stepped aside. "Wow, uh, baby, come inside."

Her lips glossed pink turned up in a pretty bow, she sailed through the door.

"Here," Wolf said, "let me take your coat. I mean, you are staying, for…the party?"

He helped her out of her coat and handed it to Absolom who finally showed to answer the door.

The dour, austere Absolom gave Wolf a wink then morphed his face back into an unsmiling, haughty blank mask.

Absolom said a stiff, "Good evening, Miss Katherine. It is a pleasure to see you back at the estate." He turned away as both Wolf and Keti gaped at the normally austere, severely quiet man, not prone to any kind of pleasantries.

Wolf could barely extract a thought. He was so surprised, so thrilled to see Keti. It was all he could do to keep his hands off her. "You look as...gorgeous as always, Ketherine. You in the flesh always more exquisite than my memory can dream up."

He had to touch her, he stroked his fingertips on her cheek, and took the bottle of champagne from her.

"You want something to eat? There is quite a spread, people dancing, drinking, eating, we have a big party going on inside. What do you want to do first? Eat? Maybe dance?"

Her thoughtful expression traced his harsh face, the animal enigma was still present, and she smiled. "I just want you, Wolfgang. I came for you."

His brows popped, then lowered as his dark eyes heated. "Oh *jah*?" His accent thickened along with his tongue. "We can go to my...our, suite and...talk, if you would like."

Wolf held his breath. Last thing he wanted to do was share her with the others, he wanted her all to himself.

If she only wanted to talk, or chow, or whatever, whatever she wanted he was beyond thrilled she was there. He set a hand on her hip, his fingers squeezed, he forced himself not to yank her against him.

Keti's head tilted, her smile coquettish, she stroked both palms up his broad chest to wrap around his neck. "Take me to your suite."

He felt a sappy grin crease his face. "Are you sure, my sweet kitten?" Wolf needed to know she had made up her mind, and chose him. His fingers caressed her waist, they wanted to cup her butt and lift her up against the erection that started building the second he'd opened the front door and saw her standing there.

"Yes, Wolfgang, I'm sure." Keti moved closer, her breasts pressed into his ribs.

"Damn, kitten," muttering, still holding the champagne bottle, he swept his hands under her back and legs and scooped her up into his arms.

Her arm looped around his neck, Keti giggled as Wolf strode down the hall and into the grand room.

Holding the champagne bottle in his fist, he nodded to the bar set up in the corner. "Grab us some glasses, darlin' we have some celebrating to do."

Laughing, Keti reached out and grasped two champagne glasses.

All talk halted as the crowd watched Wolf stride through the room with Keti in his arms.

As he exited the room, the people broke out in cheers and clapping. Wolf grinned, something he knew he was going to be doing a lot more of.

Taking the stairs two at a time, Wolf hurried to their room before she could change her mind. He kicked his door open and kicked it closed behind him and lowered his head to capture her lips with a needy, greedy kiss.

Moaning, "Mmm," he broke off with a leery smile. "I missed that, you, so much Ketherine, so goddamned much."

He let her slide gently to the floor and took the glasses from her. "Wait just a sec, baby." He set the glasses down and popped the cork.

Filling the glasses with the bubbly, he handed one to her, and raised his to hers in a toast. "To us, Ketherine." They tipped glasses with a clink as they met, and each took a sip.

Her nose wrinkled. "The bubbles tickle, Wolfgang," she giggled.

"Uh huh," he mumbled absently, took her glass and set both back on the table. His gaze stroked down the front of her, edges of his mouth rose with an appreciative nod. "That dress, wow," he admired her dress.

It was white shimmery that hugged her curves, narrow straps with a sweetheart neckline. She wore silver stilettoes, her hair a high side ponytail that curled over her right shoulder.

"Baby, you look stunning in that dress, it takes my breath away, but," he slowly turned her so he faced her back. "Nothing is more beautiful than you in the nude." He grasped the zipper at the top of the dress and slowly drew it down the sinuous curve of her back.

She didn't protest. Wolf didn't realize he'd been holding his breath, so fearful she would say no. Afraid that he was dreaming that she was really there. If so, he never wanted to wake up.

He turned her back to face him, and his heart dipped at her sweet smile. "Okay?" he asked with a murmur, his hands on her shoulders ready to push the dress down. Once he did that she would be topless as the dress had a built-in bra.

"Yes," Keti whispered.

Wolf bent and set his lips on hers and pushed the dress down slowly to her waist and stood back. A groan rumbled deep in his chest. "Beautiful, so beautiful," he crooned, gazing at her breasts.

He checked with her, her smile told him she was more than willing and he crouched to push the dress the rest of the way down. When it pooled on the floor at her feet, he grasped one of her hands to set on his shoulder and he lifted one foot then the other and removed the dress and each of her heels.

Wolf moved to kneel and pressed his mouth against her silk panties, and this time she moaned with breathless desire. He cupped her sex, and her hips tilted into his hand with another soft moan.

"*Jah*, baby, *jah*," he muttered and removed her panties. He stroked her sex, then pressed kisses over her bare skin, licked her until her legs shook.

When he heard her breaths grow shuddering and shallow, little mewing moans sounded, he stood up and cupped her face with both hands and kissed her long, steady, hungry then hot.

Keti shivered, then stood back. Her hands went to cover her breasts in modesty, "Wolfgang," she said looking pointedly at his clothes. She was naked, he was fully clothed in trousers and a white, long-sleeved button-down and a blazer.

She caught the lapels of the blazer and pushed them back. His shoulders were too broad for her to remove the jacket.

Grinning, Wolf shrugged out of the jacket and let it fall to the floor. Keti opened two buttons on his shirt, and he impatiently reached behind his back, grabbed the material and yanked the shirt off his head and let it drop.

When she reached for his belt, he caught her wrists, holding them back and said, "Wait."

Keti furrowed her brow at him in confusion, suddenly shy. "Wolfgang?"

He gently pulled her to the bed and he sat down, then he pulled her to stand between his legs. He couldn't resist palming her breasts. He fondled them then brushed his palms down her sides to around and grasped her bottom with both big hands.

"I need to know, Ketherine, if this is a one night thing, or if…if you want to give me, us, a chance. I…" he moved his hands to wrap around her arms. "I don't think I can just…just do tonight and then, you are out of my life. I…I cannot do that, Ketherine."

"Can you look at me when you're talking to me?" she smirked. He was staring at her breasts, his tongue slicking his lips as if he was holding back from suckling her.

He smiled and raised his dark eyes, warm and lustful, and anxious to hers. "Tell me, Ketherine, tell me this is more than just a night."

Keti combed her hands through his hair then held the back of his head, bent and kissed him. Straightening, she said, "For a big bad merc you aren't very observant."

"Huh?" His eyes glazed with desire, lids heavy over them. "What did I miss?"

She stood back just out of his reach, held her hand up, and wiggled her fingers. The brilliant diamond sparkled brightly even in the low lights of the bedroom.

A dark flush rolled up Wolf's neck to the tips of his ears, a stunned smile rose shaky with it. "You, you are wearing my ring. Does that mean…?"

Keti nodded with a grin. "Yes. I had to leave you to make sure you would let me go. Make sure you would let me make my own decision to be with you or not." Her head tipped coyly.

"You proved you really loved me by letting me go. You didn't stalk me, or try to talk me into coming back, or kidnap me like I know you are quite capable of doing."

His hazy gaze painted her naked body with want. "It killed me, Ketherine." His eyes connected with hers.

The corners of his mouth nicked in. "I will not lie, if another week went by I was coming for you. I could not stand this place without you. I would have had to try to get you back."

He ducked his head abashed. "I, uh," he coughed, "I was working on a plan. But," he grinned brightly, "there is no need for a plan now, right?"

Her expression sobered. "It's probably best you don't tell me what your plan was, Wolfgang. The thing is, you live...well, I don't know where you live. I live in Gladonia. I plan to leave Blackslade. Roger will marry and it will be his home. I...I mean my plan is, what I want to do is return to Italy and complete my studies."

Wolf threw out a hand to grab her but she stepped out of his reach. "Ah, you don't want me to chase you, my little kitten prey, because if you do, I may have to punish you for challenging me." One brow arched with a sinful grin.

Her hands behind her back lifted her breasts and Keti smiled at the flush that darkened Wolf's skin. "You didn't respond to what I said. Long distance relationships don't work. The statistics of- hey!"

Wolf suddenly stood up, took a few steps, and grabbed Keti. Tossing her over his shoulder, he trod back to the bed and laid her on it.

He finished undoing his pants and removed them, his socks and boots. He grinned at her wide-eyes perusal of his erection. Bending over, he clasped one of her ankles and pulled it spreading her legs.

He climbed on the bed, his knee between her legs, he lowered himself. Moving his lower body between her thighs, he braced on his elbows beside her shoulders and kissed her.

In seconds they were both breathing heavily, chests touching with every inhale, lips locked and loaded, Wolf's erection pressed at her core.

He broke off the kiss, licked her lips then gave them a quick kiss. "Sweetheart. I can live anywhere I desire. And my desire is to live with you, wherever you are. Italy is a fantastic place to reside, ancient and modern, the sun, the mountains, the wine, the food, I look forward to living there.

We can buy a villa in a picturesque village by the sea, and raise our family."

Keti smoothed a lock of hair off his brow. She said, "What about your job? Your work?"

"Baby, I can work anywhere. Truthfully, I don't need to work. I am loaded as you Americans put it. But I need to keep busy, otherwise I get into trouble."

"Huh," she snorted, "you get in trouble? I can't imagine."

Wolf nestled between her legs, prodded her sex with his shaft. "So, we are good? Any more questions before we celebrate the New Year and our engagement?"

Keti purred as he started pushing inside her, "Tell me you love me, Wolfgang."

His eyes warm on hers he kept pushing, grunted and said, "More than life itself, my Ketherine, I love you more than life itself."

He paused, his manhood throbbing against her silken walls. "Now, you tell me, Ketherine, tell me the words I have longed to hear ever since I met you. Tell me."

She tipped her jaw up and kissed his chin. "Wolfgang Valdimar, I love you. I truly love you with my whole heart, and I can't wait to become your wife, make a home with you, have your, our, children."

Against her lips Wolf murmured, "You are my home, Ketherine. You are all I will ever need, children will only be the cherries on the top. I love you," and he took them both to heaven.

The End

Dear Reader, thank you for purchasing Wrath of Wolf! *I know you could have picked any number of books to read, but you picked this book and for that I am extremely grateful.*

I hope you enjoyed this novel, and if you did, please leave a review where you purchased it, and look for other exciting titles in my name!

About the Author

Louise Furley loves writing romance with a huge helping of suspense. She finds it exciting to study new lands and learn everything she can about the area and the natives that call it home.

Her idea of fun is researching ideas, studying enigmatic modes of science, archeology, and different ways to kill someone.

Louise Furley

Her Significant Other finds the last to be particularly notable. He remains wary yet gives Louise his full support with her writing adventures.

Sunny Florida is home where Louise is a graduate of St. Thomas University with a master's degree in Mental Health. This degree is essential for exploring the deviant soul, and understanding the mind of a killer, while finding it exhilarating, frightening and sad all at the same time. With artistic license, Louise can be judge, jury, and sometimes executioner!

Louise is the author of numerous published novels. When not researching or writing, she is dreaming of unique plots, and discovering fresh ventures she hasn't yet experienced in the world.

Ride along with her as she travels new and thrilling journeys!